CLOCKWORK

A Peter Marklin Mystery

CLOCKWORK

NEVILLE STEED

St. Martin's Press
New York

Library of Congress Cataloging-in-Publication Data

Steed, Neville.
    Clockwork / Neville Steed.
        p.   cm.
    ISBN 0-312-03305-2
    I. Title.
PR6069.T387C54   1989
823'.914—dc20   89-34840
                                                                 CIP

First published in Great Britain by George Weidenfeld and Nicolson Limited.

First U.S. Edition

10 9 8 7 6 5 4 3 2 1

For Edward,
with love

One

The radio pulsed with an old Presley classic, 'Blue Suede Shoes'. The top was down, my elbow soaked up the sun on the window-sill and the slip-stream air-cooled my brain nicely. It could have been a scene from an old Elvis movie, only Swanage sea-front isn't quite a dead ringer for Malibu or Hawaii, and Dorset girls' legs stop somewhere short of their chins (or so I'm told). What's more, I'm not exactly a Graceland guy look-alike. For a start, I can't even afford the hair oil, let alone the face lifts. And the thirteen feet of my old convertible Beetle is hardly in the twenty-foot Cadillac class.

For late September, the sun had all the shine and sparkle of spring, whilst retaining just enough lulling tranquillity about its performance to remind you it was a swan-song, not an overture. And this was the fourth day that temperatures had been in the high seventies. Everyone but Gus called it an Indian summer. Gus, of course, maintained that Indian summers must be twice as hot, as, otherwise, why did everything look brown and burnt to a cinder every time India popped up on telly? As a result, Gus Tribble is the only inhabitant of this green and pleasant land who refers to hot English autumns as Indian winters. I don't know why I bother, sometimes.

I was so mesmerized by the splendour of the day, I almost ran into the back of a Sierra in front of me. I hadn't noticed it slow to let a bull terrier, who was taking an old lady for a walk, cross the road. My sudden jabbing at the brake pedal precipitated the goodies on my rear seat into the footwell. I cursed over my breath. For the cardboard box contained some rarities I'd been more than lucky to discover and whose condition, in certain cases, was giving the adjective 'frail' new depth of meaning.

I'd better explain. I was on my way back home from having collected a box full of pre-war Dinky Toy aircraft from an old man

7

in Swanage who had answered my wanted advert in the local paper. 'Dinky Toy aircraft wanted. Must be good condition. Boxed preferred. Contact Marklin, The Toy Emporium, Studland, Dorset. Telephone number . . .' He had been a pilot with the Royal Flying Corps, then a test pilot with Shorts, then had flown commercially with Hillman Airlines and Imperial Airways. Flying had been his whole life and he had more model planes in his house than a barn has mice. But now in his nineties, he was feeling it was time to pass some of them on. So that's why I was on the road that day. I had been to do a deal and pick them up. Not for sale in my Antique Toy shop, either. These were for me, Peter Marklin Esquire, a perennially thirty-nine-year-old schoolboy and unashamed nostalgia nut.

I reached behind and prised the box back on to the rear seat, praying that the more metal fatigued aircraft inside had not powdered into pieces with the jolt. (In the immediate pre-war period, Dinky used a more than normally impure alloy which has wrought havoc with the longevity of many of their toys, especially aircraft. Hence the sky-high prices currently being asked for the latter.) By the time I looked round again, the Sierra was way down the road. As I accelerated after him, I saw an old dumpy Datsun weaving its way along the promenade towards me, as if the driver was drunk. I pulled over as far as the kerb would allow, much to the concern of a well-filled pair of Bermuda shorts sashaying along the pavement and the Datsun wriggled by, its mirror missing mine by only a gnat's whatsit.

As I glared after it, what exactly I had been glaring at didn't immediately register. Then it hit me like a ton of bricks. I could do nothing but slide into the kerb and stop. As I tried to absorb the full implications of this impossibly absurd vision, the Bermuda shorts stopped by my door and in a broad Brummy accent said, 'People like him shouldn't be allowed on the road.'

I looked up into her yard-long eyelashes and, at last, mustered, 'You got it slightly wrong, darling. People like him just shouldn't be allowed at all.'

She shaded her mascara and looked back up the promenade. 'Want his number? I can still just see his car.'

'No, thanks,' I smiled. 'Don't bother. You see I've known his little number for years.'

Even by the time I reached home, I couldn't believe what I had

8

seen. And it took me longer than usual, as the Studland road was blocked just by the Manners Memorial School. Apparently, they were holding a Jumbo Jumble Sale there, in aid of the children of Ethiopia and it was being opened by His Worship, the Mayor of Swanage, no less, and our current local claim to fame, an ex-student, a Miss Bettina Badger, whose rather unstable dimensions are making Page Four and sequitur of an infamous national daily quite superfluous.

I let myself in, answered Bing's Siamese greetings with a stroke and another dollop of Whiskas (he preferred the latter), put my cardboard box in the sitting-room, then opened up shop. Not that I really expected a flood of customers, or even a single trickle (the old toy game goes in fits and starts, mainly the former), but it at least gave me an excuse for sitting still and thinking about my seaside experience.

At one point, I caught myself in the mirror – the one strategically placed to catch any light fingers in my shop – actually shaking my head in disbelief. And I didn't blame myself. The sight of old Gus driving any car other than his old upright Ford Popular was quite as mind boggling as, say, Halley's Comet going backwards, Tom Wolfe wearing black, or a social worker admitting a mistake. For Gus is wedded to that forty-year-old bone-shaker or, at very least, it's his common-law companion. I'd never, ever seen him drive anything else. To Gus, the motor industry might well have just jacked it all in after 1950, its masterpiece created, the highest pinnacle surmounted with the steel, Rexine and rubber wonder, the two-door Ford Popular.

And yet . . . and yet, I had just seen him in a Datsun. An elderly Datsun, but nevertheless . . . I mused on't. The erratic driving was easy to explain. Gus believed that God or Henry Ford had given cars steering wheels for using – and not for letting lie idle in the hands. That works fine round bends, but on the straight? But the sixty-four-thousand-dollar question was: what on earth had prised Gus out of his Ford into any other car? It couldn't have been because his Popular was away being serviced, for two good reasons. Firstly, I've only ever known Gus have it serviced professionally once, and that was at least seven or eight years ago. Secondly, I knew he would come to me and claim chauffeur's rights, if he ever did. What's more, his car had been as right as rain (I choose that phrase carefully) the evening before. I had seen him clatter off in it, no doubt on his way to his latest 'lady friend' –

9

yet another widow, pushing sixty, who was good for the odd hot dinner and I shouldn't be surprised.

However, my musings were to be interrupted just as I was about to put a quiche in the oven for my lunch. Arabella had made two and we had scoffed the first one the evening before. The shop bell clanged and I had a customer. And not your usual, rather sheepish and cautious variety, either. Far from it. He visibly bounced in and came up to my counter right away, without the lengthy browsing and critical and analytical period that the regular old toy collector normally goes through. His eyes said it wasn't just his tender age that was the cause. I've seen teenagers much younger than him, whose eyes have been dead for years. Maybe ever since birth.

'Hi,' he chirped in a tone that spoke of viewing too many game-show hosts.

'Hi,' I thought I'd better reply.

His next statement rather floored me.

'How are you doing?'

'Doing?'

'Yea. Doing. You know. Like doing. Getting on.'

I must have frowned.

'Business, I mean. You know. Trade.'

'Oh,' I recovered. 'I see. Well. Fine. Sure. Not too bad anyway.'

He sat down on the stool I keep by the counter for customers who can't believe my prices.

'Don't mind my asking, do you?' He looked at me with those eyes that made even Jeffrey Archer's seem dozy. I reckoned he must have been only about sixteen, but he had a street-wise jauntiness about him, like a kid in the chorus of *West Side Story*, and about as good looking – though his hair was not slicked, but sandy, and his complexion typically British, without a trace of tan.

I shook my head. 'No. Feel free.'

He picked up a Tootsietoy Ford 'Trimotor' that was in a group of Tootsietoy planes on my counter and glanced at the price sticker under the wing.

'Wow,' he pronounced. 'Do you really expect to get £55 for this tiny thing?'

'Yes. You don't see that one around much these days and it's well-nigh mint.'

He appraised it again, then put it down and picked up a very

10

much larger tinplate aircraft, a DC-2, resplendent in chromium with red registration letters.

'This is only £75, yet it's four or five times the size and much more impressive.'

Now, normally, by this juncture, I would have been more than a little miffed by any customer taking up my time with naive and aimless conversation, but there was a disarming quality about this boy that made resentment seem a very churlish reaction to his frank and open questioning.

'The old toy market doesn't work that way.'

'Doesn't measure the width, just feels the quality?' he smiled.

'Not even that. Prices go partly by rarity and partly by the reputation of the manufacturer. That DC-2 is as old as the Trimotor but from an unknown Far Eastern factory, whereas Tootsietoy is one of the most famous die-cast manufacturers. They pre-date even Dinky and started the whole die-cast revolution in toys.'

He replaced the DC-2 and swung round on the stool to appraise the rest of my offerings displayed in the shop.

'How quickly do you turn a toy round? I mean, all this stock. What's your cycle?'

I couldn't believe all his marketing jargon. He sounded like someone on The Money Programme.

'I haven't the slightest idea,' I replied, my expression, no doubt, displaying my amazement. 'Some toys go within a day or two of going on display. Others linger on for months.' I grinned. 'There are one or two here that I've had for a year or two now.'

He pursed his lips. 'Ever carried out an analysis? You know, identified the fast-moving lines . . . ?'

I didn't let him finish. 'Look, you've asked me a lot of questions, which I don't mind answering, but, perhaps, I could ask you one or two now.'

He nodded, with a knowing grin on his really rather dashing features. 'Sorry. Go ahead.'

I pointed to his tie. 'Aren't you at Manners School?'

'Right.'

'I mean, shouldn't you be at Manners School right now?' I winked. 'You don't look ill to me.'

'I'm not ill. Just got the rest of the day off.'

'But haven't they got a big jumble sale or something on there?'

'Right again. It was all my idea. I organized the whole thing

11

from scratch. That's why I've got the rest of the day off. I was at the school till late last night, fixing everything.'

'Didn't you want to stick around and watch the stuff sell?'

'Not really. I'll go back later and count the final takings. Much more interesting. And the Mayor, who I fixed to open it, is a right bore. How he gets elected, I can't imagine. And that Page Three girl I got to open it with him. Christ. I'd never met her till this morning. She's got the I.Q. of a dumpling.'

I laughed. 'Come now, you didn't invite her for her brain.'

'No. But even those were a bit of a let-down.' He grinned and added, 'Or would have been, if she wasn't wearing a bra.'

'I bet she's entertaining some of the dads, anyway.'

He shrugged. 'Guess so. Myself – I don't go for pneumatic types. I like, well . . . you know, something . . . less obvious. Like my current girlfriend. She doesn't have inches, but . . . everything else.'

I thought it was about time to switch back to toys.

'So you've got some hours to spare. Why did you come along here? Interested in old toys?'

He got off the stool and moved over to a cabinet, where I keep my stock of mint, boxed, post-war Dinky cars.

'Saw some of these on telly the other night.'

'Oh? What programme?'

He came as near to blushing as I guessed he ever would.

'Er . . . Blue Peter.' Then he hastily added, 'Normally never watch children's programmes. Patronizing little lot they are on that. But someone told me they were going to do a bit on old toys . . . and their value and so on. So I tuned in, just for that bit.'

'Did you switch on for the toys or for the chat about their prices?'

He looked back at me from under his sandy eyebrows.

'Both. You think I only looked for their value, don't you?'

I shrugged. 'So you like old toys?'

'Some. Only cars though. And then really only the expensive makes.' He pointed into the cabinet. 'Like that Bentley convertible there. Or the Jags. Mk X, Mk II, that kind of thing. And the big Americans, of course. De Sotos, Plymouths, Cadillacs. You know . . .'

I knew. Many collectors bought models of the kind of cars they knew they would never be able to afford to own.

Then he stunned me by adding, 'You see, I'd better start soon

12

to lay in a store of these things, before they're all gone. So I've got models of cars I'm going to buy one day.'

'Yea,' I floundered. 'Yes. Of course. Good idea.'

He pointed back to the cabinet. 'How much is the Bentley convertible? To me, that is?'

I frowned. 'To *you*?'

'Yes. To me. Preferential rate.'

I added another frown. 'Because . . .?'

'Because, I can see that I can be of service to you.' He came back to the counter, a most earnest expression now on his face.

'I can help you turn round this business. Maybe, even double your turn-over.'

I looked at him hard. 'How old are you?'

'Sixteen. Why? Age has nothing to do with whether you have a flair for making money. You either have it or you don't.'

Curiously, his arrogance didn't stick in my craw, as they say.

'All right. So you reckon you have it? You're the Richard Branson or Donald Trump of Manners School?'

'Not quite,' he smiled broadly. 'My teeth are smaller, for a start.'

I laughed out loud. I had never met a youngster quite like him.

'All right. The Bentley is marked £55. To *you* – £45.'

His bright eyes now positively glowed. 'Mean it?'

'I'm probably an idiot, but I mean it.'

He patted his pocket. 'I haven't any money with me. I'll come back with it. Promise. Will you put it by for me?'

'I'll put it by.'

'Can I come by tomorrow?'

'Any time.'

'No, I mean, not just to pick up the Bentley. You see, I'd sort of like to bring my girlfriend round too. Let her see the shop. You know . . . Would that be all right?'

I nodded.

He went on, 'Have to be the evening, if you don't mind. We won't stay long, promise.'

'Make it after eight or so. Give me and *my* girlfriend time to grab a quick bite.'

'Of food?' he grinned.

'Of food,' I affirmed.

He seemed as happy as the perennial sandboy.

13

As he made for the door, I asked, 'If you need longer to get the money, don't hesitate to . . .'

He turned and smiled. 'Already got the money, haven't I? Had an article of mine accepted by *Computer Times.'*

I raised my eyebrows. Silly me. I should have guessed, shouldn't I?

Quiche devoured, I walked down the sea lane to see if Gus had returned. Naturally, as a fisherman, he had bought a cottage as near the water as he could, without actually rowing to the front door. But there was no sign of a Ford Popular, or a Datsun, either outside the patched and crumbling walls of what was otherwise quite a pretty thatched dwelling, or up what Gus laughingly called his drive – two lines of worn tyre tracks in an overgrowth of weeds, briars and you name it, I'd rather not.

So I walked on down the hundred yards or so to Studland beach. The sun tap-danced off a billion ripples, you couldn't call them waves, and the water just idly licked the sand as it ebbed and flowed. This was an Indian summer and a half, whatever Gus thought. And the sunbathers on the beach knew it, loved it and were soaking it up. There was a surprising lot of them too, grabbing at the season's unexpected bonus.

I found myself a space, not too hemmed in by pre-school kids and sat down. The heat from the sand shimmered my view of the sea, as if I were peering down a long camera lens, so I lay back and reviewed my encounter with this extraordinary adolescent, whose name I hadn't even thought to ask. I wondered what his school thought of him. Terrified, probably. Schoolteachers, I'm sure, pray at night to be preserved from anything but the norm. I wondered what his parents thought of him. Were they proud, or maybe, just bemused? There was only one person I could think of whose attitude towards such a phenomenon I could guess for certain. That was Maggie Thatcher. I'm sure if she had known about him, he'd have been in the last Conservative Manifesto.

As for my own attitude, I wasn't quite sure. Don't get me wrong. I liked him. His openness, vitality, industry even. At least he wouldn't be slobbing around slot machines and one-armed bandits on Swanage sea-front for his kicks, like so many local teenagers. But all the same, I wondered when he eventually got his Bentley (and, curiously, I didn't really doubt his ability to get one sooner or later) whether he'd be really happy and content or

14

be too obsessed with making his next million really to appreciate any of his possessions or even have time to look back on his achievements. I had met too many self-made millionaires in my days in the advertising game to equate financial success with any form of happiness. I'll swear all the ones I've known will die with the equivalent of 'Rosebud' on their lips and there will be no movie camera around to record their last words as a lesson for posterity.

The sun suddenly seemed to go behind a cloud. Least, I thought it was a cloud. I opened my eyes. I might have known. It wasn't a cloud. The sun had gone behind Gus.

'Thought it was you,' he grunted. 'Saw yer back disappear down the lane.'

I got up on one elbow and squinted up at him. Despite the 'Indian winter', he was dressed as he always is, in thick baggy trousers and a fisherman's sweater as bushy as his eyebrows. I reckon Gus must sweat *internally*, because he never looks hot or pants like a dog (except when beer is mentioned).

'Did it looked humped and angry?' I asked.

'What look humped and whatsit?'

'My back.'

He ploughed extra furrows in his forehead. 'Your back?'

'Yes, Gus. You didn't half get it up this morning, that's why.'

He pulled a look as innocent as a born again liar. 'What did I do, then? I haven't ruddy seen you today until now.'

I sat up straight. 'Only because I took evasive action to prevent myself suffering a Pearl Harbor from a runaway Japanese car.'

He thought for a second. 'Pearl 'Arbor? Oh ... yea ... you don't mean you saw me on my test drive?'

'Test drive?'

He kicked at the sand, luckily not towards me. 'Right, old love. Just doing a bit of evaluatin'. Going to try quite a few before I makes up me mind.'

This was enough to make me stand right up. I put my hand on his shoulder. 'Gus, you nearly evaluated me into oblivion.'

He kicked at some more sand. As luck would have it, a naked toddler, wet from the sea, was trotting past us. By the time he got to his mother, he looked like a sand sculpture.

'Well, it took me a bit of time to get used to the controls, you see, old son. Bit different from my old Popular.'

15

'Gus, don't tell me you are thinking of ditching your Ford? I'll rephrase that. Trading it in for something else?'

Gus looked at what was left of his finger-nails. 'Might do, might not. Depends if I come across something I fancy.'

'What on earth has triggered all this? I never thought I would see the day you'd consider changing that lethal car of yours.'

'Got an offer, didn't I?'

'Who from?' I grinned. 'The Road Safety Council?'

'You can laugh, old son. But my old Popular is now a "classic".'

'Who told you that, Gus? Your Popular is a banger.'

'Been done up a bit, don't forget. Had to be after you jumped down through me roof,* like a great concrete dummy.'

'It's still a banger,' I muttered.

'Not according to the chap who wants to buy it.'

A seagull seemed to shriek with laughter, as it thermalled over us. I didn't blame it.

'Someone has offered you real clinking-type money for that thing?'

'Yep.'

'How much?'

'Enough.'

'Enough for what?'

'Another car.'

'Like an old Datsun?'

He threw his great arms wide and frightened a puppy who was burying someone's sandwich.

'World's me oyster, old son. Might be a Datsun. Might be a Fiesta, Chevette, Cortina . . . I'm going to do the rounds and try 'em all before I decide.'

I crossed myself. 'God help the garage trade. I never thought I would ever say that.'

Gus turned to go. 'Well, if you're going to be like that . . . '

I grinned. 'All right, Gus. I won't be like that. But who is this guy who wants to buy your Popular?'

'Chap I met in Weymouth car-park. Found him admiring it when I came back from buying some new waders. He's an old car nut. Made me an offer there and then, he did. So I took his name and number and said I'd think about it. So I've been thinking about it, that's all.'

---

* *Chipped*, Weidenfeld & Nicolson, 1988.

16

'Well, well, well,' I said. 'And did you like the Datsun? Looked a bit ropey to me.'

'Had an 'eater,' he muttered.

He had a point. Gus had never had a car with a heater before. He just warmed himself on the fumes filtering through the rotting floorboards.

'What's more,' he went on, 'that chap's offer has given me ideas.'

'What ideas?'

'Well, I could make a sort of business of it, couldn't I?'

'Business of what?'

'Keeping cars a long time until they're classics, then selling them, buying another . . .'

I put my hands on my hips. 'Gus, you need to keep a car at least twenty years before it can ever be considered in the classic class. You are at least sixty-five now. (He has never divulged his true age. I suspect even he doesn't know it.) If you bought the Datsun, you'd be eighty-five by the time it was worth a damn and a hundred and five by the time you could collect on the next one, and a hundred and twenty-five . . .'

He waved his great hands. I could feel the breeze.

'All right, old son. I'm not an idiot, you know. You see, I thought if I sold my boat and used the money to buy a second or third car . . .'

I stopped him. 'Sell your boat? I don't believe what I'm hearing.'

'Saw a programme on telly the other night. All about making your money work for you. I've got too much tied up in the boat.'

I raised my eyebrows. 'Oh hell, Gus, what's happening to me today? Everybody's suddenly struck with a money-making mania.'

'I'm not everybody,' he murmured.

I refrained from saying, 'Thanks be . . .' Instead, I said, 'Come on back to my place, Gus, and I'll tell you all about it.'

He lifted his right hand. I nodded.

'Four left in the fridge.'

So we picked our way back over the bodies towards the Toy Emporium, where I told him all about my lunch-time customer, then ended with a homily about the Thatcher generation. I knew Gus was riveted, because he didn't fall asleep until at least half-way through.

17

Two

I turned off the switch and Channel Four News vanished into a dot. I'd had enough of the world's problems for one day.

As I went into my diminutive hall (really only an architect's hiccup between my living-room and the kitchen), Arabella came down the stairs. No longer was she in the 'glad rags' she wore to work – her editor on the *Western Gazette* believed reporters should always look as kempt as the sprucest and tidiest of their interviewees – but in what might have been called in the thirties beach pyjamas, all printed cotton and gossamer thin. The outfit may keep her cool, but it sure raises the temperature of everyone who sees her in it.

'Washed off the day?' I enquired, pecking her on the cheek.

'Some of it,' she smiled and made for the kitchen. I followed her and sat on a stool.

'One of those, was it?'

She nodded, then went to the fridge. 'Eaten the quiche?'

I saluted.

She took out some sliced ham. 'Cold meat and salad do you on a hot evening?'

'If that's what you're cooking,' I joked.

She smiled weakly. 'How was your day?'

I told her. About Gus. The boy. The whole works.

When I had finished, she commented, 'Funny he came from Manners School.'

'What's funny about it? The jumble sale they were holding today?'

She cut into a lettuce. 'No, nothing to do with that.'

'Then what?'

'Well, one of our other reporters covered that event and while he was there, he apparently overheard two of the parents whispering about some teacher or other.'

18

'So? Parents are always whispering about teachers. He was lucky. Sometimes they're shouting about them.'

She turned round to me. 'They may be shouting about him soon, if what our man overheard this morning has any basis of truth.'

I perked up my ears. 'Oh, sounds like a nice juicy scandal.'

'I wish it were that simple,' she said and ran her hand through her short dark hair. I love the way it springs back like pile on a rug.

I got up and went over to her and not just to help slice the mushrooms.

'What's the matter? You sound pretty grim.'

'Well, it's all a bit sad.'

'Tell me.'

She stopped washing the lettuce. 'Promise you won't tell anyone else, until we're sure of all the facts?'

I tipped an invisible hat. 'Scout's honour.'

'Here goes then. Tom, that's our man at the sale, heard the mothers talking about one of the teachers – he didn't catch the name – and they were saying that there was a helluva row going on between two of the schools governors over him. Both mums, apparently, sided with the one who said he should be immediately dismissed. "Before God knows what harm is done." That type of chat.'

'Doesn't sound very grim to me. There are often rows about teachers and their appointments. And parents are always siding with one faction or another. They're rarely neutral.'

'Hang on, Peter. You don't know yet what the row is about.'

'All right, darling, what's the row all about?'

'It seems this teacher is homosexual.'

I thought for a moment. 'There's more, isn't there?'

She nodded. 'Yes. The rumour that prompted the mums to talk at all has it that he's . . .'

'. . . got Aids,' I reluctantly supplied. I somehow knew it had to be.

Arabella sighed. 'See now, why we've got to keep mum until we know more?'

'The mums aren't keeping mum.'

'But we have to. Especially on the paper.'

'Editor know?'

19

'Yes. That's why he's asked me to try to see Colonel Hawkesworth in the morning.'

I finished with the mushrooms and took some cold potatoes out of the fridge.

'Who's Colonel Hawkesworth when he's at home?'

'One of the feuding school governors. Or should I have said feudal? He's been a pillar of the local Conservative Club, so the editor says, since coming out of the army. And he hasn't just got a home. He's got a regular mansion. Over Wareham way.'

'Flog 'em, hang 'em type?'

'Something like that.' Arabella shook up the French dressing and trickled it over the potatoes. 'Not looking forward to the interview at all. Directly I mention such a thing as "homosexuality", he'll probably have me clapped in irons or, at least, set the Dobermans on to me.'

'You won't mention homosexuality.'

'No, I won't. Least, not right away. Just say I've heard there are considerable disagreements amongst the school governors over one of the teachers, etcetera, and see how it goes.'

I sat back again on the stool. 'Wow. I don't think sleepy old Dorset is quite ready for this.'

'I don't think anybody is ever ready for Aids, sleepy or not. I saw enough of it when I was working over in San Francisco on the *Examiner*.'

'Who's the other protagonist? Did Tom gather?'

'Not as far as I know. I'll have to try to find that out tomorrow.'

My mind went back to a well-publicized case up north, where a schoolchild, who had caught Aids through a blood transfusion, was virtually ostracized by all who knew her and was almost the cause of the school having to close down for lack of pupils willing to attend. Now a teacher whose homosexual nature was already known, who had contracted the disease . . . that could be the bombshell that blew the worst prejudices of a rural community right out into the raw and chilling open.

I crossed my fingers.

'Maybe it's all rumour. A figment of the overheated underemployed minds of mums who relish every juicy bit of gossip.'

Arabella, quite rightly, didn't comment. She just held up the salad bowl.

'Relish a juicy bit of supper?'

I slipped off the stool and picked up the two plates of cold meat. Somehow, my appetite was no longer quite what it had been.

Tuesday dawned as blue skied as the previous mornings and I regretted Arabella having to go to work. It was just the kind of day to do nothing much but mooch, stroll the beach hand in hand like new-found, tingling touch, lovers. Maybe have a picnic amidst the sand-dunes, a bottle of cool white wine never far away . . . Hey, ho, it was not to be. Arabella couldn't just lock a door, turn her 'Open' sign to 'Closed' and take the day off like I could, if I wanted to go bankrupt. Editors on newspapers sort of like their staff to turn up now and again.

I don't resent Arabella working. Nor does she resent working herself, although on that Tuesday morning she wanted to laze around in the sun as much as I did. At least her Golf is a convertible, so the rays could kiss her adorable form on the way to and, hopefully, on the way back from the *Western Gazette* offices.

Me? I passed the morning packing up a few parcels in answer to my mail-order adverts in the *Model Collector* and the *Collector's Gazette*, then, having taken them to the Post Office, I opened up shop. Luckily, the sun had not only brought out bodies in search of a tan, but the odd collector in search of a rarity. Within the space of an hour, I sold two tinplates, an early fifties MG TF by Bandai for £85 and a circa 1960 MGA by ATC for £70, to a fifties nut, who owns a small hotel in Swanage. And three mint and boxed examples of perhaps the most accurate and charming saloon car models Dinky ever made, certainly post-war, a razor-edge Triumph 1800, a Riley 1½ litre and a Standard Vanguard (early version without the rear wheel spats) to an American tourist for £150 the lot.

So the sun had shone on my Toy Emporium for once. For quite often I can go for days without a sale to keep a sparrow alive, and only my mail-order business to keep me in bird-seed. Oh, and I received quite a promising phone call. About my 'Aircraft Wanted' advertisement in the local rag. Guy said his father had some old Dinky planes in his attic, remnants of his childhood. If I was interested, he would try to get his old man to see me. So I said I was interested and he said he would ring back. I did hope he would be, as I was attempting to build up a collection of every aircraft Dinky made in its history, from 1934, when the first set of six came out, to 1979, when the whole company succumbed to the British disease of the seventies, outgoings higher than incomings. And I still had quite a few aircraft types to discover, especially those from Dinky's factory in Paris. But I didn't built up my hopes. The old toy business is punctuated with broken promises and phantom phone calls.

The afternoon, however, was a dead loss. Not a soul. So I shut up shop early, at four thirty. Lucky I did, for no sooner had I sat down in my sitting-room, than I heard Arabella's Golf pull in round the back. I went to greet her.

'You're early,' I said, after the usual buss on the lips. 'Get time off for good behaviour, or has Colonel Hawkesworth had the *Gazette* closed down for pornographic reporting?'

She grimaced. 'Don't talk to me about the Colonel.'

We went into the sitting-room.

'Okay, I won't talk to you about the Colonel.'

She subsided on to the settee and bit her lip. We were both silent for a moment, a silence she at last broke.

'Talk to me about the Colonel,' she said. 'I think I'll explode if you don't.'

I laughed. 'All right. So you went to see him?' I got up and went to the sideboard to pour her a drink. She waved her hand.

'Don't feel like a drink, thanks. I've got this article to write tonight. That's why I've come home early. To get some quiet. The offices are about as conducive to good writing as Clapham Junction in rush hour. And about as noisy.'

I sat down next to her on the settee and put an arm round her shoulder.

'What's the article about? Hawkesworth?'

'Not directly. The editor wants me to do a general piece as well about parents and teachers, and prejudice. You know the kind of stuff. What would be your attitude if your daughter was being taught by a one-eyed Jewish negro, with known ambisexual tendencies, etcetera, etcetera. And what should constitute sufficient evidence for parents – or governors, for that matter – to demand a teacher's removal?'

'No mention of Aids?'

She shook her head. 'Not in that piece. Too dangerously near what may be the truth.'

'The idea for the article came out of your Hawkesworth interview?'

'I suppose so. God, that man makes my blood boil.'

'What happened?'

'Let's put it this way. I trod carefully and he didn't. I'd hardly opened my mouth before he went into a tirade of his Fascist views on almost everything under the sun.'

I lifted my eyebrows. 'He hasn't by any chance got a small black moustache and a lock of hair that falls across his forehead?'

At last I'd raised a smile. 'No. And he's not a hundred years old and hasn't got a German accent, but, in all other respects, he's the very same, *Zieg Heil*.'

'What did he have to say about the school? Did he admit there's a rare old row going on amongst the governors?'

'Oh yes. He certainly did. That's what started it all off. He denied nothing . . .'

Then Arabella took me through the whole interviw. By the end, I felt almost as sick and tired as she obviously did. In a nutshell, Hawkesworth sounded as if he should be in a nuthouse. To say his views were right wing was the understatement of the year. He began by openly admitting the disagreement amongst the governors over the choice of teachers, with particular reference to one governor who he did name – a Miss Delia Pettican, who apparently lived over Lulworth way and whose grandfather was the 'Manners' who founded the school. She, he declared, was the 'nigger in the woodpile' and the 'liberal-minded lefty' who was the main cause of the 'decline in discipline' in the school and the 'decline in morals' amongst the staff. From his heavy hints, Arabella suspected he considered her a Lesbian to boot, all because she was sixty and still a spinster. Thence followed a heated homily on the need to protect the young from the likes of her, the likes of the anonymous teacher and the likes of anyone who wasn't white, Protestant, 'healthy', heterosexual and an admirer of the views of Enoch Powell or Barry Goldwater. If this protection was not provided by the vigilant like him, then, apparently, Great Britain would kiss itself goodbye and become a Sodom and Gomorrah by tomorrow.

By this time, she had asked for, and I had poured her, a drink.

'Then, having gone on about the need to weed out Communist and homosexually inspired books from school and even public libraries,' she said between sips, 'he ended on a real humdinger. And it's this my editor's itching to cover if and when it happens.'

23

'What's that?' I reacted. 'Hawkesworth's going to restart the Blackshirts and change his name by deed poll to Oswald Mosley?'

'Not quite. But it'll be enough to stir up a hornet's nest in this neck of the woods. He's going to insist on holding a parents' meeting to get support for his views about the kind of teachers the school should take on. And at the same meeting, he's hoping to win a vote to get Miss Delia Pettican removed from the governing committee.'

'When does he plan to do all this?'

'Any day now, he says. When he's got actual proof of the evil, heinous and inevitable consequences that follow from pursuing a so-called liberal line.'

'A reference to . . . ?' I half-asked.

She nodded. 'Felt a good bit like it. Especially as, the way he spoke, he made it sound like some Biblical plague that destroys any tribe that steps outside the straight and narrow.'

I finished my drink in a gulp. I needed to feel the burn of the scotch. Arabella looked at me with her round and ruddy marvellous eyes.

'I'll go upstairs and get down to the article.'

She made to get up. I stopped her with a kiss.

'No, stay down here. I'll be quiet.'

'Won't you want to watch something on the box? Not long to the News.'

'I'll see it later.'

'We can't see it later, can we? Aren't those children coming round? We'll have to be careful what we say in front of them. You know, that young whizz-kid and . . . ?'

I put my hand to my head. 'Hell, your Hawkesworth saga put them clean out of my mind. You're right, my darling. But they aren't due until after eight. That will give you time for some writing whilst I rustle up something to eat.'

'You rustle?' she beamed in amazement.

'Me rustle. You Jane,' I smirked back.

She kissed my smirk away. Somebody had to do it.

'You know something,' she eventually whispered to my ear. 'If they weren't coming, I think I might write my article . . . afterwards.'

'Afterwards . . . ?' my ear repeated.

'Afterwards.'

24

'But there'll be an afterwards after they're gone. A longer afterwards ...'

'How long is a longer afterwards ...?' she breathed.

'About a foot and a half.'

Suddenly she gave my cheek a playful (I think) slap and got up from the settee.

'Quit bragging, my darling,' she grinned and went out to get some papers from her car.

I was rearranging some stock in the window, trying to pretend the shop has a lightning quick turnover, when I saw it. I hadn't seen one for yonks, as, perhaps, Dorset's hills have inclined to kill the spirit of even the most sporting of its riders. I hastily replaced the Meccano Two Seater Sports car back on the top of its box, being sure to hide its price tag of £175, and watched with fascination as the riders dismounted from the tandem and rested it against the wall adjacent to the window. They didn't spot me. In the lamplight, I saw yuppy in the making take off his cycle clips, then grimace at what was obviously his girlfriend.

As they had ridden up, I had been somewhat amazed at her size, but now that she was standing next to her companion, she looked even more diminutive. I looked back at the bike. The pedals on one side were just visible and the rear one had blocks bolted to it, no doubt to accommodate her lack of leg length.

But unlike a lot of very small people, she was perfectly in proportion, so that, in isolation, one would not have been acutely conscious of her size. Just her discreet and rather fetching good looks.

I unlocked the door. 'Welcome to my second childhood,' I grinned.

He urged his girlfriend forward. 'This is Ella, Ella Eames. You know, I told you a bit about her.'

I shook her hand. 'Peter Marklin. But forget the Marklin bit.'

The boy proffered his own hand. 'Oh sorry, I've never told you my name, have I? Thorn. You know, like the prickle. But forget it. I hate that name. Every clever dick cracks the gag about my being the "thorn in their flesh" and all that stuff.'

'So ...?' I queried.

'Ah, yes, Tony,' he laughed. 'Tony's my name.' He indicated his girlfriend. 'And she doesn't like Ella, either.'

25

'I like "Lacky" worse,' she stated in a voice that was surprisingly mature.

I ushered them both inside and locked the shop door. 'Lacky?' I questioned.

'Lacky like elastic,' Tony explained. 'She is incredibly supple. Way-out things she can do with her body, you wouldn't believe.'

I changed the subject, just in case. As it turned out, I needn't have done. The way-out things she did were performed in public and wouldn't have shocked even Mary Whitehouse's grandmother.

'I like your tandem,' I observed. 'That yours, Tony?'

'No. Her dad's. He's a keep-fit fanatic and he forces her poor old mum to cycle with him all over the country on it. That is, when she's around . . .'

As I was about to ask my diminutive visitor what she really liked to be called, Arabella came through into the shop and introductions started all over again. But it was then that I found out. Arabella played my question for me.

The answer sounded like 'winner'.

'Winner?' I queried. 'Spelt with an "a" or an "er"?'

'Never spelt it. Don't suppose I'll ever have the need,' she replied quietly. 'I just like the sound of it, that's all. There should be a girl's name like that. Winner.'

I thought about it. It was quite a nice idea – that is, if your surname isn't Lot.

Tony took his girlfriend's hand. 'Just a private little name we use between us, that's all. I coined it when she won her first competition. "Winner" Eames. And it's stuck.' He winked. 'By the way, I spell it with an "a".'

'What competition was that?' Arabella asked.

Tony stood proudly next to his girlfriend. 'Oh, don't you know? Winna here is a gymnast. In fact, she's on her way to becoming the champion of Dorset. She's been on telly, has Winna.'

I could have kicked myself. I should have guessed from her diminutive size and even the way she moved and stood. It made my shuffle and stance only forgivable in a Methuselah.

'You've been in the *Western Gazette*, haven't you?' Arabella enthused. 'I should have recognized you. I've seen your picture and heard our sports editor rave about you.'

Winna blushed and turned away to look at some Schuco clock-

26

work cars arranged at the end of my counter. Tony waved his hand in a 'Why don't we all get on to another subject?' way. We obeyed the message.

'Well, feel free, you two. Have a good look around. Ask any questions you like and I'll try and fluff some kind of answer.'

I went behind the counter to a shelf where I keep my 'pending' items. Stuff reserved by customers or awaiting the mail. Any toys I've bought that need a little repair or renovation. That kind of thing. Mainly pre-war die-cast cars with snapped-off headlights or bumpers awaiting new white metal replacements or their perished and cracked tyres replaced. And sometimes, as on this day, the odd tinplate toy whose clockwork motors have jammed, broken their springs, fouled their cogs or lost their keys.

I picked up the box with the Bentley. 'By the way, Tony, there's the car you reserved.'

He joined me behind the counter.

'Great. Thanks. I can pay you now.' He reached in his pocket and drew out forty-five pounds in fivers. For the first time, I could read the words printed on the back of his sweatshirt. 'Sticks and stones may break my bones, but whips and chains excite me.' I imagined what my parents would have done to me if I had even dared to stutter that statement at his age, let alone have it blazoned across my back. I'd still be in the Chateau D'If.

As I popped the money in the till, Tony ferreted amongst the bits of a Minic Rolls-Royce, that were standing on the shelf.

'What's wrong with this?' he asked.

'Nothing,' I said. 'Once I've found a battered and broken Minic whose mainspring I can rescue to act as a transplant.'

He picked up the very basic but adequate motor mechanism and peered at it.

'Can I take this away?'

I frowned.

'Don't worry,' he went on. 'I'll bring it back. Mended, hopefully.'

I smiled. 'Don't tell me you're a whizz-kid with clockwork too?'

'Not me. No. But my father is. That's what he does all day. He sells and mends old clocks.' He grinned mischievously. 'Drives my mum crazy. There's not a room in the house without at least ten clocks. There's even a grandfather in the downstairs loo right now. She says at twelve o'clock, she might just as well be living inside Big Ben.' He held up the broken mechanism. 'So can I take it? He can probably mend it.'

I nodded. 'Why not? It would save me waiting for a Minic with a battered body.'

He pocketed the motor and went back to join his girlfriend, who seemed to be admiring a fairly rare boxed set of Dinky doll's furniture. (Yes, boys and girls, Dinky did make just a few things for the fairer sex.) I say 'seemed', because I had a definite feeling that Winna had been rather dragged to see my shop by Tony. It was nothing she actually said or didn't say. In fact, she expressed interest and curiosity about a lot of the toys. It's just that the 'eyes didn't have it'. And eyes don't lie. Hers were elsewhere, speaking of places that weren't my Toy Emporium.

I came over to her. 'See those little cracks.' I pointed to some hair lines on the very Art Deco wardrobe. 'Metal fatigue. Same with the dressing table. I haven't dared take them out of the box since I got them.'

She looked up at me with a rather incredulous expression. 'Then what good are they? No one will buy them, surely.'

'They'll sell. And quite quickly, I expect. Boxed sets always do. And you don't come across Dinky doll's furniture every day. Most of it has powdered into nothing. This little lot is in great condition compared to some I've seen.'

'But if you can't take it out of the box . . .'

'Doesn't worry a lot of collectors. They're funny people, Winna. Quite a few never ever take their finds out of the box. The magic, you see, is for the toys to remain just as they would have been originally – in the shop that was selling them.' I shrugged. 'Don't ask me why.'

Arabella put a hand on my shoulder. 'Don't say anymore, Peter,' she laughed, 'otherwise Tony and Winna will think they have chosen to spend their precious time off school in a nuthouse.'

'Not at all,' Tony chipped in with an air of authority. 'Every form of business has its quirks. It's the role of the enterprising business to capitalize on them. Now, I gather, in the City . . .'

'Now come on, Tony,' Winna interrupted, 'I'm sure Peter and Arabella don't want to listen to one of your lectures on what you've read in the back pages of your father's *Telegraph*.'

She ran her short but strong fingers through her thick chestnut hair and walked off to the cabinet containing my mint boxed fifties die-casts.

Tony raised his eyebrows and silently mouthed what I took to be 'She's in a funny mood.'

To cover the hiatus, I asked, 'Would anybody like a drink or anything?' I'd meant of the Coke, Pepsi, squash, milkshake variety, but Tony immediately answered, 'Thanks. If you're pouring, I'd love a scotch.'

I glanced at Arabella. She smirked at my discomfort and said, 'It's all right, Peter, I doubt if the police ask tandem riders to blow up balloons.' She turned to Winna. 'Same for you, or . . . ?'

The girl shook her head and blushed slightly. 'Not when I'm in training. But I'd love a Coke, if you've got it.'

I made to go into the kitchen, but Arabella stopped me. 'No, I'll get them, darling. You stay in case our friends have any questions. I wouldn't be able to answer them.'

'Can I come with you?' Winna suddenly asked.

'Of course. Come on in.' Arabella ushered her guest in front of me and for a reason I could only guess at, closed the door behind her.

Tony came and sat on the stool by my counter.

'Whew! She's been in a funny mood lately. Sorry about that.'

'That's all right. I hadn't noticed anything.'

'Getting nervy now the championship is getting nearer.'

'Understandable.'

'Yea. She's under such pressure from her father to do well. He does every sport under the sun – wind surfing, ordinary surfing, squash, competitive cycling. Used to do rugby too. How he finds time to run his garage business, I don't know. *And* he's got an old classic car he dotes on and won't let anybody touch.'

'Bit hard to live up to?'

'Very, I would imagine. I'm sort of glad my old man has never had any ambition in his life – except to live with his old clocks, that is. Leaves me a free hand.'

'I wonder who is the happier. Her dad or yours?'

'Dunno,' he said, with a certain lack of interest. His eager and all-seeing eyes scanned the shop.

'Any idea what all your stock is worth?'

I hesitated. We were off again. 'Not precisely, no.'

'Five thousand, ten thousand, fifty thousand?' he persisted.

29

I didn't want to sound obstructive, so I did a few mental (very mental) sums.

'Er . . . around your last figure, I suppose, right now. Maybe a little more. The amount's never static, goes up and down with sales and any discoveries I make.'

He picked up a model of HMS *Nelson*, made by 'T.M.' and twiddled the battleship's gun turrets round to face me. I almost put my hands up.

'What's your return on that investment, do you reckon? Five, ten, twenty, thirty . . . fifty per cent?'

'A hundred per cent,' I grinned.

He put down the ship, his face betraying how impressed he was. 'Now I can see why you're in this business.'

I felt a bit of a rat to have led him on.

'No, it's not quite what you think, Tony. I meant a hundred per cent, but not in money terms.'

He frowned.

'Human terms,' I explained. 'Hundred per cent satisfaction. Happiness. Contentment. Call it what you will.'

He looked disappointed. His toy entrepreneur had just turned into a sentimental schmuk. I went on.

'You see, Tony, I was in the rat race for years. In advertising. Where everything is counted in success or failure, percentages and profits, pounds and politics. And everyone thinks himself or herself a budding Trump, or Branson or Saatchi or Ogilvie. Or worse, on the creative side, a Hockney or Bacon or, at the very least, a David Bailey or Jeffrey Archer. Trouble is, none of them are. Worse. Most aren't even one per cent as good. They are just feeding their fictions off ham and ego. So, in the end, I got out. While I still had an ounce of soul left to feed my future.'

I stopped. 'Marklin on the Rat Race' can be a helluva bore – even to Marklin.

Tony came back to the counter. Much to my amazement, his face was now shining with enthusiasm once more.

'Great,' he pronounced. 'Great. Real cool to get out to do something you really like.'

'Cool, eh?'

'Sure. You love toys. I love figures.'

I smiled.

He winked. 'I go for those figures too. But I meant the numbers game. Profits, percentages, returns on capital . . .'

'I know you did.' Then I added, 'I admire your enthusiasm. Really.'

He sat back on the stool. 'You know, Peter,' he said with the mature earnestness of a Nigel Lawson explaining his latest budget on television, 'there shouldn't be a clash between doing what you want to do and making money.' He stopped, then asked surprisingly shyly, 'You don't think it's immoral to have money, do you?'

I laughed and patted him on the shoulder. 'Good Lord, no. Quite the reverse. I think it's immoral not to have money.'

He looked immensely relieved. 'So . . . we'd make a great team, you and I, wouldn't we?'

I hesitated. He went on. 'You look after the toy side, with me advising on the money side. That way, you can concentrate on what you really like, and I can get some practical experience of business whilst I'm still at school.'

I knew I was up against a wall. I just couldn't prick such a balloon of energy and enthusiasm.

'All right,' I said. 'Tell you what, Tony. You pop round some time next week and I'll give you one or two exercises to work on. Who knows – I may be missing a few tricks here and there.'

'You mean it?' he exclaimed, hardly believing his own ears.

I tipped my forelock. 'Scout's honour.'

He extended a hand. I shook it.

'Now, let's go inside for those drinks,' I said.

And so began my quite extraordinary days with a boy called Thorn.

It was long after our promised 'long afterwards'. Or seemed so. I guess it was Arabella's arm flopping across on to my chest that woke me up. In my somnolence, it felt like an RSJ falling off the top of the Eiffel Tower. After a few moments, I gingerly tried to remove it without waking the workman responsible, or is it workwoman? But my movement caused a grunt and then a 'What time is it?'

I performed a manual scan of my bedside table. The object of my search fell to the floor. In reaching over to pick up my watch, I pulled half the sheet off Arabella, who responded with the kindest of 'Do you minds?'

'Half past two,' I muttered.

'God,' she exclaimed and sat up on one elbow. In the moonlight

31

filtering through the gap between the curtains, she looked far too alluring for half past two, even though it was not long after the long afterwards.

'Can't you sleep?' she asked and saw my eyes eyeing her blue breast.

'Yes,' I replied, 'but not after an arm has fallen down on me out of the old night sky.'

'Whose arm?' she went on, as if there might be some dismembered person suspended above the house.

'Guess,' I said.

'Oh, her.' She forced a chuckle. 'Can't really get off somehow.'

'I thought you had several times. Or were you acting earlier?'

Unfair of me at that time of night. Or any time of day, come to think of it.

I saw the glint in her eyeballs as they were raised to the ceiling.

'Get off to *sleep*.' She sat up properly and didn't bother with the sheet.

'Worried about your article?'

She shook her head. 'No. That'll pass, I think.'

'Then what?'

'Oh, somehow, I can't get those two tonight out of my mind.'

'Tony and Winna? Yes. They aren't exactly your average downtown, down-the-line, Dorset schoolkids, are they?'

I rolled over towards her and she put an arm round my shoulder.

'But that's not the trouble. What worries me is that . . . they aren't really kids, I suppose. They seem to have skipped that bit and gone on to be . . .'

'. . . miniature adults? Yes, I felt that. They will probably regret it later, when the time for second childhood comes round. There's nothing to build on.'

She squeezed my shoulder – not too hard. Just to say 'Not everyone's like you.'

'They are both so serious about life,' she went on. 'You should have heard Ella in the kitchen. I tried to joke once or twice, but all I seemed to raise was a frown.'

'Well, she was talking about the love of her life all the time, wasn't she? Beams and parallel bars and all that paralyzing paraphernalia.'

'Not all the time.'

'Well, most, you said.'

'She did talk about other things now and again. She mentioned the school briefly. I was hoping she might have said something about the governors' row or the rumours about the teacher . . . but no. She just said everyone in the school had been very understanding about her . . . her ambitions and so on . . . and had let her use their gym when she wants it. That kind of thing.'

'Nice school,' I observed. 'Just a pity they've got Adolf Hitler as one of the governors.'

Arabella pulled her legs up to her chest and rested her head on her knees. Triangles never seemed so fascinating when I was studying geometry.

'She asked me a rather odd question at one point,' she mused. 'Right out of the blue. Didn't seem to connect with anything we had been saying.'

'What about?'

'It was more a case of "Who about?". She asked about us.'

'Us?'

'Yep.'

'Like, was she probing out whether we were going to get spliced some time, or what?'

Arabella sniggered into her kneecaps. 'Oh no, my love. She just asked whether the age difference made any . . .'

'. . . difference,' I helped.

She nodded.

'Difference to what?'

'She didn't say.'

'What did you say?'

'The usual stuff. That age didn't really matter, as long as a couple loved each other, had the same sort of ideals and interests in life, blah, blah, blah. And that, anyway, you weren't that much older than me.'

I coughed. 'Sixteen years, my love, is the whole of her lifetime.'

She ignored me and went on, 'And as long as I cut up your food very small, keep your bed-pan emptied and take you out regularly in your bath chair . . .'

She never finished, because this time the Eiffel Tower fell on top of her and not just one RSJ either. The whole caboodle.

When we at last surfaced for breath, she whispered, 'Don't you think it funny, though?'

'What?' I countered. 'Doing this again?'

She prised her lips away again, just enough to say, 'No,

dummy, her question. After all, she shouldn't have any worries. Tony is the same age as she is.'

'Maybe he takes pills and is really eighty-seven,' I chuckled. 'Would explain a lot of things, wouldn't it?'

Three

It dawned as the telly weatherman had prophesied. The sun was cracking the hedges before I had even given Bing his breakfast.

Soon after Arabella had Golfed off to her paper, I opened up shop. But instead of doing the *Independent* crossword as I often tried to do whilst waiting for customers, today I found I couldn't sit still. For a load of Tony Thorn's questions kept coming back to me. And I had to confess, he had some reason on his side. I *should* know more about my business than I do. I *should* be more analytical about what sells quickly and what doesn't. I shouldn't just rely on hunch and what toys appealed to me personally. I *should* be more conscious of my return on capital invested. Maybe I should even plan the layout of my shop, so that customers are inevitably led through to the items I really want to sell, like supermarket managers and planners do. Who knows, perhaps I should hold spring and autumn sales to clear slow-moving items, or buy cheap toys I wouldn't normally touch, just to add a come-on for the more impecunious or adolescent collector?

As my brain became more and more entangled in all the thousand and one ramifications of so-called 'scientific marketing', I became distinctly jumpy and unsettled. Suddenly, I could see bankruptcy staring me in the face, if I didn't take Tony's advice. An ignominious folding of the Toy Emporium. A pathetic and shameful future, living off the moral earnings of my beloved, until she too called the receivers in – to dismantle our relationship.

I'd just got to the bit where Marklin, now a lonely and embittered recluse, takes to the bottle, his days endless blurs, his weekends lost, his only friend a bum who looks uncannily like Ray Milland, when the shop bell clanged and brought me back to what passes as my reality.

35

No prizes for guessing who it was. Uncharacteristically, he *strode* up to my counter. Normally, he shambles.

''Morning,' Gus breezed. I don't think I've ever known him 'breeze' before, either.

I saluted. 'What's the big, Cheshire cat grin for, Gus?'

'Grass is green, sun is ris . . .' he began.

'Yea, yea,' I said, 'and I *know* where the boidies is.'

He sniffed. 'What's wrong with you this morning? Got out of bed the wrong side?' With a dirty chuckle, he added, 'Or were you thrown out?'

'Gus. My love life does not embrace in its repertoire the very muscular deviation of throwing one's partner in or out of bed. Maybe yours does.'

''Course,' he grinned and bent his arm. 'How do you think I got these muscles?'

'I dread to think,' I said.

He pointed towards the door. 'Well, aren't you even going to come out and look at it?'

I looked whither he was indicating, then clutched the counter. 'Good God,' I said, 'is that your latest test drive?'

He pulled down his sweater proudly. 'Right in one, old lad. Knew you'd like it. That's why I brought it round. Just up your street.'

Now the 'thing' parked outside wouldn't have been up anyone's street. Nose, maybe, but not street, What's more, I was surprised it could even get up one.

Biting my lip, I went outside with him. He posed by one wing. 'Big, isn't it?'

'Big,' I nodded. I didn't say 'big what?'

He tapped the bonnet. 'There's some paint on that. Not like today's rubbish. One squirt around by a ruddy robot.'

He was right there. There was some paint on it. I reckoned about four hundred coats. They were probably the only thing holding it together, besides prayer.

'Only done eighty-seven thousand,' he beamed.

I refrained from saying it had probably already run half a dozen other speedometers into the ground.

'Well, what do you think?'

I didn't tell him. I just said, 'Gus. They didn't make two-door Humber Pullmans.'

He pshawed. 'Don't be daft, old love. This 'ere car is living proof.'

'I don't think "living" is quite the right word, Gus.'

'What d'yer mean?'

I took him round the back of the huge black vehicle to the horizontally split tail-gate. I opened it up.

'Bloody marvellous amount of space in there, old son. Room for all me nets, fishing tackle, lobster pots and wotnot. Not like the Popular. Then you can fold the rear seat down too.'

He was about to climb in and do it, when I said, 'Gus, Humber never made a two-door estate car either.'

'Shows what little you know, doesn't it?'

He already had one leg raised, when I lowered it with, 'Gus. This was a hearse.'

For once, he was lost for words.

'That's why I said "living" was hardly the right word.'

When he could speak, he said, 'But 'earses don't have rear seats.'

'Not when they're hearses, Gus, no. Most people prefer to be buried lying down, rather than sitting up.'

'But . . .'

I put a calming hand on his hairy shoulder.

'Someone has converted it, see? Obviously taken out the old platform bit and the runners and put in the seat instead. After it had given up the ghost as a hearse, that is.'

He chewed his well-chewed lip. 'The man at the garage told me . . .'

'. . . a lie,' I interrupted. 'Garage salesmen are seldom heading the queue into heaven, Gus.'

He subsided down on to the tail-gate. 'Well, I'll be . . .'

I put my finger to my lips. 'Watch it, Gus. You don't know how many ghosts of the dear departed still haunt this decaying shell.'

He clenched his fist. 'When I take it back, I'll throttle that pansy poofter, who peddled me a load of rubbish about it being an estate car.'

'I wouldn't do that, Gus. I would just forget it and go to a more reputable garage next time.'

'Like who, clever dick? And remember, I don't want no Volkswagens or anything like yours. Constant phut-phutting from behind the rear seat would drive me round the bend. Ain't natural to have an engine at the back.'

I suddenly remembered what Tony had told me.

'Heard about a garage last night that might do you. That whizz-kid schoolboy I told you about came around with his girlfriend and, apparently, her dad owns a garage and he's a classic car nut as well. So he might be interested in your old Popular and do you a good exchange for something decent.'

Gus thought for a minute. 'What's the name of his place then?' He'd got me.

'I don't know. But the girl's name is Eames, if that's any help.'

'Eames ... Eames ... yea ... come to think of it, there's a garage called Eames, as you come down into Swanage from Corfe. On the left it is. Never called in, 'cos their petrol costs an arm and a leg.'

As he spoke, I vaguely remembered it. Quite a smart place, with one of those forecourts that funnel you into a car-wash.

'Worth a try,' I said. I patted the tail-gate, then added, 'You should keep your Popular and off-load this on to your latest.'

'What d'yer mean? She doesn't drive.'

'What a pity,' I grinned. 'Then you could have had "His" and "Hearse".'

I only missed his fist by a whisker.

Nothing of note happened in the afternoon – unless you call the sale of a Britain's Bren Gun Carrier (unboxed) for £45 a headliner – and by early evening I was itching for Arabella to be home, so that my intellectually stimulating conversations with Bing could be brought to an end. But following the law that fellow Sod enacted, she wasn't home till past eight, a good hour or so later than normal.

I poured her a glass of wine from the Sauterne I had started on my ownio.

'Bang goes the latest Bond,' I said.

'Bond usually goes bang,' she smiled, knowing full well what I meant.

'No, I mean, by the time we've caught the ferry to Bournemouth, it will have started.'

'We can go tomorrow. It will still be running. It's held over for another week anyway.'

I sat back on my chair. 'Was rather looking forward to it. Haven't seen a Bond picture in the cinema for yonks. They're lousy on television because you haven't got the scale of the big

38

screen and all that stereophonic sound to fool you into thinking they've got any content worth a damn.'

She mimed taking notes with a pencil. 'May I quote you, Mr Marklin?'

'You may quote me, Miss Trench.'

She offered me the imaginary pad and pencil. 'Now, would you like to take down some notes?'

'Only if it's something newsworthy.'

'It's newsworthy enough for the *Western Gazette*. That's why I was late. I had to rush over to Manners Memorial School at the last minute to interview the headmaster.'

I put down my glass and leaned towards her.

'Ah, so the word is at last out, is it? Is the truth as dramatic as the rumours running round those mums?'

'That's not why I had to go. It was about something entirely different.'

'The headmaster is really a woman in drag . . .?' I hesitated, then added, 'Come to think of it, can a woman ever be in drag?'

She sipped her wine. 'Do you want to know or not?'

'Want to know.'

'They've had a burglary.'

'Burglary? What was taken? Usual school stuff? Silver cups, plaques . . .?'

She shook her head.

'Remember the Ethiopian Jumble Sale?'

'Of course. Opened by the mayor and that Page Three trembler.'

'Well, all the proceeds have been stolen. A cool eight hundred and thirty-two pounds.'

'Now, no doubt, a *hot* eight hundred and thirty-two pounds.' I got up from my chair. 'When did this happen?'

'Last night, apparently. Some time between eight in the evening when the caretaker locked up and seven this morning when ditto opened up again.'

'I'm surprised the takings weren't banked already.'

'I asked the Headmaster that. He said he expected a few more cheques to come in, 'that various parents had promised', and was waiting for them before he banked the lot.'

'Did he say where the money had been kept meantime?'

'In a small safe that lives in a cupboard in his room. I asked to see it, but he said the police had taken it away for examination.'

'Did it have a combination lock?'

'I believe so.'

'Was his room locked?'

'Apparently not. He says he has nothing else much of value in his room, so he doesn't usually bother locking it. He regrets it now.'

I thought for a minute. 'And the caretaker? Didn't he hear or see anything during the night or doesn't he live on the premises?'

'He lives in an annexe. Man called Boxall. Andy Boxall. I saw him too.'

'What was he like?'

'Like . . . a caretaker, I suppose. Around sixty or so. Smallish. Neat. Looked honest enough.'

'Married?'

'No. He lives on his own. Widower, I think.'

I sighed. 'He won't be too popular right now with the Headmaster. Or the governors, for that matter. Caretakers, after all, are meant to take care. By the way, how did the burglars gain entry?'

'No one knows. It's a complete mystery, according to the Headmaster. Nothing seems to have been forced or broken into. No keys have been stolen recently, or even lost. He says the police are baffled by it too.'

'Inside job, perhaps. Who knows, your smallish, neat caretaker may have been Raffles in his youth . . .?' I stopped, because I suddenly realized what was happening. I was allowing myself to get too interested in crime again, albeit at a fairly trivial level. Such weakness had cost me dear in recent years and I had no intention of repeating past and almost fatal mistakes.

'Anyway,' I went on, 'thank God it's got nothing to do with me.'

This time Arabella sighed. 'Well, it still has with me, unfortunately.'

'How so?'

'In the morning, I've got to interview the dear lady governor Hawkesworth so hates. I tried to get hold of her today, but she was off fossil-hunting somewhere in the Charmouth area. Apparently, that's her hobby. The question of the burglary is bound to come up while I'm with her. No doubt, Hawkesworth will use it as yet another example of a too liberal and lax management at the school. So I may have to see him again as well. Hey ho.'

40

'Hey ho and off to work you go,' I Disneyed, then offered her some more wine, which she declined.

'We ought to eat.' Arabella got up to go into the kitchen. I put my hand on her arm.

'Like to eat out?'

She put on her knock-me-down-with-a-feather act.

'Hey, what's got into you? When we go to a restaurant, it's usually only because I've dragged you.'

'Don't know. Just thought, as we aren't now going to Bond, you might still like a change. Get your mind off your work and all that Manners School brouhaha. Nothing like good food to make fossil-hunters and Hitlers instantly forgettable. Tip I got from Churchill.'

She took my hand and squeezed it nicely.

'Okay. You're on, Winston. Where shall we go?'

'Well, Chartwell is too far, so we'll make it the Swan's Down at Tolpuddle.'

'Bit pricey, isn't it?'

I threw my arms in the air. 'Who cares, Clemmie! Its beauty and tranquillity weave the backcloth against which the world's greatest dishes take on new meaning. Says so in their brochure.'

She grimaced. 'How do you know?'

Laughing, I replied,' I wrote it when I was in advertising. The Swan's Down was our smallest client. We only took it on because we got great food every time we had a meeting.'

So off we innocently trotted. Hell, how outrageously misleading advertising can prove to be, even when you've written it yourself.

It started well. Despite the yucky copy in their brochure, the Swan's Down is quite a place. All beams and thatch, long and low, and if you don't hit your head, rather magical. Americans lap it up.

So, after a couple of opening drinks and a nice dry foil for our first course – a combination of fish and liver taramasalata that melts on the fork, let alone in the mouth – Arabella and I had shed a couple of years or so and were right back where we had started. Sort of amazed at our luck at finding each other in this trampled and trampling world and holding tentative hands across the table, foot whispering naughty things to foot below. The waiter had been forced to repeat himself on at least two occasions

41

already during the meal and was, no doubt, busy rehearsing in the kitchen to double do so again.

However, as I have hinted, this idyll was not to last. Any moment, that brochure was about to be laid at the door of the Advertising Standards Authority. For, just after the waiter had cleared away our first course, I saw Arabella's usually mobile face freeze.

'What's the matter?' I asked.

'Don't look round,' she Alec Douglas Humed under her breath.

My lips didn't move either. 'Why?' I exhaled.

'It's him,' she smiled fixedly.

'Him who?' I now knew why ventriloquists never say things like that. I made to look round. She shook her head and started to hum the Horst Wessel song. I didn't even know she knew it.

''Awkesworth?' I whispered.

She raised her eyebrows and then extended her arm. I was somewhat bemused and about to shake it, when it was shaken for me and a voice boomed from behind me.

'Ah. The young lady from the *Western Gazette*, if I'm not mistaken.'

Now I guessed I could look round. What I saw was rather different from what I had been expecting. For a start, he wasn't tall. About five nine in his, no doubt, khaki socks. No colonel moustache, either. Florid, maybe, but shinily clean shaven. And recently too, I could detect. He must have taken a bath in after-shave and splashed on water. Probably he himself couldn't smell it, because his nose, his most prominent feature, looked as if it had been broken at some time before booze had done its best to puff it out to hide the kink.

He totally ignored me and went on, 'Delightful place this, isn't it?' followed by a question I thought was never asked outside comedy programmes, 'Do you come here often?'

I couldn't resist it. 'Only in the mating season,' I said, getting up.

He looked surprised, as if, up to then, he'd thought Arabella was dining with a corpse.

'Have we met?' he smiled, extending a hand.

'Not outside reported speech, no,' I smiled back and shook what I'd been offered.

'Hawkesworth, Colonel Hawkesworth.'

'Marklin, Peter.'

He turned back to Arabella. 'Well, Miss . . . er . . . er . . .'

I came to his aid. 'Trench. Arabella Trench. As in "trench warfare". Went down like a lead balloon.

'Well, Miss Trench, I hope I'm not interrupting your . . . er . . . evening.'

I noticed upon what his rather bloodshot eyes were settling. I cursed Arabella's dress designer. He would never have cut it that low if he'd known.

'No, that's . . . all right,' Arabella lied, and having noticed his eyes too, inclined further back on her chair. In response, he leaned forward and said, 'We will be meeting again, anyway, Miss Trench, in your professional capacity, as I prophesied to you, but perhaps, you and . . .' he turned to me, '. . . Mr . . . er . . . er . . . er . . .'

I let him 'er'. After all, it's only human.

'Marklin,' Arabella laughed. 'Peter Marklin.'

'Perhaps you two might like to join me for coffee and perhaps a drink, before you leave. I'm only having two courses, so I won't be keeping you.'

Arabella and I played 'snap', both indicating our watches.

'Love to, Colonel, but . . .' she began, then floundered. I put her back in the water.

'. . . we're expecting a phone call from New York. Coming through at ten thirty,' I beamed. 'Got to be home for it. American chappie wants some old toys from me. Tanks, guns, Bren gun carriers, toy soldiers, stuff like that. Daren't miss a sale. Sorry, old boy.'

He screwed up his eyes, as he tried to understand what the hell I was wittering on about.

'Oh, yes, well then. Another time, perhaps.'

He gave a slight bow, more to see Arabella's boobs, I guess, than as a mark of respect, then made off to his own table.

'Whew.' I wiped my brow with my serviette. 'Saved by the bell, dring, dring.'

'Thank God for that,' Arabella grinned. 'Pompous, pushy sod.'

I jerked my head towards the window. 'Funny – coming to a place like this to eat alone.'

'He's been divorced years, I gather. Though I've heard he's been through quite a list of ladies since.'

'The Colonel a ladies' man?' I said in considerable disbelief.

43

'So the gossip goes. The editor warned me before I interviewed him, that he might well make overtures to *me*.'

'Did he?' I frowned.

She held my hand once more.

'No, Marklin, Peter.'

I took mock umbrage. 'Why on earth not?'

She raised her lovely eyes to the ceiling. 'You're getting more like Gus every day,' she sighed.

'Rubbish,' I countered. 'My sweaters don't smell of fish.'

'They do now,' she chuckled, pointing to a daub of pink down my Marks and Sparks best. 'You've been a trifle careless with your taramasolata . . .'

Four

Thursday dawned as Indian as the previous days. I was tempted to play truant from the shop and laze around on the beach for the morning, but conscience pricked – what's more, Tony Thorn pricked. I knew he wouldn't have approved.

It was a slow morning. Two gawpers and touchers and a man with a stutter who bought a mint boxed 'Avengers' set by Corgi. I was glad when twelve thirty didn't ding and I could take a stroll in the sunshine and maybe, share a 'jar' (that's a collective plural) with Gus; that is, if he wasn't out test-driving some other strange vehicle – like a white estate car that was really an ambulance.

I was just crossing the road to get to the sea lane, when I was startled by a medley played on a car horn. I whipped round, expecting it to be you know who. But no, it was a Golf convertible, with a rather delicious short-haired girl at the wheel. She slewed to a stop beside me.

'Don't you know it's anti-social to blare your horn like that in a sleepy village like this?' I asked, with some severity.

'Sorry, officer,' she grinned. 'I'll come quietly.'

'Should have come quietly before,' I reminded her.

She reached across the open car and grabbed my arm.

'Now, listen, darling, I haven't really got time right now for gags. I've got to get back to the paper.'

'Just dropped by on your way back from the Colonel's favourite lady governor? Must have been a long interview.'

She shook her head. 'No, I finished with Delia Pettican some time ago.'

'Then where've you been since?'

'That's what I've just dropped by to tell you. I thought you would like to know, so you're prepared if that boy Tony gets in touch.'

'Okay, wingèd messenger. Give.'

'Headmaster called a press conference, didn't he?' she raised her elegant eyebrows.

I sighed. 'Oh God, the rumours aren't true, are they?' Then I brightened. 'Or maybe, has he found the missing money? Hidden behind a cistern in the girls' lavatory, I bet.' I crouched down (or is it Grouched?) and pulled at an imaginary cigar. 'If so, what was he doing in the girls' loo? You have sixty seconds to answer . . .'

She took the cigar out of my mouth, broke it and threw it on the ground.

'Now be sensible,' she said. 'Because I think the proverbial has just hit the fan at Manners School.'

'Aids?' I said, then nervously looked up the street, in case anybody heard me. 'Aids?' I then repeated in a whisper.

'Yes. He said he called the Press in so that the real facts could be known, before they were amplified by rumour.'

'Hell. I can imagine what's going to happen now. The school will be like Dawson City tomorrow morning. Not a pupil in sight.'

'That's what the Headmaster is trying to obviate. The teacher in question has been suspended. A fellow called Alistair Folland, apparently.'

'He had all the blood tests?'

'Yes. No doubt, it would seem, about the diagnosis.'

'What did he teach?'

'French and, hostage to fortune, Scripture.'

'God,' I said, 'of all subjects. Prejudice will have a field day.'

She nodded. 'I know. But there's more and it doesn't get better. Folland seems to have been quite an athlete in his university days. Ran and rowed for his college. All that bit. So he was the swimming and tennis coach at the school . . .'

' . . . in close physical contact with the kids.'

'Exactly. I saw his photograph taken at the Inter School swimming gala. He's quite the body beautiful. Like something out of "Muscle Beach".'

'I wonder if he is now.' I patted her arm. 'Thanks for coming over and ruining my lunch-time tipple.'

'Off to see Gus?'

'To see if he's in. But I'd rather down one with you.'

She looked at her watch. 'Wish I could. But I daren't. Got to write up all my notes.'

'But you've got to eat.'

'I'll grab a sandwich. Eat it in the office, with a plastic coffee.'

She started up the Golf. 'You know, I feel rather sorry for that Headmaster. First the burglary, now this . . .'

'I wonder what the third thing will be.'

She frowned.

'Disasters are often three-packed, aren't they?'

She crossed her fingers.

I crossed mine and kept them that way, until the vw was lost to sight.

Didn't do much good, as it turned out.

There was no car (of any description) outside Gus's place. And no Gus inside. I kicked my heels for ten minutes or so by pumping up the tyres of my 1966 Daimler V8 that I keep in one of Gus's barns and generally flicking dust off its fairly recent respray. I don't use it often. Just enough to keep the moths out and the engine from seizing. For its work-horse days are long over and it drinks enough petrol to double the standard of living in every Gulf state. I bought it for a song a good few years back, when the super smooth and rounded Jaguar shape was regarded as distinctly old hat compared with the contemporary vogue for sharp creases, straight lines and, pardon me, I'm yawning again.

As I locked the barn up again, I thought of Tony Thorn. I guessed my old car, at least, would be one purchase of mine of which he'd approve. For its return on capital invested wasn't too bad, judging by the 'Collectors Car' adverts at the back of the *Sunday Times*. I wondered what he would think of the Aids announcement. I imagined it wouldn't be long before I knew. I expected hourly to get a call from him to set up our next meeting, for I couldn't see him passing up an invitation to get involved, albeit on the fringes, with my business – or any business, for that matter.

Somehow, I had the feeling he wouldn't be too fazed by the tragic affair. He would probably dismiss it in a few words, as one of those things that, as our transatlantic friends say, 'rolls down the pike' occasionally and if you know how to take the necessary evasive action, needn't touch you, either physically or, maybe, even emotionally. For if Tony was anything, he was single minded. And where he was looking, human suffering had a low profile.

His girlfriend, Winna, I reckoned might be a little more concerned. But only 'might'. For after all, she had a million other
pressures on her right then to worry too much about a teacher
stricken down by the dread disease. That is, unless she believed
all the mumbo-jumbo about Aids being transmitted by touch or
breath, or even pure proximity. But she seemed too intelligent to
embrace such loony and unscientific ideas. As, indeed, did Tony.
But then, today's brood of kids can often be more analytical and
canny than their parents. I just hoped Tony and Winna's families
didn't embrace the 'loo-seat' lunacy and try to infect their off-
spring with the same unfounded phobias. But a degree of hys-
teria would, no doubt, surface now amongst some of the parents,
fanned by at least one of the school governors, bless his little
khaki socks.

Gus, of course, didn't turn up until I'd given him up. I was
half-way back along the sea lane to draw a pint at the pub, when I
met him – or rather, his Popular. To my amazement, I was glad to
see the old upright shape again (the car, I mean). For I suddenly
realized that rattle bucket was as much a part of Gus as his bushy
eyebrows, his marine sweater, his Incredible Hulk hands and
assorted grunts and groans.

'Lifting elbow time?' he grinned out of the car window.

'Could be, Gus, could be.' I pointed at the Ford. 'Surprised to
see you still in it. Didn't that Eames fellow come up with anything
to your liking?'

He sniffed. 'Got plenty there, but all a bit pricey.'

'So, no go?'

'Don't know about that. Eames said he might have something
in later in the week. An 'illman H'Avenger.'

I patted the bonnet and instantly regretted it. Instead of patting, I should have tried frying an egg. I sucked my third degree
burns.

'So he's interested in this thing?'

Gus sniffed again. 'It's not a thing. You don't call that old
Daimler of yours a thing, so don't call this.'

'Her or him?' I grinned.

'Shut up,' he said. 'Yes, he'll do a deal, he said. But I'll believe it
when I hear it. He's a bit of a strange one, that Eames.'

'Strange one?' I queried. 'I thought he was the all muscle, all
sports, all hero type. Boardsailing champion and all that.'

'Oh, he's got muscles all right. Built like a brick sh . . .'

48

'Yes, thank you, Gus, I've got the picture. So why is he strange?'

'Not strange looking, you berk. Except p'raps his eyes. They're a bit sunk in his face and sort of stare at you, like. No, it's his manner, old son. Bit strong. I heard him tell off one of his mechanics for getting a lady customer's seat dirty.'

'She shouldn't have sat on him,' I laughed. Gus ignored me. Quite right.

'Tore him off a regular strip, he did. Didn't you say Eames had a daughter? Wouldn't want to be in her shoes. One step out of line and wallop, I'd imagine.'

Gus slapped the sill of his door. The whole car rocked. Then he graunched into gear. 'Still, wasting good tippling time, sitting here talking to you. I'll put the car away and see you up there.'

And with that he was gone.

I walked on up to the pub, my mind fancying what I'd be like if I had any children. By the time I was in the bar, I had convinced myself I'd be ruddy marvellous – a parent for the whole of man and woman-kind to emulate and envy. Indian winters do that to the brain, or so Gus maintained later, after more than a few Heinekens, 'Boil every ounce of common sense out of you, old son.' Maybe he's right, blast him.

At five thirty on the dot, what I had been expecting, happened. Tony Thorn turned up.

'I thought I'd leave it until you'd shut up shop,' he announced, when I had unslipped the door bolt I'd only that second slipped.

'On the dot,' I smiled and ushered him over to the counter. When he had sat down and before he could start his 'Young Businessman of the Year' act, I remembered, 'I hear there's a bit of drama over at your school.'

He looked at me, then said, somewhat guardedly, 'What have you heard?'

'Oh, not very much. Arabella attended your Headmaster's Press conference this morning.'

'Oh, that,' he said, as if Aids could ever be an 'Oh, that.' 'The old Head's got his knickers in a twist over Mr Folland.'

'Shouldn't he have?'

Tony shrugged. 'Not really. Every kid in the school has always known what Mr Folland is like. It's never worried us what his . . . bent is. It might have done, I suppose, if he had ever shown any

49

signs of ... you know ... getting too friendly with any of the boys, but he never has. Kept his personal life right out of the school.'

'So you're not worried about his having contracted Aids, then?'

He took a breath. 'Me? Worried? No. Sorry, more like. He's a nice chap, Mr Folland. Everyone enjoys his lessons. He makes French interesting, sort of come alive, you know.'

I didn't know, actually, but could imagine. When I was at school, teachers seemed to stun subjects to death the instant they raised a piece of chalk.

'So you'll miss him?'

'Yea. S'pose so. He was ruddy good at sports too.' He looked at me hard. 'Tell me, Peter. Has anyone ever recovered from Aids? My dad says it's always a death sentence, sooner or later. And those telly films ... God, they scare you half to death on their own, don't they? Winna can't bear to watch them any more. She reaches for the remote control the second she sees one coming.'

'They're meant to scare people, Tony. Scare you into being careful.'

Tony sat back on his stool. 'Well, I *am* careful, aren't I? I've never taken drugs and never will. So I'm not likely to share a needle. And when I'm with Ella, I always ...' He stopped suddenly and blushed. 'Well, you know.'

This time I did know and I nodded to show him his secret was safe with me.

'In answer to your question,' I said, to get over his embarrassment, 'there's no known cure for Aids yet. Doesn't mean there won't be one, though. They're working like stink to find a vaccine right now.'

'Could be years, though, couldn't it? They haven't found a cure for cancer yet and that's been around for ever.'

He had a point. I was now regretting having raised the brouhaha at Manners School at all.

'Big meeting tomorrow. We're all being given the afternoon off. Can I come round and watch what kind of customer comes in?'

'All right. But some afternoons, no kind of customer comes in.'

'So I'll ask you some questions, make notes on your stock and start on a bit of analysis.'

'What's the meeting?' I asked, anticipating the answer.

'Parents' meeting.' He cocked his head and put on a Lord Snooty voice. 'Old Fuddy-duddy's called it.'

'Colonel Hawkesworth?'

'Who else? Do you know about him, then?'

'Met him the other night, that's all. In a restaurant. Ruined my appetite.'

'We all reckon he's only doing it to try to get rid of old Miss Pettican. I'll be sorry if he succeeds. She is a nice old biddy. She's been responsible for a lot of good things at the school – like Adventure Camps in the holidays and sailing lessons in school time. And she changed old Hawkesworth's choice of caterer, so that our meals are now half eatable.'

I laughed. My stomach has never forgiven my school cooks. And I still can't look a piece of liver in the face.

'So you don't want to see her go?'

He shook his young head. 'Not on your life. She gives the Headmaster a bit of backbone in standing up to the Colonel. Without her, he's a bit of a spineless creature. Nice enough, but weak. Besides, she's always gone out of her way to help Winna. They like each other a lot.'

I didn't comment. 'What do you think will be the result of the parents' meeting?'

'A vote, of course. Maybe several. On how the school should be run, I guess. Fuddy-duddy will work on the parents' emotions. I can hear him doing it. And bingo, the school curriculum will go back a hundred years, and the whole relaxed style of the school will disappear. If it happens, it's enough to kill Miss Pettican. Her grandfather founded the school, you know.'

'So I've heard. But maybe it won't work out like that. Enough sensible parents . . .'

He suddenly reached into his pocket and withdrew what I saw was the 'Minic' motor he had taken home to his father to be mended.

'Got a key?' he asked. I handed him one from my shelf. He applied it to the mechanism and started to turn.

'It'll be like this,' he grimaced. 'The Colonel will wind the meeting up and it'll all happen. Go like clockwork. You mark my words.'

I marked them. A reluctant ten out of ten.

Arabella was late again, as I had rather expected. Tony had gone by the time she staggered in, for which I was quite grateful. For he'd given me quite a grilling on the assignment I had given him – compare and analyze my monthly mail-order stock lists over the five years I'd been in business, to spot the quick and slow movers and see what, if any, changes I'd made over that time in the kind of items I was offering. In addition, he himself suggested he should plot a graph of the increases in my prices and compare it with one for inflation and another for the rise in the Stock Market. Who was I to argue? So he left around seven, clutching a mass of papers and promising to let me have some answers early the next week.

'No hurry,' I said.

'How did Tony go?' Arabella asked, as I pressed a cooling glass of white wine into her lovely but sticky hand.

'Fine,' I said. 'Like clockwork. He even got his dad to mend that broken Minic motor.'

She smiled. 'I can see you will be taking a partner soon.'

I kissed her on the equally sticky forehead. 'I've got one.'

She laughed. 'I don't mean a sleeping partner.'

'Nor do I.' I gulped, rather than sipped my wine, as the evening temperature was still pretending it was high summer. 'How was your day? Tony told me Hawkesworth is holding a Nuremberg Rally tomorrow. Armbands will be worn.'

She ran her fingers through her short hair. It was too damp and hot to bounce back. 'I know. The editor has told me to attend and pretend to be a parent. Do I look like a parent?'

'Sure,' I grinned. 'I found you on one of my New Guinea expeditions. Married you in a mud hut when you were thirteen. Had a baby before you were even back in England. He's now ten and is in Mr Folland's class, or what was Mr Folland's class.'

'Oh, thanks. I wondered what I was going to say.'

'Any time. Now, this Delia Pettican. What was she like when you interviewed her? Tony told me he quite likes her. So does Winna, apparently. Miss Pettican seems to have a soft spot for her.'

She looked across at me. 'Don't you fall for old Hawkesworth's hints and innuendoes about her.'

'I'm not. Really. But it sounds as if you like her too.'

'I do. I sort of expected a kind of Margaret Rutherford or the latest Miss Marple actress. But not a bit of it. She's a bustling, busy, lithe sort of lady. Sinewy rather than slim, if you know what I mean.'

'Lauren Bacall, *vieille*.'

'*Exactement*,' she winced. 'And just as downright and forthright as Bacall is, but without getting up your nose at all. There's no doubt she holds fairly liberal views, especially about education, but they aren't loony left or anything. Not half as extreme, as the Colonel's right-wing blather.'

'Thank the Lord for that. You interviewed her before this Aids news broke, though, didn't you?'

'Yes. But I think I know what her reaction will be.'

'What?'

'That you wouldn't stop employing heterosexual teachers just because they might catch VD.'

I thought for a second. 'But it's not quite the same. VD isn't fatal. Least, not any more.'

'Fatality doesn't determine morality, surely?'

'No. But it sure as hell puts a different complexion on things.'

'Complexions are superficial.'

There was no answer to that.

'Sounds as if you discussed the subject of teacher choice, then?'

She finished the last of her wine. 'Yes. She said she knew what all the fuss was about and, if she had the choice all over again, she would still appoint a homosexual, if he or she were the right person for the job. She said her grandfather had set up the school on liberal principles. And that he had once taken on a divorced teacher who was known to have an illegitimate child, when no other school in the West Country would have him. She said, a couple of years back she herself had recommended a black applicant for the post of science teacher, but that time, the Headmaster had sided with the Colonel and the idea had been squashed. I don't think she reckons the Headmaster much. I got the impression she thinks he's a bit of a weed.'

'Tony intimated the same. You've met him. What do you think?'

'Don't know really. Don't forget that the times I've seen him, he's been worried sick with his problems. First the burglary. Now Aids. Not been his autumn.'

'No sign yet of the money, I suppose?'

'As far as I can gather, no one even knows how the money was stolen, let alone where it's gone.'

She got up. 'Anyway, let's forget about Manners School. I've had enough for today.'

She held out a hand and prised me from my chair. 'Before we settle down, let's go for a walk along the beach. I feel I need some fresh air.'

'In the gloamin'. That would be nice.'

She relinquished my hand. 'Let me go upstairs for a second and take my make-up off.'

'Shall I come with you?'

She pulled a school ma'm frown. 'No, Mr Marklin. My make-up is the only thing I plan to take off . . . that is, right now.'

So we gloamed. Everybody should have a Studland Beach. Then psychiatrists could pack up their couches and go home.

Next morning, Friday, dawned sunny, but the TV weatherman had warned that the Indian summer was about to be a British autumn again. 'Take your umbrella, if you're going out in the afternoon,' he'd advised. 'Thundery showers are spreading up from France and will reach southern coastal areas soon after midday.' So in case he was twelve hours out, I'd put the top up on my Beetle before I had gone to bed the night before. Not a shrewd move, romance-wise, though. Arabella was in bed and in the land of Nod by the time I had finished. I didn't blame her though. Just the weatherman.

I had hardly finished going through my mail and then packing up a couple of parcels to satisfy a couple of postal orders (an Italian Mercury Fiat airliner of the early fifties and a 'Minic' steamroller), when I was alarmed by the vigorous shaking of my still bolted shop door. For a second, I thought the thunder had come early. But it was the next worse thing – Gus. I let him in.

'Couldn't sleep?' I muttered, as I ushered him forward.

He took me literally. 'No. Slept like a baby.'

I've heard Gus sleep. No baby has ever sounded like that. Human, that is.

'So what's on your beautifully rested mind, Gus? Let me guess. You want me to come fishing with you. Or chauffeur you somewhere. Or you'd like to borrow some readies until the banks are open. Or maybe your cottage is on fire again?' (A couple of weeks back, Gus had set the dark and forbidding cupboard under the stairs alight, by striking a match to look for his wartime gas mask. I had never got round to asking him why he suddenly needed that gas mask. Still, knowing the state of his larder, it wasn't too hard to make one guess.)

'Wrong, wrong, wrong, wrong, old son. Just nipped over to see if you would like a ride to Swanage with me.'

I should have known.

'Going to see that H'Avenger?'

'Yep. Thought as how you might like to come with me.'

'Afraid to deal with steely eyed muscle-bound Eames on your own, eh?'

He ran his huge hand along the counter. 'Nothing of the sort, you silly sod. Just thought you might give the car the old once-over, seeing as how you know a bit more about the things than I do.' He looked up. 'Won't take long. Then you can play with your tin-pot toys all the rest of the ruddy day.'

I had to go, didn't I? Seeing as how he'd asked me so nicely.

The Avenger wasn't in the showroom. It was round the back. And I could see why when I clapped eyes on it. Not that it was rusty. It wasn't. Or, at least, not shoutingly so. In fact, the blue paintwork shone in the last of the weatherman's sun. Nor was the interior ripped or ravaged. The plastic seats looked as bad as new. It was just the whole air of the vehicle that let it down.

'Well, what d'yer think?' Gus beamed. 'Looks nice and tidy, doesn't it?'

'Certainly tidy, Gus.' I walked round it twice and felt I was at a funeral.

'Now. Come on, old son,' he urged. 'Before ruddy Eames surfaces and starts his sales talk.'

I kicked a tyre. All I did was hurt my foot.

'How much is it?' I ventured.

'Only a couple of hundred more than me Popular.'

I opened the driver's door. You needed Gus's gas mask to filter out the stale smell of damp and decay. I did not need to get in.

'Well. Gus. I hate to say it, but I'd stick with your old Ford.'

Gus looked as if his crest had not only fallen, but was smashed to smithereens.

'Why on earth . . . ?' He pointed through the still open door. 'See, it's got an 'eater.'

I closed the door. It sounded like a tin-can on the tail of a wedding car.

'Gus, heaters aren't the be-all and end-all of the art of choosing a motor car. Besides, every modern vehicle has a heater.'

Gus was about to come back, when a 'How do you like it, Mr Tribble?' boomed out. I turned round and instantly saw what Gus had meant about Eames. It wasn't that he was at least six feet four or built like that specialized house to which Gus tends to allude. It was his manner. I had a feeling that if Gus didn't buy that Avenger, we might be in a spot of trouble. No wonder he had wanted me with him, the sod.

'This 'ere's me friend,' Gus offered. 'Come to have a dekko too.'

I extended my hand like a fool. 'Marklin. Peter Marklin.' The 'M' bit was said between my teeth, before I unclasped and tried to force some blood back into my fingers.

'Well, what's your "dekko" say, Mr Marklin. Smart, isn't she? Especially for her age.'

I didn't comment. After all, it was Gus's decision, not mine. Unfortunately, that detached attitude lasted all of a second and a half, as Gus came up with, 'I'm leaving it all to me friend. Knows more about cars than I do.'

Eames turned his deep-set eyes in my direction.

'Car buff, Mr Marklin?'

'Not exactly.' I could have killed Gus. And a second time when he said, 'Got an old classic car, he has.'

Eames half-shut his eyes against the sun.

'Really, and what would that be, Mr Marklin? I've got a 1948 Jaguar 3½ litre saloon myself. I'll show it to you later, if you like.'

'Daimler,' Gus took the word right out of my mouth. 'The V8 thing that looks like a Jag. Got a Dinky toy of it too in his shop.'

I saw Eames' eyes switch from interest to disdain. So much for macho-me. A grown man with Dinky toys.

'In your *shop*?' He thought for a second. 'You wouldn't be the owner of that old toy place in Studland, would you? My daughter told me about it the other night. I think she and Tony Thorn visited you, didn't they?'

I nodded. 'They did.'

'My daughter very much liked your . . . er . . . girlfriend, is it?'

'Arabella,' I replied, leaving her designation open.

'Ah, how interesting,' he said. A phrase I've found that's never used except to cover complete indifference.

He patted the Hillman's roof. 'Would you like a test run? I can go into the office and get the keys . . .'

I looked at Gus. Gus looked at me. By the time we looked back, Eames' attention seemed to have been diverted. For he shot out a muscular arm in the direction of the forecourt and boomed, 'Ella. Come here. Come here at once.'

Now I could see her. She was still on her bicycle. She got off and propped it up carefully against the wall of the garage shop and nervously approached her obviously irate father. I knew what he was going to ask. The same question framed in my own mind. What was she doing coming home in the morning? The parents' meeting was not until the afternoon.

Eames turned back to us. 'Excuse me for a minute.'

We were thankful to excuse him. He walked a little way towards his daughter, but his voice still carried as if his voice box had been built by Sony.

'What the devil are you doing back at this hour?'

I saw him grab his daughter's arm and remembered my own numb fingers. Winna suddenly burst into tears and tried to back away.

'Are you playing truant? That cursed meeting is not until this afternoon and you know it,' he shouted.

She shook her head and I could see the sun glistening in the tears now pouring down her cheeks. She looked pitifuly vulnerable and even more minute alongside the vast frame of her father.

'Answer me, girl, or I'll . . .'

She suddenly looked up at him. 'Leave me alone. I've done nothing wrong.'

He shook her arm. I thanked the Lord I hadn't been born an Eames.

'So what are you doing home?'

She tried to get her breath between sobs.

'They've closed the school.'

His shaking continued. I looked back at Gus, who raised a fist. I shook my head. Gus has many failings, but physical cowardice is not one of them. He rushes in where even devils fear to tread.

'Closed the school? Who's closed the school?'

She shook her head, squeezed her eyes shut and wailed, 'The police.'

57

Her father let go her arm. 'The police? Why? What on earth has happened at that bloody school now?'

'They've found . . .' she began, then rubbed her eyes with her hand.

'Found what? Come on, out with it.'

'Mr Folland.'

'Found him? What do you mean? He wasn't lost, you stupid girl. Just suspended.'

'He's dead. They found his body this morning . . . in the gym.'

Five

'I crossed my fingers too,' I said, as Gus bounced me home in his Black Peril.

'What about?'

'Manners School. Not having a third disaster.'

He negotiated a bend with his usual deftness. I looked back and sighed. Still, Dorset should have known by now. You don't grow flowers in beds adjoining the road.

'Might not be a disaster. Might be a Godsend,' Gus muttered.

'A death? A Godsend?'

'Well, he didn't have long to live, did he? Not with that there Aids. Taking his own life has probably saved everyone a load of trouble and worry.'

'She didn't say how he died,' I pointed out. 'Just that he had been found dead.'

'Obvious, isn't it?' he sniffed. 'Doesn't take an 'Ercool Parrot to work out how he died.'

I didn't comment. After all, Gus could well have been right. I fervently hoped he was. Manners School needed a murder like a hole in the head. (Maybe I should rephrase that.)

'She was pretty upset,' I said.

Gus yanked the long lever into second. By the terrible grinding noise, I thought it might have been into oblivion.

''Nough to upset any child, death is. Worse than for adults. Noticed it before. Takes the wind out of their young souls something rotten. Reminds them that life isn't all foppy fairyland and happy endings, after all.' He turned to me. 'It's our own bloody fault. We shouldn't feed kids all this pansy pap.' His expression performed one of its famous turns from deadly serious to impishly provocative.

'Still, saved us dying a death with that H'Avenger, her turning up did. Gave us a chance to sneak away.'

'Gus,' I remonstrated. 'One shouldn't actually need a death to intervene to allow one to escape from a second-hand-car dealer – although, I admit, it helps.'

'Oh, listen to you,' he scoffed. 'All those "ones". What are you up to? Rehearsing to meet that Prince Charles?''

We didn't speak much after that. Not because we'd started to bicker. But I guess because we'd both begun to think. Least, I had. And by the time Gus had deposited me and sped off home, I was more than a mite depressed. (No, I didn't invite him in for a jar and he didn't ask. I don't think either of us was quite in the mood for a quick carouse.)

Bing caught my mood immediately and started yowling the house down. I stilled his tongue with some silver-top, then pulled a Heineken for myself, more to take the dry taste out of my mouth, than to inject stimulant. I had just sat down to imbibe it when the phone call I had been expecting came through.

'I've heard,' I said. 'I was over at Eames' garage with Gus when his daughter came home.'

'Oh, well I needn't have rung,' Arabella said. I felt a rat for anticipating her. 'Can't be long, anyway. I'm late already to get to that parents' meeting.'

'Sorry,' I said.

'About what?'

'For jumping your gun when I picked up the phone.'

'Oh, that. I thought you meant about Folland's murder.'

I took a breath. 'Murder?'

'Yes. But you said you knew . . .?'

'All I know is that Folland has been found dead – in the gym.'

'Correction. Folland's been found murdered – in the gym.'

I shut my eyes. Suddenly I could see what the next few days, maybe weeks, might bring, if I wasn't darned careful. I just prayed Tony had not heard about my odd amateur sleuthing forays and that the police would solve the crime in double-quick time.

'How was he killed?'

'"Blunt instrument" is all the police are saying.'

'Who is on the case?'

'Guess.'

She didn't need to say more.

'Have you seen Digby Whetstone?'

'No, the dear Inspector is incommunicado at the moment. I've only seen the Headmaster so far.'

'Do they have any idea how it happened? Like what was he doing back at the school and why he was in the gym? And even better, who did it?'

'Not a clue. I mean, I haven't. The police may have, but they're keeping stumm.'

'Ah well. Let's hope Digby won't take for ever to solve it. Maybe he already has.'

'Maybe. The caretaker found the body, apparently, when he opened up this morning.'

'Not his week, any more than it's the headmaster's, is it?'

There was silence for a second. Well, comparative. All I could hear was the clacking of typewriters going on somewhere in her office.

Then Arabella asked, 'Has Tony turned up yet?'

'No. I expect, when he does, he'll be all bright eyed with theories as to who killed the poor blighter.'

'Got to go. Mustn't be late for the Colonel's meeting. Imagine what he's going to say now, with his bête noire bludgeoned to death.'

I cleared my throat. 'Maybe he'll now soft pedal the whole thing.'

'Why? Because he feels he has to exhibit some kind of respect for the dead?'

'No. Because – hasn't it occurred to you? – he may well have done the bludgeoning.'

I had just finished lunch when Tony arrived. But his first words were not about murder, but the weather. He was British, if nothing else.

'Seen it out to sea?' he asked, the instant he came in.

'Seen what out to sea?'

'Clouds as black as ink. And they're rolling in. I heard a clap of thunder rumbling away over the water, as I cycled over.'

'Brought a mac?'

He pointed out to his cycle's saddle-bag. 'Sure. Always prepared. Tony Thorn, boy wonder.'

I smiled. He had a marvellous knack of making arrogance seem acceptable, rather charming, even. Maggie Thatcher could learn from him, as well as be proud of him.

He came up to the counter and sat down.

'I haven't done your graphs and all that yet.'

I waved my hand. 'Didn't expect them this week.'

I wondered when he would get round to the murder.

'Had a successful morning?'

'Haven't been open today yet, if that's what you mean.'

'Stock-taking?'

'No. Gus accompanying.'

I told him who Gus was and all about our trip to Winna's father's garage and her unexpected return home.

'So the Avenger was no good?' was his only comment. I couldn't quite believe his seemingly deliberate avoidance of the subject of murder.

'We never really discovered. Your girlfriend seemed so upset, we thought we'd better leave.'

He sighed. 'Oh, that's Winna all over. Recently, the slightest thing sets her off.'

'Murder is hardly the slightest thing, Tony,' I admonished.

His bright eyes burnt into mine. 'Do you really want to talk about that, Peter?'

'Well, it's up to you. But I'm surprised you don't seem to want to.'

He pulled up closer to the counter and his whole attitude suddenly changed. 'Oh, I'm bursting to. It's just that . . . well, you won't get cross at what I'm going to say, will you?'

I winked. 'I can be an ogre when I'm roused. Strong men blanche . . .'

He went on, 'You see, my Mum has vaguely heard about you. She knows someone you know.'

'Oh? Who's that?'

'I think she's a cousin of Arabella's. Runs a garden nursery over Owermoigne way. My Mum buys all her bedding plants there. Swears they're better and cheaper than anywhere around.'

'So your mother knows Lady Philippa, does she?'

He blushed. 'Well, not really "knows", you know. Just buys stuff from her.'

'So what has that got to do with your not talking about poor Folland's death?' I asked, but I guessed I knew the answer.

62

'Well, my mum heard about that thatcher case, you know.'*

'Did Philippa tell her?' I asked in considerable disbelief.

He shook his head. 'Oh no. Nothing like that. Just that it was the talk of all her customers for a while. You know . . . and your role in it all.'

'So?' I sighed.

'And my Mum says that from what she can gather, you don't like getting involved in things like that, really, I mean . . .'

I helped him out. 'No, she's right, Tony. I don't. Trouble is, you see, you get type-cast. Once an amateur sleuth, every Tom, Dick and Harriet thinks you're itching to get involved again. Can't wait for the next crime.'

'So that's why I didn't mention Folland's death. I thought you might think I was trying to embroil you into it in some way.'

This time I looked hard at him. 'You're not, are you?'

He looked hurt. 'No, why should I? Anyway, the police are crawling all over the school right now, so they'll probably have it all sewn up in no time.'

'Let's hope so.'

There was an awkward silence. Then he said, 'I just hope they don't come to any wrong conclusions.'

'About what?'

'Oh . . . nothing.'

Sod him. He was being too clever.

'Conclusions about what?'

'Well, about old Andy Boxall, for a start.'

'The caretaker, you mean?'

'Yes. He's a lovely old guy. All the kids like him.'

'You, especially?'

'Me included. Trouble is, he's so naive . . .'

'What are you getting at?'

'Well, doesn't look too good for him, does it? First, he discovers a burglary that's just the kind of thing he's employed to prevent. And now he discovers a body. He's not the strongest of characters. Half an hour's grilling by someone out of "The Professionals" and he'll believe himself that he's the guilty party.'

'And you know he's not?'

Tony hesitated before replying. 'And I know he's not.'

---

* *Chipped*, Weidenfeld & Nicolson, 1988.

'How?' I asked. 'Not that I'm implying you're wrong.'

'Instinct. And like I've got to know him quite well, and I reckon he's mega-honest.'

I laughed to myself. I hadn't heard the word 'mega' preceding an adjective since the mega-hype of my advertising days. This Tony was even more equipped for the rat-race than I had imagined.

'Any ideas as to who might have killed your teacher, then?'

'It could be any number of people, couldn't it, after all the bad-mouthing that's been going on? There are a hundred and twenty-five kids at the school. That makes two hundred and fifty parents who are possibles, for a start.'

Trust Tony to start with numerical figures, rather than human ones. 'Other than the two hundred-odd parents?'

He pursed his lips. 'Well, there's old Fuddy-duddy. Not hard to see him . . .' he affected his Lord Snooty voice once more, '. . . clubbing someone to death, is it? What's more, he's got a set of school keys. All the governors have. He could have let himself in without Mr Folland hearing a thing.'

'What do you think your teacher was doing in the school at all? Wasn't he supposed to stay away while he was on suspension?'

'Yea. Suppose he was. Hadn't really thought of that. Maybe he came back in the evening to clear up some of his personal things. Like from the teachers' common-room. Or his desk in Five A.'

'But he was found in the gym, wasn't he?'

Tony looked at me and smiled.

'I'm not a Tom, Dick or Harriet. I'm Tony, remember, Peter?'

I got up from behind the counter. 'Hell, you're right. I'm falling into a trap, this time of my own making.' I pointed at the toys around the shop. 'Anyway, it's all this stuff you've come about, not your unfortunate teacher. Now what would you like to know?'

So, for the rest of the afternoon, he told me. By the time Arabella came home, I knew what a lousy life a dishcloth leads. And what's more, that I needed to reputty some of my shop windows. For the storm had now broken over Studland with a vengeance and quite a few of the cats and dogs were finding a way in.

Arabella came in looking like she'd swum back from Bournemouth.

'Hey? What happened? Car break down?' I asked, helping her off with her now ten-gallon blazer. (She'd looked 'absolutely ripping' when she had left that morning. In her striped blazer and white linen trousers, she'd been more luscious than the strawberries and cream devoured at Henley Regattas.)

She shook herself. The spray was, at least, warm on my face.

'No, the top.'

'Wouldn't go up?'

She nodded and licked away a dribble of water running down from her hair. 'I tried for about quarter of an hour. One of the supports has jammed open, or something. Couldn't budge the thing more than quarter way shut. All I needed after that dreadful meeting.'

She took off her shoes and put them by the boiler.

'How did it go? Badly?'

She wiped away another dribble. 'Look, darling, I must go up and get out of these wet things. Might as well grab a bath too while I'm at it.' She took my hand. 'Wend your way up too and I'll regale you while I'm lathering.'

'Will that be nice?' I grinned.

'Up to you,' she replied, dead pan. 'Totally up to you.'

It was rather nice. But it took a bit longer to reach the 'regaling' part than either of us had anticipated. Still, we did get squeaky clean.

Eventually, I lay back between the taps and said, 'So, what about that other meeting? Did it come to a vote?'

'Unfortunately,' she sighed, wiggling her toes between my legs. 'No prizes for guessing how it went.'

'What was the Colonel's motion?'

'Many were discussed, including, as you may imagine, the removal of Delia Pettican from the board of governors. One parent even suggested the Headmaster should be removed and replaced by Hawkesworth himself.'

'I take it the men from the funny farm took him away in one of those shirts that does up at the back?'

'No. He even got a round of applause for the suggestion.'

'So what was the final motion that obviously pleased the baying majority?'

She stopped her submarine hunt for the soap and replied wearily, '"That the meeting totally deplored recent events at

Manners School and condemned the excessively liberal policy that had quite clearly given rise to them." Something like that. The second clause went on, "As a result, it is the meeting's view that the whole philosophy of the school be revised, especially in regard to the appointment of staff and the composition of the governing body." And, surprise, surprise, the Colonel got himself unanimously elected as the custodian of the parents' views and the leader of the wolf pack. Wow!' She shook her head in frustration and disgust.

'Wow, indeed. So was a motion to remove Miss Pettican ever voted on?'

'Not finally. I think the Colonel was rather surprised how well liked she seemed to be. Even some of those who criticized her so-called "liberal" views, expressed their respect for what she and her family had done for the school over the years, etcetera, etcetera. All much to my relief. It was the only redeeming feature of the whole ghastly affair. I would have had a bath the instant I came home, whether I'd been soaked by the storm or not. Just to wash myself clean of the bigotry, bad-mouthing and . . . ugh!'

This time I wiggled her toe. 'I'm glad you did.'

She reached for my hand. 'I'm glad *we* did.' We were silent for a moment, then she said quietly, 'You know, listening to some of the parents made me wish I had never grown up.'

'I never have,' I smiled.

'Maybe, that's why I like you. You know what I mean. We're sort of fun together. Like it was when we were kids.'

'Not quite like it was when we were kids.'

'Promise me you'll never lose the child in you, Peter.'

'Promise. Ditto?'

'Ditto.'

She looked around the bath. 'For a start, why don't you bring some of your toy boats upstairs, so that we can play battleships and submarines and all that? John Lennon played ships in his bath in that Dick Lester film.'

'Two good reasons,' I laughed. 'One, most of my ships are lead or die-cast and would sink the instant they felt water. Two, the ones that wouldn't, the tinplate clockwork jobs, Hornby and the like, are too valuable to get rusty.'

'Can't I have just one?' she pouted. 'I could wind it up and send it up your end. Then you could send it back to me.'

I clasped her leg lovingly and laughed again. 'I wonder what Tony Thorn would think if he could see us now.'

She frowned. 'What do you mean?'

'Adults playing as children. It's the direct reverse of what he is doing.'

She smiled. 'He's a phenomenon, isn't he? By the way, how did it go with him?'

So I told her. By the time I'd finished, she had begun looking distinctly shivery.

'Think I'll get out,' she said. 'The water's starting to get cold.'

As I watched her swing her long legs out of the bath and reach for a towel, I said, 'I don't know. I have a sinking feeling the water is only just starting to heat up.' As I finished the sentence, a clap of thunder directly overhead almost blew me out of the bathroom.

The next morning, Saturday, I had to go to see a guy about the next Bournemouth Toy and Train Swapmeet to be held in November. I don't normally get involved in the planning, setting up and promotion of these events, but this time I couldn't avoid it. He had asked for every regular stall-holder's views on the policy towards the ever-increasing domination of these events by *new* toy dealers, who sell nothing but acres of Lledo and Yesteryear vehicles, both regular and promotional. (The latter is where a toy commercial vehicle, say a van or truck, carries advertising signs on its coachwork that differ from those of the normal production runs from the factory. These are produced in limited and usually, but not always, certifiable numbers, for brief periods and, in my view, have become the plague that may eventually kill the toy collecting mania. There are just far too many of them.)

As you may gather, I'm a purist (in this respect, anyway). I believe old toy swapmeets should be just that. Where old toy enthusiasts can meet each other and swap, sell and buy toys of at least a creditable vintage. My cut-off point is 1979, the date of the final closing of the original Dinky Toy factory in Binns Road, Liverpool. Not that long ago, maybe, but it's a date hallowed and goodbyed by every collector with blood rather than shekels in his veins. A message I delivered to the Bournemouth promoter that Saturday morning in no uncertain terms. But I doubted my views would count for much. Money speaks louder than words.

By the time I got back to the old Toy Emporium, there was a car parked outside. And a car I, unfortunately, recognized. Sighing mightily, I let myself in the back way and went straight into the sitting-room, where Arabella was about to bless a giant fist with the lager that gets to parts of Gus that other beers can't reach.

After receiving the usual garbled grunts of welcome, I asked, 'Gus, what possessed you to go near that ruddy Avenger again?'

'Well, old love, we 'adn't taken it out, had we?'

I looked at Arabella, who couldn't help laughing.

'Because it wasn't worth taking out, Gus, that's why.'

'Yea. But I didn't know it till I'd tried, did I?'

I brightened. 'So I'm vindicated. It's clapped, right?'

'Right, old son. If clapped means a bloody great rattle from the engine. Expired twice, it did, on the way here. Had to get a push both times to start it.'

Arabella raised her elbow. I nodded. She disappeared into the kitchen.

'So why did you bring it here, if it wasn't any ruddy good? Why didn't you take it straight back?'

He hesitated and filled in time by slurping half his lager.

'Well, old son, it's ... er ... like this 'ere.'

'Like this 'ere what, Gus?'

'Like this 'ere fellow Eames.'

'What about him?'

'He was ... well ... in a helluva temper this morning. Much worse than when we saw him with his daughter.'

'You annoy him?' I grinned.

'No, you berk. But some mechanic had, by the sounds of things. And "sounds" is right. He bellowed at him like a ruddy bull. Reckon it could be heard as far away as soddin' Cornwall. And all because his Lordship reckoned he'd been messing with his precious old Jaguar.'

'Old car nuts are like that,' I said. 'They don't like anything on their precious vehicles mucked about with.'

'Felt sorry for that mechanic, I did,' Gus went on. 'He should have given that muscle-bound bully as good as he got.'

I took the Heineken from Arabella's returning hand.

'Cheers. Anyway, Gus, it still doesn't explain why you bothered to bring that Avenger all the way over here, when you knew you weren't buying it.' Then I added, 'Or does it?'

Gus nodded, self-consciously.

Curse him. That was the rest of my morning gone.

68

'You want me to come with you to add moral support to your "No thanks, Mr Eames, it's a sodding awful car."'

Gus looked away. 'Nice pub near there. Thought you and Arabella might like to come and share a Saturday noggin, that's all.'

I glanced at Arabella. She gave me a 'how can we get out of it?' look. I had to admit, I didn't have any answer to that one and was about to respond, 'Oh well, as long as we're back for a late lunch', when I heard the bell clanging in the shop. I trudged wearily through, anticipating some regular customer, irate that I was not yet open. But no, it was Tony Thorn and for once, his eyes weren't so much bright, as distinctly agitated.

I unlocked the door.

'Tony. I didn't really expect you today.'

He grasped my arm and said rather breathlessly, 'I'm sorry, Peter, to interrupt your weekend, but I couldn't think of anything else to do. I just had to cycle right over.'

I ushered him into the shop. 'Now, calm down, Tony and tell me what the trouble is?'

'It's Andy Boxall. Remember? The caretaker.'

'Yes, I remember.'

'He's in a terrible state.'

'What's happened to him? Has he been attacked?'

Tony shook his head. 'No, nothing like that. It's just that he's sure the police suspect him.'

'Of what? The murder?'

'Of both. The murder and the robbery. They've told him he could have stolen the jumble sale money and then murdered Mr Holland because he found out about it.'

Hell. I could see it all coming, but nevertheless, asked, 'So why have you come round here?'

He looked so distressed, I wished I hadn't asked.

'Oh, I'm sorry . . . I don't know . . . I wouldn't have come, but . . .' His voice trailed away.

I patted his shoulder. 'You want me to see him?'

His eyes brightened for the first time.

'Will you? Honest?'

'You had better come on in. There may be a few questions I ought to ask you before I see him.'

'Anything,' he smiled.

We began walking towards the counter.

'For starters, how do you know all this?'

'I popped round to see Andy about ten o'clock. Thought he might know how the investigations were going, you know. Well, he looked awful and he's terrified out of his mind. He had only got back from the police station at two this morning. They have been interrogating him all night.'

Just as we got to the sitting-room door, Tony tapped my shoulder.

'You don't mind too much, my coming, do you, Peter? You know. I remember all you said . . .'

I shook my head.

'No. Forget it. Really. You see . . . as you told me, you're not a regular Tom, Dick or Harry, now are you?'

Six

First, we conveyed Gus back to Eames' garage – the 'we' being yours truly, Arabella, Tony and his bike and the convoy vehicle, Arabella's Golf, still with its hood jammed down. For the bike wouldn't fit under my Beetle's bonnet, unless I'd been willing to steer by periscope.

In contrast to the last sublime days, the air was distinctly nippy and still pregnant with the threat of more rain. So by the time we got to Eames, Gus was the only warm one, cosseted as he was with the H'Avenger's 'eater. On the way I worked out why he wanted me with him. It wasn't that he was afraid of Eames physically – Gus is by no means averse to throwing a punch – but he does fight shy of slick salesman spiel, with or without ranting admonitions.

But Gus didn't need me after all. Eames was out, having taken Ella to her gymnastics coach and then gone sail-boarding, according to his mechanic. Upon such felicitous news, Tony asked him if he could fix the Golf's top, which he effected in under ten minutes, much to my chagrin; I had spent a fruitless hour on the thing before breakfast.

'He's a nice guy,' Tony smiled, as we motored out of the forecourt. 'Always willing to help. Winna and I often chat to him when her father's out. Doesn't do it, of course, when he's here.'

'Father raise the roof?' I asked, quite innocently.

'No, it was the mechanic who did that.' Tony winked at me in the rear view mirror, as he tapped the inside of the Golf's now cosy top.

It wasn't far from the garage to the school and I was relieved to see the road outside was free of flashing Rovers and Granadas.

'Pull in here,' Tony suggested. 'He's got a separate gate just round the corner.'

I followed his advice and parked in a narrow side road. Ara-

71

bella opted to stay in the car, in case three was a crowd for a man who was already half-terrified.

The iron-barred gate, narrow and high, was unlocked and we let ourselves in and walked up a short concrete path to the door of what proved to be a small whitewashed extension at the back of the main science block.

'Not very big,' I whispered.

'It's enough,' Tony whispered back as he rang the bell. 'At least for now.'

'Is he thinking of moving, then?' I asked, prompted by his last remark.

'Not unless something miraculous comes up, no. He doesn't earn much as a caretaker.'

Further exchange was cut short by the sound of sliding bolts and the door was opened cautiously.

'It's okay, Andy. It's only me, Tony.'

The crack widened, and I peered into a pair of eyes like foxes must see in rabbit warrens.

'Don't get alarmed,' Tony reassured,' I've just brought a friend along who might be able to help you.'

'A friend?' he queried, in a low crackle.

I extended my hand. 'I'm Peter. Peter Marklin. A friend of somebody you've met. Arabella Trench. The lady from the *Western Gazette*. Remember?'

'You're not from any paper, are you?'

I shook my head. 'No, no. Don't worry. I'm just somebody who Tony Thorn thought might be able to help you, that's all.'

The door was still only half-open. 'How?'

'Well, I've . . . er . . . had a little experience of . . . er . . .'

I didn't quite know how to phrase it. After all, what were my qualifications? Only Sweet Fanny Adams knew for sure.

'. . . redirecting policemen, seeing they don't waste time with innocent people, when they should be getting after the guilty . . .'

Lousy as that was as a placebo, it seemed to do the trick and a second later, we were inside the very small, but amazingly neat, annexe. He led us through into a tiny sitting area – it could hardly be termed a room – totally dominated by an overblown sofa, whose stuffing had moulded itself into a series of hard lumps, and a twenty-six-inch TV, which I assumed came as a set with his pebble glasses.

72

He took a deep breath, then exhaled. 'Tony is a good boy. Hope he isn't wasting your time, Mr . . . er . . .'

'Marklin. Peter,' I smiled. 'I hadn't got much planned for today, so . . .'

'Peter has solved other cases,' Tony interrupted proudly. 'Haven't you, Peter?'

I waved my hand. 'Don't let's worry about those. Let's talk about this one.'

Andy Boxall indicated I should sit down on the settee amongst the lumps. I obeyed. 'Like a coffee or anything? It's no bother.'

He pointed to a bead curtain through which I could just see an electric hob complete with kettle.

'No, thanks. Now Mr Boxall, tell me exactly what's been happening, so that I know all the background.'

So he did. In essence, he told me very little that I hadn't gleaned already. He confirmed that he had neither seen nor heard any intruders on the nights of the burglary or the murder. He added, however, that he was surprised at the jumble sale money still being on the premises more than a full day after the event and that he had assumed it had been banked on the first morning. As to the murder of Folland, he was totally at a loss. First, he was amazed that the teacher was on the premises at all that night. Second, he could not see how anyone could have got into the gym without Folland knowing or hearing something. In answer to my question about the number of sets of keys to the school, he replied that there were six, as far as he knew. Colonel Hawkesworth and Delia Pettican had a set apiece, the headmaster had two (one for himself and one to lend out to other members of staff as he saw fit), he himself had one and, interestingly, Folland.

'Why was Folland the only member of regular staff to have a set of keys?' I'd asked, to which I received the reply I should have guessed from Tony's previous descriptions of the dead master's roles in the school.

'He did some physical training, as well as class-work, did Mr Folland. Fine figure of a man he was, despite what they now say about his . . . er . . . being a bit, you know . . .'

'I know.' I was intrigued by the obvious dichotomy in his mind between the concept of being homosexual and being ruggedly athletic. I guess we have popular comedians to blame for the stereotyped homosexual image being effeminate and weedy.

73

'Well, he conducted some of his classes outside normal school hours. Extra swimming lessons, tennis coaching and especially gym work. That kind of thing. So he needed a set of keys, really.'

'He used to help Winna after school sometimes,' Tony cut in. 'Let her use the apparatus on the evenings her regular coach had other pupils.'

Boxall rested back against the arm of the settee. 'Nice man, Mr Folland, whatever his faults. I can't imagine who'd want to kill him . . . unless . . .'

'Unless what, Mr Boxall?'

His small neat mouth twitched at one edge. 'Nothing, really . . . I mean . . . unless, well, you know . . . the Aids thing.'

'Someone killed him because he had Aids?'

'Could be, couldn't it?' he brightened, no doubt seeing the conjecture as a way out of his own obvious dilemma with the police. 'I read a case the other day – in London it was. Fellow killed another fellow, he was living with, when he heard he'd got Aids. Sort of revenge for not having told him, like.'

I brewed on it, then asked, 'Did Folland live with anybody?'

'No. At least, not as far as I know. Not permanently, anyway.'

'Where did he live?'

'In a flat in the town. Never seen it, but I'm told it's very nice. Small, but full of, you know, antiquey things. He had taste, did Mr Folland.'

'Any landlord or landlady on the premises?'

He shook his head. 'No. It's a big old house, just back from the sea-front near Victoria Drive. All divided up now into flats. No landlord or commissionaire or anything.'

I sighed to myself. So there was nobody I could easily quiz about Folland's private life and the comings and goings to the house.

'Did Mr Folland ever mention any particular friends of his?'

Boxall thought for a minute. 'Not that I can rightly remember. Kept himself to himself a bit, did Mr Folland.' He shook his head woefully. 'Oh, it's terrible, terrible, what's happened to him. The school will never be quite the same, you know, Mr Marklin. I can see changes coming that will . . .' He stopped suddenly, then went on, 'Still, it ain't none of my business, any road. I just hope I don't lose my job, that's all. This little place may not be much, but it's my home.'

'You'll be all right,' Tony encouraged. 'Especially now Mr Marklin's on your side.'

I looked round at him.

'You are on Andy's side, aren't you, Mr Marklin?'

The need for an instant reply was eradicated by a knock at the door. I saw Boxall's eyes lose what little hope I had managed to restore to them.

'I'll go,' Tony offered, sensing the caretaker's fear that it might be the return of the boys in blue.

From where we were, we could hear every word exchanged at the door.

'Oh, hello, Miss Pettican,' Tony's voice betrayed his own relief. And then a cheery, 'Hello, again,' from him.

I didn't have long to wait to discover who the second visitor was, for after a 'Andy is in. Would you like to see him?', a few footfalls brought them into sight.

As I rose from the settee, Arabella came over and stood by me.

'Miss Pettican saw me waiting outside,' she said. 'Said it might help if I came in and heard her news too.'

I was about to say, 'What news?' when a slim, sinuous arm was extended towards me and a firm hand grasped mine.

'You'll be Peter Marklin, I presume.'

I smiled back. 'I'm glad to meet you, Miss Pettican. I've heard a lot about you.'

She smiled ruefully, laughter lines joining the other etchings on her tanned and slightly leathery face.

'Never mind. I'm not as bad as I'm often painted.' She turned to Boxall. 'But Andy, you're the man I've really come to see.'

The caretaker, still looking like a frightened rabbit, shook her extended hand and offered her a seat.

She sat down and crossed her trousered legs. 'I hear the police have been giving you a bit of a grilling, Andy. That so?' Her voice was authoritative, but kind.

He nodded. 'They have a bit, Miss.'

She made a steeple with her long, lean fingers. 'Well, that's why I've come. All that's come to an end now, Andy. You can relax.'

He looked at her in surprise. 'Why, what's happened? Have they found who did it all?'

She shook her head. 'No, not exactly. But they now know who didn't. And that includes you.'

75

I looked at Arabella. She'd anticipated me and smiled encouragingly.

'You see, Andy,' Delia Pettican continued, 'I went down to the station this morning with some new information – new to them, that is.'

She turned to Arabella. 'That's why I invited you in too, Miss Trench. Everything I say now is fit to print in your newspaper. In fact, I would welcome the publicity to lift the cloud of suspicion off people like Andy here. There's nothing worse to live through than unfounded rumour and vicious gossip.' She pursed her lips. 'And I should know . . .'

'I'm glad to hear it Miss,' Boxall perked up. 'It's been a living nightmare ever since the jumble sale robbery.'

'What's the news?' I asked.

She turned to me. 'Well, Mr Marklin, it's all my fault, really. You see, I had totally forgotten about it.'

I frowned.

'Simple,' she said. 'When a tragedy like Mr Folland's death occurs, the mind seems to go numb and tends to obliterate all the little minor worries and occurrences that have gone before. And that's what happened with me, more's the pity.'

'How so?' Arabella asked.

Miss Pettican recrossed her legs and leaned forward. 'I was returning from Bournemouth after giving a little talk on "Fossil remains on the Dorset Coast" – I'm often asked to address various gatherings on my hobby; this time it was to a Rotary Club ladies' night. It was about ten thirty or so, I suppose, on the evening before poor Mr Folland's body was found. And I had to pass the school on my way home.'

'Did you see something?' Tony interrupted, his eyes wide with curiosity.

'Yes, Tony, I believe I did.'

'What? The murderer?' the boy quizzed.

'I can't very well say that yet, Tony, can I? But in my headlamps – it was very dark by then – I saw a figure . . . a sort of large black shape atop the wall that runs alongside the playground.'

'A man?' they asked.

'By his size, it must have been. A big man too. I slowed and looked again. But the shape had gone, disappeared. So I thought I must have been tired and seeing things. Or it was a big black dog or something. Didn't give it another moment's thought, until I

76

was driving past the school this morning. Then it all came back to me. I gave up on my shopping expedition and went straight to the police in Bournemouth. Told them the whole story and they took me in to see the Inspector on the case.'

'Digby Whetstone?' I queried.

She nodded. 'Yes. Do you know him?'

'We've crossed paths on the odd occasion. Tell me, Miss Pettican, do the police now know the approximate time of Mr Folland's death?'

She held up a bony finger. 'Good question, Mr Marklin. I can see you read crime fiction, like I do.'

'A little,' I replied, relieved that she had attributed the question to fiction rather than fact.

'Well then, that's exactly why the Inspector was so interested in what I had to say. Apparently, they reckon poor Mr Folland died somewhere during that time, between ten and, at the very latest, midnight.'

Andy Boxall subsided down onto the settee, next to his visitor.

'Thank God you remembered seeing somebody, Miss Pettican. At least, it shows it was most likely an outside job.'

'It would look like it now, wouldn't it?' she said, with a reassuring smile. 'I've always known you were completely blameless, Andy. Now I think the police are thinking that way too. Especially after I mentioned the other little bit of information.'

'Other bit of information?' Andy repeated, now obviously rather dazed by a governor of the school becoming his fairy godmother.

'Yes, Andy. You see, Mr Folland used to confide in me, a little, now and again. I think he was somewhat of a lonely man. Not many friends really – at least, not round here in Dorset. And he knew my part in getting him selected as a teacher here in the first place . . .' She glanced at Arabella. '. . . against considerable opposition, I might say.'

'I know that, Miss,' Andy agreed. 'Mr Folland always talked about how he liked and respected you.'

'Well, we came to know each other quite well. He used to come round some weekends to my cottage. Have tea and a chin-wag. Even came with me on a fossil-hunt once. Anyway, on one of his recent visits, he told me about a friend he had made some time ago. In Weymouth, I think he said, and I gathered he was French and sailed across the Channel quite often. Never found out whether on his own boat, a ferry or merchant ship, I'm afraid.'

She looked round at me. 'If I had foreseen the tragedy that was about to befall us, I'd have asked him. Still, it's no good being wise after the event, is it?'

'You think this Frenchman may have some bearing on Mr Folland's death?' I asked.

'Yes,' she said positively. 'Could well have. And Inspector Whetstone seems to agree with me. You see, Alistair – that's Mr Folland – confided in me that he now very much regretted his friendship with this man and had tried to break it off. But the Frenchman wouldn't take "no" for an answer, apparently. More than that, he had become quite aggressive. Alistair seemed very apprehensive about the whole affair and asked my advice about it.'

'What did you say?' Arabella queried.

Delia Pettican shrugged her rather wide shoulders. 'What could I say? I think I mumbled the old cliché about time being a great healer and that his friend would gradually see the folly of trying to breathe life into a relationship that was now dead.'

'What was Mr Folland's reaction?' I asked.

'As I remember, nothing much. But I had a feeling at the time, that he regarded my comments as being a little naive in the circumstances. And I was pretty certain that he wasn't so much concerned about this Frenchman, as afraid of him, somehow.'

I thought for a moment, then said, 'So you think the black figure you saw at the school could have been Folland's ex-friend?'

'I don't know. But it could have been, when you come to think about it, couldn't it? The police seem to think so, anyway, and said they would now extend their enquiries to the Weymouth area.'

Tony moved across to the caretaker and put his hand on his shoulder.

'Well, there you are, Andy. Sounds as if the police won't be bothering you again.'

'Still leaves the burglary, young man,' he muttered. 'Unless this Frenchman friend of Mr Folland's did that as well.'

Andy Boxall had echoed my own thoughts, but I couldn't see why any French seafarer, hurt by his lover's rejection, would burgle his school – unless, of course, to incriminate his ex-lover in some way. But that didn't seem to have been the outcome.

78

I took Arabella's hand and moved towards the door.

'I guess you won't be needing me now, Tony. I'll just pop out and get your bicycle out of the boot.'

He came over to us, dragging Boxall behind him, like a dog on a lead.

'Thanks for coming, anyway, Peter.'

'Yea, thanks,' the caretaker echoed. 'Much obliged. And to you, Miss Pettican.'

She rose from the settee and joined us at the door.

'I had better be going too, Andy. Get my shopping done at last. Now don't you worry about anything, will you? There's no need, now.'

He smiled. 'No, Miss. I'll try not to.' But his eyes still retained a whisker of their warren look.

So we left. Miss Pettican to her matt green and sea-gull-spotted MG Midget, mid-sixties vintage, Tony to his bike and us to the Golf. As we were about to get in, Tony remarked, 'Thanks again for coming, Peter. You must be relieved.'

He instantly reacted to my expression. 'Aren't you?'

'You mean, that I don't have to get involved or that Andy Boxall doesn't need to get so hot and bothered?'

He propped his bicycle up against the kerb. 'Both, I guess.'

'It's not over yet,' I said. 'Still, it's not really my worry any more, for which I *am* thankful.'

'See you next week, then,' he grinned. 'I'll have those graphs for you then.'

'No hurry. Take your time.'

As we U-turned and drove away, I noticed in the rear-view mirror that Tony Thorn was pushing his bike back up the road towards the caretaker's annexe.

'Nice lad,' Arabella remarked. 'He's obviously going to stay with Andy for a bit. Must be a lonely old life he leads in that pokey place – especially at weekends when the school is closed.'

'Yes,' I nodded, turning out on to the main road. 'Maybe I've misjudged Tony. He's proving not to be all facts and figures, flow-charts and profit margins, after all.'

That evening, we at last caught up with the latest Bond. But somehow, all the glamour, gadgetry, safe sex (safe enough, that is, not to merit an X certificate), exotic scenery, vast sets, laser-firing Aston Martin and a back-firing plot, paper thin but convoluted, like it was written by an origami expert, failed to lift my spirits more than a hair's breadth.

Arabella noticed my mood the moment we stepped back on to the hard reality of a Bournemouth pavement.

'You were shaken and not stirred, weren't you?' she grinned. 'You never like them. I'm always surprised when you suggest going to another one.'

She took my arm. 'And I'd be very happy to bid the ludicrous piece of cardboard known as Mr Bond a permanent goodbye, so don't go for my sake.'

'No, I didn't reckon it much,' I muttered, as we walked across the road to the car-park. 'But maybe I'm not really in the right mood tonight for schoolboy "bang-bang" movies.'

'It's a schoolboy that's worrying you, isn't it?'

I sighed. 'I don't know. Maybe.'

We reached the car and I ferreted around in my pocket for the keys.

'You don't think you've heard the last of Andy Boxall, do you?'

I opened up the car. 'I don't know about Andy Boxall, but I've got a nasty feeling that . . .'

'. . . you'll get dragged in again.'

I got in and slipped the latch of the passenger door. 'Something like that.'

We sat beside each other for a moment, not saying anything, just staring at the street light glinting on the parked cars in front of us.

'You don't need to get involved,' she said, at last. 'Not if you don't want to.'

Hell, she'd hit upon it. I should have known she would. My unease was not so much about the whole Manners School affair, but about myself. I'd never had a case where I had started to get involved and then stopped – for whatever reason. And my tiny problem was, I didn't really like it. I guess it's like the sleuth's equivalent of coitus interruptus. Your adrenalin is up, your juices are flowing, then . . . nothing, goodnight already. Well, I could just about deal with my adrenalin and my juices, but I couldn't stop my brain working, my instincts instincting or whatever. Good God, I was already starting to amass more theories about the Manners School case than scientists have about the extinction of dinosaurs from our pleasant planet. None of them right, maybe, or even near the mark, but . . .

'No,' I sighed. 'I can always say "No".'

She reached across for my hand. 'You don't have to say "No", for my sake, if the need arises. It's like going to a Bond picture. Don't feel you have to do it for me.'

'Well, let's hope old Whetstone finds the Frenchman or whoever and solves it on his own.'

I started up my old Beetle engine and, as Gus would have it, 'phut–phutted' out of the car-park, as the heavens opened.

Seven

The next week started wet and chill, and autumn was now well and truly with us. Bermuda shorts, bikinis, lilos and loungers were all packed away for their six-month winter hibernation, and the tinkling cacophony of ice-cream vans was now heard only rarely in the land.

Come to that, the tinkling of my shop bell was not being heard that often, so my attempt at a new lay-out for my Emporium – prompted by Tony – was not being afforded much of a test. Not that it was a 'mega' break-through in marketing. All I had done really was to dress the window about ninety per cent with proven die-cast sellers, like fifties and sixties Dinky and Corgi vehicles, instead of the almost even split between die-cast and tinplate items of all vintages that had been my wont. I had also at one end of the window, made what I called a 'Collectors' Corner', where I offered rather exaggerated reductions on toys that the spiders in my establishment now regarded as old buddies – 'come-ons' or 'loss-leaders', as Tony would term them. It went against my grain a bit, not the reductions per se, but the whole idea of brash and breezy cut-price labels being blazoned in any part of the Toy Emporium. But Tony was getting to me and I certainly needed some kind of stimulus to my turnover.

Inside the shop, I rearranged the display cabinets, so that anyone wanting to come to the counter would have to pass most of my merchandise, and I grouped my toys much more strictly into categories and typed little cards to indicate what price ranges the rows of items covered. The thinking behind the latter was that people have read so much in the media about the huge prices old toys now fetch, that they might be pleasantly surprised to see how inexpensive some of them can still be. (The thinking, how-ever, proved to be as effective as the famous Edsel marketing plan. For I discovered collectors actually like to handle the product and turn it over to find the price. Somehow, that way, they feel more involved and more committed to its purchase. So gawping and touching, the bane of the vintage toy trade, has its plus side, after all.)

Gus was quite taken aback with my changes, when he popped by late the next Monday afternoon and went through an elaborate and over-long charade about how sorry he was to have come into the wrong shop and had Peter Marklin moved, and if so, could I give him his new address?

However, I eventually managed to interrupt his Oscar-winning performance, by pointing to the strange pink vehicle parked outside.

'Oh that,' he mumbled. 'Got it till tomorrow, haven't I?'

I went out to give it the once-over. The year 1961 is renowned in motoring history for having given birth to the Jaguar 'E' type and has now been forgiven for the befinned fairground object I saw in front of me.

'Cresta,' Gus grinned.

'Runs well, then, I expect,' I grinned back.

He pulled a face. I started to explain. 'Cresta Run, get it?' He didn't and he was probably right.

I looked inside and regretted not wearing dark glasses.

'I like the Lurex-thread seat covers. Very Liberace.'

Suddenly, a massive weight crashed down on my left shouder. It was Gus's hand.

'Well, you can quit your leering and sneering, old love, 'cos I'm not buying it. Might as well get some use out of it, though, before I take it back to Sampson Motors in the morning.'

'What's wrong with it then?'

'Don't fancy myself, somehow, in a pink car. People might start thinking I live off . . . you know . . . a string of girls. What d'yer call it? Moral earnings.'

'Almost,' I said. I was going on to point out that pimps gave up pink cars yonks ago, but thought it might confuse the issue – worse, wean him back on the car. And I couldn't bear the thought of Gus poncing around in a pink Lurexmobile, even if it did have an 'eater.

Gus rubbed his chin. I knew what that meant and there was still some sixty minutes to yard-arm time.

'Nar. Came round for a natter, not to show you that poofy thing.'

'About any brand in particular?' I asked, as I ushered him back indoors.

'No. Don't be like that. I only came to see if you've heard any more about that murder over at Manners School, seeing as how that schoolboy is always with you these days.'

So over a couple of Heinekens, I told him, ending on my coitus interruptus with the caretaker and the leathery but likable Delia Pettican.

It took quite a few slurps before he reacted.

'Well, they're never likely to catch him, then.'

'Who?'

'The Frog.'

'The Frog? The French sailor friend?'

'Yea. They're often a dime a dozen in Weymouth, they are. In for a few hours, then they hop off across the Channel and go home. And home needn't be just France, neither. Could be the Channel Islands. Be like looking for a ruddy needle when you don't even know where the perishin' haystack is.'

He had a point.

Poor Mr Folland's sailor friend was hardly going to be easy to trace and, for that matter, I reckoned, if he was the murderer, let alone the burglar, he would give England a wide berth, so to speak, until Folland's death was just a forgotten file or a computer name and number that no one punches up any more.

Gus held up his empty glass with his usual subtlety. I pulled him another Heineken.

'So that was a quick off and on,' he grunted. 'Cheers.'

I raised my own, still half-full, glass.

'Certainly was,' Gus grinned.

'So it's all up to our dear Digby Whetstone now, is it?'

I nodded.

'Lucky Froggie.'

'If it is him.'

He looked at me. 'You don't think it was?'

I shrugged. 'Don't know. It's just . . . well, that burglary worries me for a start. I can't see how it fits, somehow.'

'Maybe it doesn't. Maybe someone read about the jumble sale or even attended the ruddy thing, then thought of popping back and pinching the takings. Then someone else, on another night, maybe this sailor fellow, takes a dislike to Folland for some reason

84

or other, or has a violent argument with him and, Bob's your uncle, bops him on the head.'

'You may be right, Gus. But there is something that links the two events.'

'What?'

'How they got into the school. Apparently, it's a complete mystery. There's no sign of breaking and entering.'

'Just entering.'

'Right.'

'Well, either that someone had been given a key or had one made, or someone else already inside the school let them in. F'r'instance, if it was this Froggie fellow, then Folland could have let him in, couldn't he? After all, he was his . . .'

I was interested that Gus could not bring himself to say 'lover'. Wrong generation, I guess.

'Possible. But still leaves the burglary . . . unless Folland carried out the burglary himself. I can't quite see how the other key-holders, the Colonel or Delia Pettican, could be involved in a robbery. And the headmaster would hardly be likely to jeopardize his twenty thousand a year or whatever for a measly eight hundred pounds or so.'

'What about that there caretaker? He's got keys. Eight hundred would interest him.'

'Probably would. But he came across to me as too timid, somehow, to conceive of robbing the school, let alone carrying it out. Besides, he looked honest.'

Gus cackled. 'You'd buy a second-hand car from him, then?'

I took his point. Only about one in a million of the population came across as that honest.

'He doesn't have one to sell,' I laughed, 'Luckily for you, Gus. By the way, when are you going to stop all this borrowing of other people's cars, on the specious pretext that you might buy one?'

'Dunno,' he smiled. 'Still, it's a good lark, isn't it? Think of the mileage and petrol I'm saving on me Popular. And now the weather is nippier, their 'eaters are at least keeping me wotsits from falling off . . .'

My exposure of Gus's motives was interrupted by the clanging of the shop bell.

I looked at my watch. It was two minutes to closing time of half past five. A late collector, no doubt, rushing home from work to buy a goody before it was too late. Late collector, my eye. It was an early schoolboy – Tony Thorn. And he was already in the shop.

I hello-ed, then went on, 'I wasn't expecting you so early with the graphs, but you're very welcome.'

But as I said it, I could see from his expression that I was on quite the wrong track.

'Sorry, Peter,' he puffed from his exertions in pedalling over, 'but I'm not here about the shop.'

I ushered him to the counter stool. 'What's the trouble, Tony? The police aren't after Andy Boxall again, are they?'

'I don't think so,' he answered and took a deep breath. 'But I think someone's after me.'

'After you?' I queried, distinctly puzzled. 'Who do you mean, the police? Why should the Law be . . . ?'

He cut me off. 'No, it's not the police. Least, I don't think it is.'

I took a hard look at him, then took his arm.

'Come on in, Tony. You look as if you need a drink. And I don't mean school milk.'

We went through into the kitchen and I poured him a scotch, a modest tot for an adult, minuscule for Gus, but fair for a teenager. He took a longish draught, then grimaced.

'Now, Tony, start at the beginning. What makes you think someone is after you?'

He peered into his drink. 'It started yesterday. I had a day on my own, because Winna spends nearly all her time with her coach at weekends, now the championships are getting so near. And anyway, she is really preoccupied when she is free nowadays. So I cycled over to the Tank Museum at Bovington, where I know a guy who works there restoring the old armoured cars, tanks and stuff they have there. Anyway, it was his Sunday off, apparently, so I stayed around for a bit, then started cycling back. It was just before Wool that I saw him.'

'Who?' I interrupted, but he parried me and went on.

'His motor cycle was parked in a gate opening. I noticed the bike as I passed by, because it was one of those mega-big BMWs, like the police use on the Continent. You know, all brute force and "dee-da, dee-da" or is it a siren they use out there? Anyway, I forgot about it, until I was through Wool and on the Lulworth road.'

'You didn't go straight home?'

'No. The rain had held off and I had nothing better to do, so I thought I'd detour round by Lulworth Cove for a bit.' He took a much smaller draught of his scotch. 'Well, my gears began acting up – teach me to have a mountain bike with fifteen – and I stopped to fix them. I happened to look back and there was this mega-bike BMW stopping just up the road from me. Same guy, I could tell by the black helmet with the silver lightning flashes.'

'See his face?'

'Not a hope. He had a tinted visor and I never saw him with it up.'

'What did you do?'

'At this point, I wasn't all that worried, despite all Mum and Dad have told me about strange men who follow after boys. So I fixed the bike and rode on. This time, I heard him start up after me. So about a mile further on, I stopped again and pretended to play with my gears. He'd stopped too, about a hundred yards behind. You know, that was when I started to get really worried, Peter.'

'Wasn't there anyone else around?'

'Not a soul. Not surprising with yesterday's weather forecast. Anyway, all I could do was ride on, which I did. At Lulworth Cove, there were two or three people on the pebbles, so I hung around them. But he stayed around too for quite a bit. I could see him just back from the jetty. Then after twenty minutes, I looked and he was gone. I waited another half hour, then pedalled like mad for home. Luckily, there was no sign of him then.'

'Did you tell your parents?'

'No.'

'Why not?'

'Because it would have made me look a right twit, wouldn't it, if he'd turned out to be just an innocent motor cyclist out for a spin on a Sunday afternoon.'

'That what you think he was now?'

He shook his head.

'Why not?' I asked.

'Because I saw him as I cycled home from school tonight. Least, I saw his bike. It was parked up an alley.'

'Sure it was his?'

'Pretty certain. It had some kind of pennant on the front mudguard.'

'Mention it to your parents today?'

He sighed. 'Nope. I can handle it. Least, what can they do about it, anyway? Follow me everywhere I go, all day and all night?'

'No. But you and they could mention it to the police.'

He drained the last of his scotch. I didn't offer him another.

'I'd rather tell you, Peter,' he said, self-consciously. 'You won't laugh or think I'm just an over-imaginative kid.'

I smiled. 'Can you describe the man at all? I mean other than that he was wearing a helmet and, I assume, leathers of some sort.'

'All black,' he said. 'The leathers, I mean. But he was a big chap. I know because those BMWs often seem to dwarf their riders. This guy almost dwarfed it.'

I remembered Delia Pettican's description of the big black shape atop the school wall, but kept the thought to myself.

'I really think, Tony, you should tell the police. It may be important.'

He shook his head and turned away.

'Want me to tell them?' I asked quietly.

'Then they'll only want to see me, won't they?'

'Maybe.'

He thought for a second, then looked up. 'Wait until I see him again.'

'Think we should?'

'I'd feel better. I'd be sure then.'

I sighed. 'Okay. But you know my view. Any delay . . .'

I stopped, as I could see I was only upsetting him. I put my hand on his arm. 'Anyway, I'm flattered that you want to tell *me*.'

He smiled awkwardly.

'What did Winna think when you told her?'

After a second's hesitation, he replied, 'I haven't told her yet.'

'Why not?' I immediately added, 'Not that you need to tell me.'

With a shrug, he turned away again. 'Well, Winna and I are not quite as . . . close as we were, that's all.'

I guessed at what 'close' meant. 'It's probably those championships coming up. Before big events, athletes often . . .'

'. . . stop screwing,' he surprisingly cut in. 'I know. I know. Just my luck, isn't it? I'll have to take up a sport myself, I guess.' He smiled for the first time. 'Tell me, did John Lloyd take up tennis before or after he met Chris Evert?'

And with that, after a few cautionary words from me, he left.

By the time I got back to Gus, he'd left too. For Never Never Land. The Heineken and the sandman had just been too much.

The thunder Gene Krupa-ed on into the distance and the first raindrops tap-danced on the bedroom window. Arabella snuggled closer to me.

'You feel half in and half out, don't you?'

'Pardon?' I said.

She smiled at me out of one eye.

'The Manners School murder case.'

'Sounds like the title of a thirties crime novel.'

'You should know,' the eye smiled again.

Now what did she mean by that? So I ignored it.

'I wish I was both halves out, or better, had never heard of Manners School at all.'

'Too late now. What's more, your schoolboy Virgin . . .'

'He's no Virgin,' I cut in quickly.

'I meant Virgin Records, Richard Branson, entrepreneur is bound to maintain a blow by blow account of developments, with or without accompanying BMW rider.'

She rose on one elbow and her nipple tickled my arm. I didn't laugh.

'What are you going to do about that motor cyclist, by the way? Tell the police?'

'You tell me. As you know, Tony has asked me not to, until he's absolutely certain he's being tailed. I don't like to let him down. On the other hand, if he's right, then I don't want him found dead in some ditch, or abducted, all because I didn't speak up.'

'Heads you lose. Tails you lose.'

'Some penny,' I muttered and drew her down on to my chest, as Gene Krupa started up again, only this time his drums were only a mile or two away.

When she could hear herself speak, Arabella mouthed into my chest, 'Think the motor cyclist could be Folland's French boyfriend?'

I gave a lying down version of a shrug.

'Could be. What's more, you could bring a bike over easily on a boat. I should have asked Tony if it had French plates.'

'He'd have told you if it had. His eagle eyes wouldn't have missed a thing like that.'

I ran my finger through the pile of her hair. This time it sprang back.

'It makes him easier for the police to find if he does bring the bike across with him – that is, on a regular basis, anyway.'

'That'll be a relief.'

I herrummed. She herrummed back. We are the archetypal twentieth-century conversationalists.

After an interval of another drum solo, I said, 'But what beats me, other than the thunder, is why Folland's ex-lover and maybe murderer, should be following Tony Thorn. Why trail a schoolboy?'

She hurrummed again.

'All right,' I said. 'I know, I know. But don't you think it's a bit strange. There are almost a hundred boys at that school and he chooses Tony.'

She fluttered her eyelashes. 'There were more than a hundred girls in the world, when you . . .'

I put my hand over her mouth. Big mistake. She bit it.

'No. Ow! Be serious. It interests me why he should choose Tony; that is, if he's not just an innocent BMW rider who just happens to be around every time Tony ventures out of doors.'

She rose up off my chest, her eyes suddenly illuminated by a lightning flash.

'You don't mean, darling, that your nasty little mind has Tony mixed up in this whole affair, somehow, do you?'

'Didn't say that, did I?'

'Not outright, you didn't. But . . .'

'But. You're right, Harriet Vane, you're right. But . . .'

'I don't believe a non-existent word of it. Tony may, in years to come, turn out to be a devious millionaire, I'll grant you, but he's no teenage murderer, nor an under-age Raffles – especially when it comes to funds that were going for Ethiopian famine relief. No, sir-rio.'

She marked out a big 'x' on my chest with her finger and it didn't stand for a kiss. 'You're barking up the wrong tree, Lord Peter, I'll tell you now.'

'I'm not doing anything up any trees. I just think it strange that Tony may be being followed, that's all. I can't believe it's a motor cycling child molester, lying in wait, somehow.'

'Why not?'

'First of all, Tony is a bit big and a bit old for that kind of

90

attempt. Secondly, you can tell a mile off that he's far too street-wise to fall for any "Your mother's phoned and says you're to come to my place to wait" routine.'

'So why is he being followed?'

'That's my question.'

'It's mine now.'

I hugged her to me.

'It's neither of ours, actually. Because I've suddenly decided I'm going to see old Digby Whetstone in the morning.'

'Can't take the risk of waiting?'

'Not really. Tony's life could be at stake. Why, Lord knows? It's over to Digby to find out.'

'He'll be surprised to see you.'

'I don't think the word will be "surprised", quite. Choose from "horrified, aghast, irate, purple in the face, disgusted, sick, mortified" and anything but "struck dumb", and mark your choice with a tick in the margin.'

She started to tick my margin. I didn't interrupt. After a while, she said, 'It's the right decision.'

'Glad you think so.'

'You couldn't just leave it.'

'Over to Digby.'

'Lord Peter . . . ?'

I managed a 'Yes?'

'Thanks for saving me from the hangman.'

'That's all right, Miss Vane, any time, any time.'

To my utter surprise, it did not turn out the way we prophesied. Number one, Digby Whetstone did not keep me waiting on his rock-hard ante-room chair. He saw me right away. Number two, he didn't have me brusquely ushered in by some macho-moustached constable, but actually deigned to emerge from his office himself to greet me with a Number three, rarely seen and rarely used smile on his red face. For a moment, I wondered if Bournemouth CID had substituted a wrongly programmed clone.

Once seated opposite his steely anonymous desk, I wasted no time in getting down to the subject of my mission, just in case Digby's mood changed. He listened with fat freckled fingers held in a v close to his ginger moustache and he didn't let his reclining chair creak once during my performance.

At the end, he did recline and, to my surprise, someone must have oiled that too.

'Well, well, well,' were his first words, followed by, 'This is a turn-up for the book, Mr Marklin. You coming to me with information and wanting to involve the properly constituted forces of law, rather than acting on your own. It's taken time, but I think the penny must have at last dropped.'

I thought of bending down, searching the floor and asking, 'Where?' but decided his remark wasn't even worth that. I brushed an imaginary speck off my Marks and Sparks jeans instead.

'Well, that's all, Inspector,' I said. 'I just thought you should know. Both to protect Tony Thorn and maybe, help you in solving the Manners School affair.'

I got up to go, but – and I've lived to see it – he did not want me to; he waved me back to my seat, with a second smile.

'If you're in no hurry, Mr Marklin, would you like some coffee?'

I shook my head, more in disbelief than to reject institutionalized coffee.

'In that case, I'll get right down to brass tacks.' He leaned forward. 'I've seen your girlfriend, Arabella . . .'

'Trench. As in coat,' I smirked. 'You know that.'

'Ah yes, Trench. I've seen her at Manners School recently. Covering events for her paper, I gather.'

'You gathered.'

He pursed his lips.

'So that means you are being kept up to date with all the latest.'

'I don't know. What is the latest?' I tried. 'Found the Frenchman?'

'Ah, you know about him, then. Someone has been talking to Miss Pettican.'

'That's why I came to tell you about the motor cyclist following Tony Thorn. In case it could be the same man.'

He patted his moustache, as if it was coming off.

'Ah . . . I see.'

'What . . . er . . . is all this leading up to, Inspector?'

'All what?'

'You are not really given to idle conversation. Police time is too valuable, I'm sure. So I'm guessing this conversation is the reverse of idle, whatever that is.'

'Industrious, Mr Marklin. That's the reverse of idle.'

Oh God, how patronizing could he be?

He went on, 'I'm being very industrious about this whole Manners School affair. Checking every lead, every possible source of information.'

I suddenly twigged what he might be getting at and why he had been acting so totally out of character with me from the start.

'Do you mean source of information or of ideas, Inspector?'

This time I leaned forward. He immediately leaned back.

'You're stuck, aren't you, Digby? You've got a burglary you can't solve. You don't even know how the thief got in or away again, from all accounts. You don't know whether the burglary fits in with the murder or is on its ownio. You haven't recovered the money, or I'd have heard. You don't know who murdered Folland or, I bet, why he was killed, either. Or how the murderer got in and out, for that matter . . .'

Digby Whetstone closed his red-rimmed eyes and took a deep breath. 'Finished, Mr Marklin?'

'Not quite,' I hurried. 'I'm going to surprise you now. I'm going to sympathize with you, Digby, for once. If I were in your shoes, I would be well and truly stuck too, unless you've got more information than I've been fed by Miss Trench and Tony Thorn. You've got a stinker of a case to solve and I don't blame you tapping every brain you come across for ideas. Sorry, old boy, for not being more help. Right now, I'm fresh out of ideas, unless you call suspecting everyone in the case, Hawkesworth, Pettican, the Headmaster, the Frenchman, the motor cyclist, even . . .' I stopped there. Odds were, if I mentioned the 'evens' of the caretaker or Tony Thorn, albeit in jest, I might land them both with visits they could do without. As it was . . .

Whetstone took the words right out of my brain.

'You realize I'll have to follow up on your information, don't you, Mr Marklin? Go and see this boy.' He held his hand up. 'It's all right. I'll tread softly and, if you like, attribute my knowledge of this motor cyclist to observations by some of my men.'

'As you will,' I said. 'But I'm perfectly willing to own up I told you.'

He reclined further, until his face was only just above the level of his desk. Somehow, I think they'd not only oiled the chair, but weakened it too.

'So you have got none of the ... famous Marklin theories, then?' he went on. 'No flashes of insight, intuitive hunches ...?'

I shook my head. 'Not this time.' Then I said, 'I know it's a silly question, but I assume you have checked everyone's whereabouts at the time of the burglary and murder and that their alibis stand up?'

He sniggered. 'Everyone you've mentioned, except the Frenchman, of course. And quite a few you haven't.'

I held up my hands. 'Well, all I can offer you is good luck, Inspector.'

'So you're keeping out this time?'

His eyes brightened like Herbert Lom's in the *Pink Panther* series, whenever he hears Inspector Clouseau has been taken off a case.

I got up. 'Remember that penny?' I said.

His ginger moustache twitched, then he forced another smile. 'Whilst we are totally against private individuals taking action as their own private police forces, Mr Marklin, we don't frown on the same individuals sharing any information they mave have come by, or even offering us their own theories and ideas. So, Mr Marklin, if you think of anything that might be relevant to this Manners School case, regard my door as ever open, won't you?'

I tipped my forelock and left, being very careful to shut his door behind me.

Eight

I felt somewhat better after seeing Digby Whetstone. It wasn't anything he did or said. It was just that I had taken the weight of Tony's fears of being followed off my own shoulders and transferred them to where they really did belong – with the boys in blue. After all, I had no resources to protect Tony or even put a tail on him. My only regret was that now Tony would undoubtedly get a visit from the law during the day. I just prayed Whetstone had the tact to leave it until after school hours. The thought of a constable appearing in the classroom to whisk him away in mid-lesson shivered my timbers.

The day, Toy Emporium-wise, was only so-so, so much so that I rather despaired over the scientific re-siting of the stock in my shop. A sixties Dinky Rambler Station Wagon went to a middle-aged man with a basset-hound face for forty-five pounds, and a lady in her mid-thirties, with a mouth the size of a railway tunnel, bought a boxed pre-war Dinky 'Flying Fortress' bomber for ninety pounds for her husband's birthday present. (He had seen it in my previous unscientific window display and had asked his wife to get it for him.) The only high point came in the early evening with a telephone call. It was from the guy whose father had the old Dinky planes in his attic. It appeared the old man was now prepared to sell, if the price was right. I wasn't willing to haggle on the telephone. Besides, you have to actually behold pre-war Dinky aircraft before buying, for the metal fatigue reasons I've already described. So I asked whether the guy could bring the collection in for a valuation. He said he would, if I could see him one evening and should he bring the French ones too? My ears perked up at the last piece of information, as my own personal collection was short of many of the aircraft produced by the Dinky factory in Paris, as they are very hard to come by. But I kept my enthusiasm to myself as I coolly made a date for the next evening at eight.

Meanwhile, I was looking forward to a quiet Tuesday evening with Arabella, for they were showing Woody Allen's *Zelig* on the box, a film I had missed in the cinema, as it had suffered a very patchy general release.

The credits had only just rolled, when the noise I had been dreading, jangled above the soundtrack. Arabella looked round at me.

'Tony?' she queried.

I sighed. 'Probably. I've been half-expecting it. He has probably come to berate me for telling the police.'

I dragged myself through into the shop. Parked outside the window was an old but immaculate Vanden Plas Princess 1300 (you know the one, basically a tarted-up Morris with leather and walnut). Parked at the shop door were two figures, only one of which was Tony.

I hesitantly opened the door. Before I could utter a word, he said, 'Peter, I'm sorry to come round like this, but my father . . .'

The taller figure extended a hand. 'Mr Marklin,' it said, in a very precise voice. 'I am Tony's father.'

I reciprocated the gesture.

'Oh . . . er . . . do come in, Mr Thorn.'

'Reginald,' he pronounced. 'Everyone calls me Reg.'

I couldn't get over his voice, or manner for that matter. Tony had told me he was a clock enthusiast, but this was ridiculous. He moved like one of those clock figures that chunder out of little doors on the hour to strike little bells to mark the hour. And, as if that wasn't enough, his voice had the measured rhythm of the old telephone TIM, but with the added measure of a kind of echo. If he hadn't been Tony's father, I might have laughed.

Directly I had shut the door, Tony said urgently, 'We won't be long. Dad just wanted to meet you and . . .'

'. . . thank you, Mr Marklin,' Pater took over, 'for the time you're sparing for my son and for the trouble you took to tell the police about his being followed.'

I looked at Tony. 'I'm sorry, Tony, but I felt I had to inform them. I didn't want you to run any further risk of . . .'

He nodded his head and smiled. 'It's okay, Peter, really. You see, I saw him again this morning. As I was cycling to school. He was in a layby. So you see, I'm glad you went to them.'

Well, that was one weight off my mind, anyway.

'Like to come on through?' I indicated the door into the house.

Mr Thorn waved his arm, like he was about to strike the quarter. 'No, thank you very much. I don't want to take up your evening. I just wanted to express my gratitude, that's all.'

His large, brownest of brown eyes scanned the shop.

'Interesting selection of toys you have. Takes you back in time, seeing the toys of childhood.'

'Oh, by the way,' I suddenly remembered. 'Thank you so much for mending that Minic motor of mine the other day.'

His long, rather lugubrious face broke into a smile. 'Think nothing of it. I love tinkering, as my boy here knows. Drives the rest of the family mad, I'm afraid.'

'You have old clocks the way I have old toys,' I ventured.

'Yes, I'm afraid I do.'

'But yours aren't forever ticking and chiming, Peter,' Tony chipped in. 'We're used to it now, but overnight visitors in our house look mega-exhausted by the morning.'

I laughed. Not a mega-laugh, though.

'Hope my boy is not bothering you too much with all his theories, is he, Mr Marklin?'

'No,' I half-lied. 'I'm intrigued with some of them enough to give them a try. Like I have rearranged the shop according to the best supermarket rules.'

Reginald Thorn put his hand on his son's shoulder. 'Tony, here, is brimful of theories as to how to make money. We get them over breakfast, lunch, tea and supper. He thinks that there's always a formula to be successful. Follow the right rules in life and, bingo, the jackpot. Everything will follow like . . .'

'. . . clockwork,' Tony grinned. 'And so it will, Dad. Just you wait and see, when I can put a few of my ideas into practice.'

Thorn looked across at me. 'Life's not quite like that, is it, Mr Marklin? Too many unforeseen hiccups, I'm afraid.' He re-adjusted his tie.

'Anyway, we should leave you in peace now. Thanks, once again, for helping my Tony. We do appreciate it.' He turned to go.

I turned to Tony. 'Did the police come round?'

He nodded. 'Yes, about half past five. I was in the middle of tea.'

'Digby Whetstone?'

He looked puzzled. 'Digby who?'

So the dear Inspector hadn't turned up himself.

'Oh, Digby Whetstone is the Inspector in charge of the case.'

'The man you saw?'

'The man I saw.'

'No, this was a Constable Harrington, I think he said his name was.'

'And you told him all about the motor cyclist?'

'Everything I know, which isn't much. He took it all down and said they would follow it up.'

Reginald Thorn patted his son's back. 'Meanwhile, I am taking Tony to and from school for a bit, in the car. At least, until things . . . get sorted out over the tragic happenings at his school. It's one of the advantages of working from home, you see, Mr Marklin,' he smiled. 'You can always be on call to be the family chauffeur.'

He held out his hand. 'Anyway, I'm very glad to have met you. Remember, don't take any nonsense from Tony.'

'Haven't heard any yet,' I said. 'And I'm glad to have met the man who has such a way with clockwork.'

'Any time you've got trouble with a toy . . .' He propelled his son towards the door.

Tony looked back. 'I'll bring the graphs, Peter, in a day or two. Okay?'

'Okay,' I grinned. 'No mega-panic.'

Tony took my meaning and winked. I let them out. From the back of the shop, I watched the streetlight dance over the small car's immaculate paintwork, as it drove away. Mr Thorn was patently as much of a fanatic as his son, in his own, much quieter, way.

When I got back to Arabella, I was delighted to see she had slipped a tape into the video recorder to catch the bits of *Zelig* that I'd missed.

'Tony come about the police?' she whispered out of the corner of her mouth, without her eyes leaving Woody Allen.

'Not really. He brought his father along.'

She shot me a glance. 'His father? What on earth for?'

'Ostensibly, Dad wanted to thank me for all the time and trouble I'm taking with his son.'

'And without an ostens . . .?'

'I think he really just wanted to check me out.'

Now she'd given up whispering. 'Check you out? What for?'

98

'To see I wasn't another Folland or even that motor cyclist after his son.'

'You?' she exclaimed.

'Shut up,' I smiled between my teeth. 'Look, Zelig's about to meet Hitler.'

Wednesday dawned as an autumn day should. Brisk but bright. And Arabella actually lowered the top of her Golf, before she accelerated off to her paper. I read mine cover to depressing cover (the pre-Christmas three months seems to bring out the worst in the world's populations, somehow), then sorted out my mail and opened up shop. Almost immediately, I felt like closing up again, as, would you believe it, an orange Bond Bug three-wheeler jerked to a stop outside. No prizes for guessing the driver.

He came in, with a taunting grin on his face.

'Gus. This has to be the living end,' I gasped. 'A Bond ruddy Bug. They couldn't even give them away when they were new in 1970.'

My stool creaked under his ungainly frame.

'That's as maybe, my son.'

'Don't tell me you're thinking of . . .' I began, but he cut in, 'So I won't tell you.' And he shut up like a clam, sod him. There followed a most un-Gus-like silence. For even when he's asleep, Gus is guilty of noise pollution.

When I'd tapped my fingers on the counter a few times, I said, 'Okay, Gus, give. You haven't come over here just to wear out my furniture rather than your own, have you? I mean, it's only really a small extension of your current habit of wearing out other people's cars.'

He suddenly guffawed and the stool rocked.

'Me last time, I reckon, old lad. When I take back that Bug.'

'You mean . . . you've decided to call all this free-wheeling a day?'

'Probably,' he sniffed. 'I'm starting to get fed-up with having to learn new controls every five flipping minutes.'

'Well, well, well,' I said. 'And you're going to stick with your Popular, after all?'

'Maybe. Maybe not. Still a bit worried about not making the most of me assets.'

I raised my eyes to the heavens. All I saw were the cobwebs

embracing a Meccano Constructor biplane that dangled on a fishing line from the ceiling.

'You and Tony Thorn would make a wonderful pair. But pair of what, I'm not willing to divulge.'

He leaned forward, so I had a fine close-up of his mass-market stubble.

'Ere, talking of that there schoolboy, brings me to why I dropped by.'

'So it wasn't to show me the Bug?'

'Naa. Not showing you no cars no more, I'm not. Snobby sod.'

'So . . .?'

'Well, when I picked up that three-wheeler yesterday evening, guess who I saw eyeing a brand new Vauxhall in the showroom?' His rheumy eyes did the next best thing to sparkling, as he attended my reaction. I didn't keep him waiting.

'Duke of Edinburgh? Colonel Gadaffi? Terry Wogan? The Ayatollah? Or – I know – it has to be Joan Collins.'

This time *his* eyes went to the cobwebs.

'Thank you, Mr Marklin,' he grunted. 'Now, do you want to know or not?'

'Want to know. Promise,' I smiled.

'That fellow from Manners School. You know, the caretaker chap.'

'The caretaker, Andy Boxall? But you've never met him.'

'Saw him, didn't I, when they interviewed him on local telly after the teacher's body was found? 'Sides, salesman recognized his face too. Cracked a joke about him, he did. Said, maybe he'd done the jumble sale burglary and was going to use the money as a down ruddy payment.' He laughed, then looked at me.

'Thought you'd like to know, old lad, that's all.'

'Why should I want to know?'

''Cos . . .'cos . . .,' he leaned forward once again, 'you're sort of caught up in the case, aren't you?'

I denied it. But not seven times.

''Course you are, old son, whether you like it or not.'

I came round to Gus's side of the counter.

'You are a sod, Gus. Do you know that?'

He looked as innocent as anyone with that much stubble can look. 'Me? A sod?' he said in an almost falsetto voice.

'Precisely,' I snapped. 'Because you ruddy want me to get up to my neck in this case, don't you?'

He grinned. 'That would make two of us then.'

I pointed an accusing finger. 'Now, look here, Gus, I know your game. You want *me* to get involved because, if I do, then you think I'll farm out odd juicy assignments to you to liven up your long and weary days. Well, sorry, Gus, but you should have realized fishing was boring over half a century ago.'

He rubbed his sandpaper chin.

'Old Digby Whetstone's not going to solve it, is he? Stands to reason.'

'Why not? He must have solved hundreds of cases I've not been involved with.'

'This one is different. You can smell it.'

He had a point. If I followed my nose, I had to agree with him.

'He'll solve it,' I wishfully thought.

Gus looked at me hard. 'Why, what do you know that I don't?'

I sighed and looked towards my shop window for help. But customers were there none.

'Got time for a natter,' he announced, 'if you have.'

So there was no escape. We nattered. And when we had finished over an hour later, we had explored just about every nook and cranny of the Manners School affair. And for once, bless old Gus, I felt distinctly better for doing so.

At the end, Gus said, 'Know something?'

'Wish I did,' I smirked.

'The key to it all, I reckon, is what links the burglary to the murder.'

'If they *are* linked at all,' I reminded him.

'Bit of a you-know what, if they're not. One day a burglary, next day a murder.'

'Coincidence?' I suggested.

'Yea. One of those,' he grinned.

'Maybe. I thought you were going to say that the key to it all is quite literally that. A key. The key that must have let the burglar in and the murderer in. Whose key was it? Or maybe there were two different keys. We know all the official key-holders, but it's pretty simple to have duplicates made, if you can snaffle a bunch for half an hour or so.'

Gus thought for a moment. 'That boy's father. You say he's a clock repairer?'

I nodded. Wasn't hard to see what he was getting at.

101

'He'd know all about keys, wouldn't he, chap like that? And have a ruddy great pile of them, wouldn't wonder.'

'Clock keys are different,' I pointed out.

'I bet he's had to make a key for an old clock before now. Works with metal, anyway, doesn't he? So he could turn his hand to making a copy now, couldn't he?'

'If he could get hold of the originals for a time, probably.'

'Well, then.'

'Well, nothing,' I said. 'I can't see any ruddy reason why Tony Thorn's father should rob his son's school or murder the French master.'

'Maybe Tony hasn't told you it all,' he sighed.

'You mean . . . ?'

'Yea.'Fraid so, old son. I mean, he might not own up to you that teacher had made advances, like. But could have told his dad.'

I was starting to regret Gus's visit all over again.

'I'd rather stick with the French connection as a theory.'

'The sailor with the bike?'

'Well, the sailor, anyway. We don't know the motor cyclist is the same fellow.'

Gus chewed his lip. 'Then there's that caretaker, remember? Bit funny a chap like him hanging about car showrooms.'

'It needn't be funny. Maybe he daydreams . . . like Walter Mitty.'

'Walter who?' Gus frowned.

'Oh, he's a . . . forget it, Gus. All I meant was that window-gazing at expensive things doesn't make you a thief.'

'Well, then there's that Colonel Bogey character. He has keys, you say, and has a thing about chaps like Folland, without bloody Aids.'

I threw up my hands. 'That's the trouble with this school affair, Gus. There's no end to the there's-es. There's Delia Pettican. Who knows, she might have a skeleton in her cupboard that Folland perhaps found out about and she needed the Ethiopian money to keep his mouth shut.'

'Fossil, more like,' Gus laughed, and noticing my look of puzzlement, explained, 'Not skeleton, old love. Fossil, get it? She collects fossils.'

I ignored it and went on, 'Then there's the girl's father, old Eames. We know he's got a temper. Maybe he was so incensed about the Aids thing, he made an appointment with Folland and did him in.'

'Then there's always your whizz-kid,' Gus added quietly. 'Never know. Maybe he robbed the school. You say he's money mad. Then Folland found out and he murdered him.'

I shook my head, not because I was absolutely positive Tony Thorn couldn't have done such a thing, but because I didn't even want to think about such a possibility.

'I didn't say he was money mad, Gus. I just said he was obsessed with ways of making money.'

Gus shrugged. 'Big difference.'

'There *is* a big difference, whether you can see it or not. Tony is obsessed with the mechanisms of making money, rather than with money itself. That's why so many successful businessmen don't stop when they've made enough to last them and their families a couple of lifetimes, but go on and on and on. It's not for the millions. Their real turn-on is not so much making a buck, as making a deal.'

Gus exhaled slowly and looked at me. Sod him. There was no real answer to that, whatever my wishful thoughts.

'Hope you're right, old son,' he said at last, then looked at his watch. I looked at mine. It was quarter to Heineken.

'Dropping down?' he asked as nonchalantly as he could.

'Don't think so. Got some parcels to do up and post.'

He sniffed. 'Must be important parcels.'

'Only toys. Direct mail orders.'

'Take you all lunch-time?'

'Some time.'

He moved round on the stool, as if he was about to get up. I loved it.

'Think I might drop by. Nattering gives you a bit of a thirst.'

'Along with everything else,' I said.

Silence, followed by, 'Well, I'll be off then.'

'Give my love to the regulars.'

'Won't be many in today. Not Wednesdays. Quiet day, Wednesdays.'

'Well, give my love to the landlord, then.'

He squirmed around on his stool. 'Sure you're not coming?'

'Positive,' I said.

'You might do your parcels quicker than you think.'

'Might do. But still won't be going down to the pub.'

'Why not?' he looked aghast.

'I'll tell you why not, Gus,' I laughed out loud. 'I'll be too bloody busy here, pouring Heinekens down the gullet of a stupid old bastard who's taken fifty years to discover he prefers sleuthing to fishing . . .'

I think if I'd said it any later, he'd have had a heart attack.

I made Gus walk home, after I'd poured him out the door. I didn't like the idea of him and that Bond Bug weaving their way into trouble so he left it outside the shop, vowing he would return for it before close of play. But I knew he wouldn't. That garage wouldn't be seeing its orange peril back until the morn and I didn't suppose for a minute they would really miss it. After all, they had Gus's Popular, which had to be worth more than the Bug. Everything is.

Within minutes of Gus's departure, I saw Arabella's Golf pull up behind the three-wheeled wonder and noticed the convertible top was now up, though the day was still bright. Directly she dinged into the shop, I could see something was wrong – and that something was her. Her forehead was damp with sweat and her tan was starting to look like a poor top-coat over deathly white. As I took her hand, I could feel she was running quite a temperature.

'Can't stay long,' she muttered. 'Got to go over to see old Hawkesworth.'

I shepherded her into the sitting-room.

'You're not going anywhere but bed, my darling.'

She collapsed on to the settee. 'I have to go. He's drawn up a new credo and curriculum for the school and has called in local Press and TV to publicize his plans.'

I felt her forehead. I could have fried an egg on it.

'Look, Arabella, you've got a mother and father of a fever. I'm going to see you go straight up wooden hill to blanket bay.'

'But . . .' she began.

'No buts. I'll ring your paper and say . . .'

'. . . that you will cover Hawkesworth,' she cut in with a weak smile.

'Pardon?

'You'll cover Hawkesworth.' She took my hand. 'Will you? Not hard. Just take my little tape-recorder and a notebook. Easy as . . .'

104

'. . . getting flu,' I sighed. 'Bet you got it when you came home drenched the other day.'

'You haven't answered me, Peter. Tiny favour? When I'm better, I'll do one for you.'

I forced a smile. 'An interview?'

'No, moron.'

'Like what, honey chile?'

'Like taking Gus off your hands once in a while. Who knows . . . ?'

'Oh . . . I see.'

'Well, will you?'

I sighed. 'Okay. This once. But only if you go up to bed with two man-sized Paracetamols this instant.'

'Go to bed with two Paras?' she smiled.

'Well, not the whole battalion,' I said, raising her up from the settee.

Nine

When Arabella had first suggested it, I'd imagined I would be going to Hawkesworth's impressive home. But no. He'd had the gall to call the conference at the school, though it soon became evident that his educational plans and philosophy were entirely personal and had not been discussed with the staff or Delia Pettican. Only the Headmaster seemed to have been privy to his thinking and then only some thirty minutes before the conference began. (Which the Headmaster was at pains to point out.)

However, I had to admit the Colonel, ruthless and misguided as he might be, was a considerable speaker and, as was the reported practice of the legendary Field Marshal Montgomery, assembled and displayed the facts and arguments that suited him with martial discipline and, thus, with stunning clarity. And like all cunning politicians, he paraded exaggerated alternatives to the new school philosophy and curricula, thus taking most of the wind out of the sails of the disbelievers or challengers. ('Let's get back to the good old discipline of the 3 Rs. And ditch the 3 Ls that are infecting our education system: Loony, Left Wing, Laisser-faire. And if we are not careful in our selection of teachers, our children won't grow up to be proud examples of homo sapiens, but be encouraged to entertain notions of quite a different homo . . .' etcetera, etcetera.)

The members of the media, to my disappointment, seemed to be more interested in encouraging Hawkesworth into more and more extreme statements than really querying his credo. I guess they thought that made for better copy.

I kept my eyes on the Headmaster, a Mr Henry Beamish, a lot of the time. But he rarely looked up, as if he was embarrassed by the whole affair. He just sat there on the school platform, his podgy hands folded over his equally podgy stomach. His normally beetroot complexion was perfect camouflage for any blushes that might be triggered by the Colonel's rash and radical statements. So there was no way of knowing what his thoughts were, except about personal survival, that is. The few comments he did make were so hedged with qualifications and trimmed with platitudinous phrases – such as 'thought provoking', 'basis for discussion' and 'the process of rethinking must, of necessity, be a catholic one before decisions are finally taken' – that he lost me, which, I suspect, was his intention. However, my disrespect for his obvious cowardice in not taking a stand was somewhat balanced by my sympathy for the trials and tribulations he had endured recently. A major robbery and a murder in quick succession would have fazed even Quilp of Dotheboys Hall.

The meeting that had begun with a bang, ended somewhat in a whimper as questioning tailed away and the media started to pack up to go home. I switched off my recorder and waited for the television people to get out of the way before I made a move. The Headmaster left the platform pretty smartly, having shaken hands with the Colonel, who was still shuffling papers at the lectern. I watched him as he marshalled them into a neat pile and then stowed them away in one of those wine-red leather 'I'm an executive' cases. As he looked up, his eyes caught mine and I could see the chips in his electronic memory working overtime to work out where he had seen me before. I looked away, but by then he'd got a read-out.

His voice boomed: 'You're Miss Trench's friend, aren't you?'

He'd descended from the platform and was coming up my aisle, before I could make my escape.

'Now, your name is, again?' he smiled unctuously.

'What it was before,' I replied. 'Marklin. As in ... nothing.'

'Ah.' He held out his hand. I had to shake it.

'Didn't see Miss Trench,' he frowned.

'She wasn't here. I came in her place. She's in bed with a flu bug.'

'Oh, I'm so sorry. Do give her my warmest regards and wishes for a speedy recovery.' He looked at me, as if I was something the cat had brought in.

'You a journalist too, then?'

'No.'

My long and elaborate reply seemed to take him aback.

'Just helping out ... a friend?'

I nodded.

'Word has it, Mr ... er ... Marklin, that you make a bit of a habit of helping out ... friends.'

I looked at him. The conversation had taken an unexpected turn.

'Good Samaritan, me,' I smiled. 'But you would know all about that. Your knowledge of the Bible this afternoon was most illuminating.'

He fingered his sometime broken nose. 'Can never read the Good Book too often. But I was really referring to your reputed activities as a ... how can I put it ... amateur private eye.' Guess which word he emphasized.

'Oh. What little birdie settled on your shoulder and chirped you that?'

'A little birdie, as you put it, that flies around in a white Rover, Mr Marklin. You know, the one with the red stripe.'

'One of the beaks of the brigade?'

'Precisely. I had some questions asked about you.'

'By a big, burly boiler with a ginger moustache?'

He didn't smile. 'Inspector Whetstone asked if you had been round to see me.'

I sighed. Trust Digby not to take my word that I wasn't involved.

'"Ferreting around" were the exact words he used,' he went on. 'Warned me you might get up to what he called "your usual tricks" and to ring him if you did. And now, Mr Marklin, I find you here. Quite a coincidence, don't you think?'

'I told you,' I replied irritably, 'Miss Trench has flu and I'm just standing in for her paper.'

'I might believe you, Mr Marklin, but a million others might not.'

'I didn't know there were a million people with freckled hands and ginger moustaches ...' I began, but was promptly interrupted, not by Hawkesworth, but by a shout from the back of the school hall. I looked round at what was now a practically deserted hall and saw a lean and purposeful figure striding towards us, her eyes flashing laser beams of anger. I stood back.

'You've gone too far now, Colonel. Too bloody far.'

I stood further back.

'Why, Miss Pettican,' Hawkesworth patronized, 'I don't remember inviting you.'

She stopped, some three feet from me, yet I could feel the physical vibrations of her anger.

'I was over Weymouth way, when I heard about this little shennanigan, otherwise I'd have been here sooner and put some backbone into Beamish to refuse to hold it on school premises.'

'Mr Beamish is his own master,' Hawkesworth smiled.

'He's the lackey of the last person who speaks to him and you know it.'

'Tut, tut,' the Colonel scolded. 'What will everyone think of our school, if you go around bad-mouthing its head like that? Mr Marklin here, for instance. And he says he's come on behalf of the *Western Gazette*, no less.'

She turned to me for the first time.

'I'm sorry, Mr Marklin, to have to wash a little of our dirty linen in public. But it's been forced upon me by this . . . this . . .' she hunted for a word and then found two quite good ones, '. . . antediluvian bully. For your paper, you can say, quote, "Miss Pettican was deliberately kept in the dark about the conference by Colonel Hawkesworth and upon arriving too late either to stop it or to contribute to it, expressed her utter contempt for the inexcusable unilateral action taken by one of the school governors and will see that no further meetings of this type can be held without due consultation between the governors and staff of the school."'

Unfortunately, I only managed to get from 'no further meetings' etc. on tape, as she had taken me by surprise and anyway, I'd pressed the wrong button.

The next thing I knew I felt Hawkesworth's heavy hand on my shoulder.

'I think it may be time for you to go, Mr Marklin. What Miss Pettican and I have to say to each other is no concern of amateur pressmen, or indeed, amateur sleuths.'

Miss Pettican gave me a leathery look. 'Sleuth?'

The way she said it, it wasn't quite a question, really. It was almost an invitation. I picked up the nudge.

'As you already know, Miss Pettican, I'm a friend of Tony Thorn's.'

'And a friend of that nice Miss Trench,' she smiled.

I nodded. 'She would have been here but she's got flu.'

'Oh, I'm so sorry. Do wish her well for me. And don't bother to explain about Tony. I've heard all about it from his girlfriend,

Ella. And all about you, Mr Marklin. Thank you so much for trying to help out the other day.'

'What on earth did you do the other day?' Hawkesworth barked, but we both ignored him.

'Lucky, in the end, you weren't needed,' she continued. 'I should have remembered about the figure on the wall and Folland's French friend before.'

'Tragedies tend to numb the mind,' I offered.

'There were quite a lot of policemen in Weymouth today, I noticed. Inspector Whetstone is obviously taking my information very seriously. Let us hope we soon have news of an arrest.'

'Let's hope so,' I nodded and then felt the heavy hand of the bore once more.

'Please, get out, Mr Marklin. And get back to your paper, or Miss Trench, or wherever you're going. I can't waste time listening to you two all day . . .'

Miss Pettican shrugged and clasped my hand firmly.

'Hard to believe "Gracious" is his second name, isn't it? Anyway, give my regards to Miss Trench. I liked her awfully when I met her. And tell her I do sympathize. Flu is such a lowering thing.'

'Will do,' I said and started to leave.

'And keep out of affairs that don't concern you,' Hawkesworth bellowed after me.

I turned round at the door. 'I thought you said this afternoon, "Education should be the concern of every man Jack and woman Jill in our green and pleasant land."'

I think if looks could kill, he'd have been up for first-degree murder right then and there.

Despite a forehead that felt like like hot lead and which, apparently, drummed like you know who, Arabella wrote up a fair old piece for her newspaper from my garbled notes and crackling tape-recorder. Mind you, I had to sit beside her on the bed to guide her through the jungle of non sequiturs, yawning gaps and barely decipherable comments, but all the same for an Indian-winter flu victim . . .

After taking her paper and Parker from her, I offered to make some supper which she declined in favour of some hot sleep. So I tiptoed downstairs, fed myself and Bing (who seemed far less interested in his Whiskas than normal – I prayed Arabella hadn't

110

contracted some form of cat flu by mistake), then let some television wash over me in an effort (vain) to cleanse myself of my ever-nagging concerns over the dramas at Manners School. Concerns that my afternoon encounters with the dear Colonel and Miss Pettican had only inflamed. I only wished I could totally identify with the seeming 'goody' of the two, for man is never happier than when he's chosen sides and is rootin' and tootin' for a cause.

But there was some little thing about Delia Pettican that niggled me, and, try as I might, I could not put my finger on it. In the end, I put it down to the fact that I'd been frightened to death of ageing spinsters ever since my 'knee high to a bee' days, when my mother had taken me to visit an elderly aunt, who lived near Wookey Hole. During an endless afternoon visit, she had pronounced me guilty of the heinous crimes of 1) having dirty finger-nails. 2) Speaking when not spoken to. 3) Not speaking when spoken to. 4) Staring at the goitre on her neck. 5) Leaving finger-prints on the gloss of her baby grand. 6) Not double flushing the toilet and 7) Not double chewing her anchovy paste sandwiches before swallowing.

It was whilst I was pondering on Miss Pettican that the doorbell jangled me back to then and now. I looked at my watch and knew who it would be.

He was a tall, willowy man with the perpetual stoop that seems to go as a set with adjectives that describe him. I guessed he must live in an old cottage, because he ducked automatically every time he went through my own seven-foot-six doors.

'I hope these may be what you are looking for, Mr Marklin,' he said in a voice too light for his body, and patted the large cardboard container under his arm. We went through into the sitting-room and sat down. Moments of discovery like this need to be savoured slowly and in a relaxed atmosphere. Bing promptly left the room, for though the container had '24 Kitekat' blazoned all over it, he wasn't fooled.

'Like a drink?' I offered, as he opened the lid of the box and took out the first object wrapped in what could only be the front page of the *Guardian*.

'No, thanks,' he smiled. 'I've still got another appointment tonight.'

I must have frowned or something, for he went on, 'For you see, I'm a bit like you. I'm in the antiques business. But not toys.

Almost everything else, curiously, but not those. Victoriana mainly.'

I should have guessed. There was a musty quality about him that went with horsehair sofas, antimacassars and oleograph pictures.

'Can be a slow old game,' I said, 'anything to do with antiques.'

He finished unwrapping the first item and I knew his visit had not been in vain – unless, of course, he wanted a king's ransom for the contents of his Kitekat box.

He handed the small die-cast aircraft over to me.

'Good condition, isn't it? My father has always been meticulously careful about his possessions.'

"Good condition" was the understatement of the year. The "Arc en Ciel" trimotor was mint beyond belief, its red and gold paintwork as bright as when it had first left the Dinky factory in Paris some fifty or more years before. And not a trace of metal fatigue.

I watched with bated breath as he proceeded to unwrap the rest. First a tiny Breguet Corsair, then a blue and silver Potez 56, a Hanriot 180T, a Dewoitine de Chasse with French Air Force roundels, then a yellow and grey Potez 58. All as mint as the "Arc en Ciel".

I put them all down on the small table beside me and tried to conceal my utter delight, for fear it might give lofty men lofty ideas on their worth.

'These are all the unboxed items,' he smiled. I liked the sound of that, for it made me itch for what might be boxed. I wasn't disappointed. For a moment later, he withdrew pure gold from amongst the other pages of the *Guardian*. I recognized the box lid immediately. It depicted a small boy excitedly shouting out about the assorted collection of French Dinky Toys assembled in front of him. In the top right-hand corner, it bore the small label I was praying it would. 'No. 64 Avions.'

He took the lid off and handed the box to me. This time, I did not manage to conceal my excitement.

'Like them?'

'Er . . . yes . . . er . . . I like them . . . amazing,' I stuttered.

'Never been taken out of the box,' he went on. 'Still got the original string holding the aircraft in place.'

There were five models, as there should be, each one resplendent in its pristine silver finish, from the large trimotor Dewoitine

112

338 right through to the very rare, twin-engined Potez 63 attack bomber with French Air Force insignia. A set of sets, produced immediately prior to the German invasion of 1940, and thus rarely seen in Britain.

'I don't expect you to be interested in everything I've brought, naturally . . .' he began, but I waved my hand.

'I'm interested,' I said, then added quickly, 'but obviously, as you know from your own business, only if the prices are right.'

He stuffed the old *Guardian* pages back into the container and put it down by his feet.

'Naturally,' he enigmatically smiled. 'We all need to make a profit.'

I cleared my throat. 'They're not going to be for sale. They're for my own private collection.'

'Of Dinkies?'

'Of Dinky aircraft. At least with the aircraft, you have some chance of owning an example of every casting, whereas they made far too many cars and commercials . . .'

He leaned forward in his chair. 'Will these help you own them all?'

I nodded and waited. It's at times like this I wish I bit my nails.

'Perhaps we could do a deal,' he smiled.

'What kind of deal?'

'Well, you must visit quite a few houses in your search for old toys, don't you? Attend a lot of auctions.'

'Of course.'

'Well, maybe we could come to a reciprocal arrangement. When you spot a house full of Victoriana or attend a house clearance sale where decent Victorian items are likely to go cheap, give me a ring. And when I spot any old toys, I will reciprocate.'

Sounded reasonable to me. So I agreed and he handed me his card. "Duncan Noble. Victoriana et al. Market Street, Dorchester. Tel: Dorchester 79646."

'Like a price for the lot?' he asked.

I nodded.

'Well, as you're going to be helping me, how about . . . four hundred pounds?'

I was glad I was sitting down. I pretended to give it some thought.

'Three fifty?'

'I think they're worth four hundred.'

113

He was wrong. At a good auction, they could well be worth four times that amount.

I got up and took a cheque book from my pocket.

'All right. Cheque do, or would you prefer cash?'

'Cash, if you've got it.'

'Come through into the shop and I'll see if I have enough.'

I ushered him ahead of me and noticed he took very small steps for such a tall man. Whilst I opened up the till, he wandered round my shop, his stoop even more apparent as he inspected the merchandise. As luck would have it, I had only £389.

'I'll have to go upstairs and see if my . . .' I was going to say girlfriend, but, with a guess at his inclinations, decided against it, ' . . . see if I've got the other eleven pounds hidden away somewhere.'

He came back to the counter.

'Don't bother, Mr Marklin. Any time, any time.'

Before I could reply, the stillness of a Studland evening was shattered by a police siren and headlights flared by outside the window. As the wailing subsided, he sighed.

'Dear old Dorset had to succumb at some time, I suppose. The rest of the country apparently has.'

'To crime?' I queried.

He nodded. 'I've had two break-ins in my shop this year. Been in Dorchester eight years. Never had one at all before these.'

'Burglary is on the increase everywhere. Unfortunately, it's often kids who are at a loose end – who can't find employment.'

I offered him the notes which he accepted without bothering to count them.

'Talking of children,' he remarked, 'this Swanage school affair is pretty dreadful, isn't it?'

Just my luck. Good news – I had come upon a trove of Dinky aircraft, that had made me forget Manners School for once. Bad news – messenger with treasure chest has to remind me, etcetera, etcetera.

'Dreadful,' I agreed, hoping to close the conversation. No such luck, even though I started to walk him towards the shop door.

'I knew that schoolteacher, you know. Not all that well, but he used to come into my shop occasionally. Poor Alistair . . .'

Not 'Mr Folland', I noted.

' . . . to be struck down like that, just as he was about to . . .'

114

He stopped abruptly and looked away. 'But, perhaps, I shouldn't betray any confidences . . . especially of the departed.'

I waited a moment. People who come out and say they shouldn't betray confidences usually go on to do so. It's those who say nothing, say nothing, if you follow me. Eventually, he looked back at me.

'But, maybe, it can make no difference to Alistair now.'

'So just as he was about to . . . what?' I gently encouraged.

'Well, he always used to have a bit of a natter, when he dropped by the shop. Used to tell me about the school and how he was doing. A bit about his background, upbringing – very strict, apparently – in the Midlands, and how he loved France and all things . . . French.' He bit his lip. 'Then one day, in the spring I think it was, he seemed to be much more . . . well, boyish, if you like. More exuberant. Happier. Normally, he was just a little on the quiet, almost sad, side. He talked about life in a different way too – seemed to be much more optimistic about the future, his prospects – even talked about moving and buying a house somewhere. I thought perhaps he might have come into money or something, but didn't say anything until the next time he popped by.'

'Still as . . . boyish?'

'Yes. That's what prompted me to comment on it. He told me that something rather marvellous had happened in his life, which might dramatically alter his whole future. That's all he would say. Wouldn't tell me what it was. But he continued to talk of moving out of that dreary apartment block he lived in and buying something somewhere. A house of his own . . . that kind of thing.'

'You still think he might have had a windfall or come into money somehow.'

He pursed his lips. 'Could be. Or, perhaps, he could have found a new . . . friend.'

'Rich and generous friend?'

The antique dealer rasped his thin fingers together, as if they might spark his reply.

'Well . . . er . . . yes. He told me once he had a few quite wealthy acquaintances. There was some titled fellow in Surrey and a chap in France, who owned a big yacht, I remember, and a . . .'

I interrupted him. 'You don't know if this French yachtsman owned a BMW motorbike, do you?'

He frowned and then laughed. 'What a funny question, Mr Marklin. Why do you ask?'

'Oh nothing,' I said. 'Go on.'

'Well, there's nothing more really. The next – and last – time he dropped by was a few days before he was found dead.'

'Still ebullient?'

'No. Far from it. All the life seemed to have gone out of him. I didn't know then what I know now.'

'The four-initial word?'

It took him a little time to get it. 'Oh, yes. I see what you mean. The disease that kills not only people, but everything in its wake. Reputations, goodwill, tolerance, justice. Hell, Mr Marklin, I don't think God afflicted us with its scourge as a punishment or retribution for our ways, but as a means of exposing our pretensions, our hypocrisies, our paper-thin liberalism.'

He stopped in full flight and turned towards the door.

'He must have suspected something then,' he said quietly, then added, 'before it was even confirmed.'

I went over and opened the door for him.

'Sorry to end my visit on such a depressing and downbeat note, Mr Marklin,' he smiled self-consciously, as he shook my hand. 'Anyway, I'm glad you like the toys.'

'I like the toys,' I said.

'Ah, that we all could be as innocent as children again,' he sighed. 'Perhaps in the next world . . .'

'Perhaps.'

In the lamplight, I watched him get into his Volvo estate, required transport of all antique dealers, and drive away. Then I went back to my new-found French collection. And fantastic as those tiny aircraft were, they couldn't quite fly me away from the mysteries of Manners School and the new revelations about its disputed and departed French master.

'Happy?' Arabella sniffed.

'Only two more to go,' I parried and handed her a steaming cup of Lemsip.

'What are they?'

'A big black Junkers 89 and a Leopard Moth.'

She looked up from her Lemsip.

'I thought you'd got a Leopard Moth.'

116

'I have. Now I want the rare camouflaged version they produced for only a few months in 1940.'

'Oh,' she sniffed again, 'so paradise is still two away.'

'Isn't it always?' I grinned. 'That's what makes it paradise.'

I leaned over and kissed her forehead. It was still hob-hot.

'When you've drunk that, you should turn over and get some sleep.'

'Aren't you coming to bed, now?' Sniff, sniff.

'Will soon.'

'Why not now?'

'My sandman phoned to say he would be later tonight.'

'I think I know who your sandman has gone out with.' Cough.

'Oh?'

Sniff. 'Poor Alistair Folland.'

I now regretted having told her about the antique dealer's comments.

'He's not exactly lively company,' I grimaced.

'Sandmen aren't choosy.'

She reached for a tissue and I waited out the trumpeting.

'I'll be up soon. You get some rest.'

'Why not now? It's Digby Whetstone's problem, not yours, to work out who the teacher's friends were and from whom he seems to have had great expectations.'

I plumped up her pillows. 'I know.'

She looked at me and coughed out, 'You think Folland pinched the jumble sale money?'

I shrugged. 'Eight hundred pounds doesn't seem quite enough to change a man from quiet and downbeat to boyish and buoyant. Anyway, according to our visitor, the change took place a good time before the burglary.'

'By the time the money was stolen, he was back to despondency.'

'Wouldn't you be, with those four initials hanging over you?'

There was no need to answer that. I handed her another Kleenex.

'All we know is that Folland seems to have been expecting some good fortune. How? From whom? And when, we know not.'

'It couldn't have been that far in the future. You said he was thinking of moving and buying a house.'

'Maybe he had saved up enough money of his own for that. He

was single, after all, with no dependants that I've heard about. He could have stashed away enough, at least for a deposit on a small property. And banks are bending over backwards to lend money these days.'

She blew her nose.

'Maybe this French yachtsman was going to lend him the money,' she suggested. 'Or even buy the house for him. Then Frenchie would have a solid pied-à-terre in England, whenever he was bored with rocking about on his ... bo ... bo ... bo ... bo,' she gave an almighty sneeze, ' ... BOAT.'

I mimed wiping my face and clothes down.

'Stranger things have happened,' I said.

'Like forgetting Manners School and coming to bed to comfort a sick friend?'

I looked down at her, perspiring and propped up on the pillows, her eyes now starting to stream to keep pace with her nose. She was downright irresistible. I took off my jacket.

'You enchantress you,' I smiled. She handed me a jar of Vick vapour rub from the bedside table.

'My mother always used to rub my chest with this when I was a child,' she said, straight-faced and twinkleless.

After all that, Arabella insisted we actually spend the rest of the night in separate beds, not so much, she said, to protect me from the virus, but to prevent my waking up in the morning hard boiled from the oven heat her body was generating. There was sanity in her suggestion, so I spent a lonely bachelor night in the spare room, much to Bing's amazement.

As a result, I overslept and was only awakened by the clanging and banging filtering through to me from the shop. I shrugged on a dressing-gown and groaned downstairs, expecting it to be Gus, parading another fugitive from the scrapyard. But to my amazement, it was no elderly fisherman I let in, but a highly agitated youth.

'Tony. What on earth are you doing here at this hour? It's only five past eight.'

He touched my arm and said breathlessly, 'I'm sorry, Peter, but I just had to come now. It couldn't wait.'

I sat him down by the counter. 'What couldn't wait?'

'Andy's in trouble.'

'The caretaker?'

118

He nodded. 'The police took him away last evening and didn't release him until six this morning.'

I frowned. 'How do you know all this?'

He hesitated, then replied, 'I cycled round and saw them taking him away. I kept phoning last night and again this morning. Oh hell.'

I put a hand on his shoulder. 'Now calm down, Tony. The police have released him, haven't they, so . . . ?'

'So nothing,' he cut in. 'I've talked to Andy and he says they spent the whole night trying to get him to confess to stealing that money. But worse, Peter. To murdering our teacher. Andy – murdering our teacher. It's unbelievable.'

'The police are linking the burglary with the murder.'

'Andy says that they tried to get him to confess that he murdered Mr Folland because he'd found out that Andy had stolen that money. Oh God, Peter, what are we going to do? Andy didn't do it. *Didn't* do it. *Didn't* do it.'

Tony looked so ashen, I considered offering him a pre-breakfast scotch, but felt that a whiff of alcohol on his breath during morning lessons might not go down 'summa cum laude' with his teachers.

'Tony, before we go any further, I want to ask you a serious question.'

'All right,' he said. 'Anything. But we've got to hurry if we're going to . . .'

I cut him short. 'Now hold your horses. Answer my question first.'

He took a deep breath.

I went on, 'There's something that's been worrying me for quite some time now.'

His eyes flashed both fear and annoyance. 'What's that?'

'Why you're getting so het up about a guy I assume you hardly really know, who happens to be the school caretaker?'

He fidgeted on his stool. 'Because . . . because he's . . . nice. I like him. A lot. He's always been kind to me. He's kind to everyone at school. Someone has got to help him, you see. You've met him, he's not all that bright . . . can't really help himself too much.'

He was blushing now as he looked up at me; a far cry from the cool and confident Thatcherite entrepreneur I'd known.

119

'Is that all, Tony? Are you sure that's all? That you are all hot and bothered because you like him and want to help.'

'Why else?' he asked.

That was really my question.

'Someone's got to help those who can't help themselves,' he added. Now he sounded like the Opposition.

'Anyway, Peter, I've answered your question. Now can I ask you one?'

'I know what it is. And the answer is "Yes", but within strict limits.'

He sighed with relief. 'Oh thanks, Peter. I'll never forget it. When I'm . . .' He stopped suddenly and blushed once more. I was sure his next words were going to be 'rich and famous . . .'.

'Hold it,' I said. 'I haven't done anything yet.'

'But you will,' he said excitedly, then frowned. 'You mentioned limits. They're not mega-ones, are they? I mean you will really try to help Andy?'

'I'll try,' I said. 'But the limits are the limits of the law. I don't want to tread on any big, black, shiny toecaps.'

'The police?'

I nodded. 'They're only trying to do their job.'

'But they're making a huge mistake accusing Andy . . .' he began, but I interrupted.

'Are they? How can you be so certain?'

'I know. That's all . . . I just know.'

I waited, but he didn't offer any more. So I posed a question. 'Supposing, in the course of trying to help Andy, I actually discover he *is* guilty. Not necessarily of both crimes. But, say, of one, the burglary.'

'You won't. Because he isn't. The problem's no problem, because it won't come up.'

I changed the subject. 'Tell me, Tony, is there any specific reason why the police have returned to Andy as their chief suspect? When I last heard, they were keen on following up the Frenchman lead. And then there was the guy on the motorbike who followed you. Has he stopped, by the way?'

'Yes. I haven't seen him for a bit. Probably got wind of the police watching out for him. But they're after Andy again because they've . . . been checking up on him.'

'So? He's got nothing to hide, has he?'

'Well, it seems that someone reported to the police that . . .
Andy was . . . thinking of buying a house.'

'Buying a house?' I said, incredulously. 'Andy hasn't got that
kind of money, has he? Anyway, who is it who reported him?'

'Someone from Brinkham and Tellors in Bournemouth.'

I had heard of them. Seen their signboards. 'The estate
agents?'

'Yes.'

I thought for a moment. 'Has Andy been in to see them?'

'Seems so,' he sighed.

I remembered what Gus had said about the caretaker eyeing
new Vauxhalls in the showroom. Now he seemed to have gradu-
ated to window-shopping for houses.

'Does Andy say why he went to the estate agents? I mean, is he
really thinking of buying a house for himself? Or, perhaps, he
was looking for someone else.'

'I guess . . . he must have been . . . looking for someone else.'

'Because Andy doesn't have that kind of money? Is that why
the estate agent person reported his visit to the police?'

'S'pose so.'

'But supposing Andy *does* have that kind of money? After all,
you don't know how much he might have stashed away somewhere . . . or do you?'

He got up from his stool and turned away. 'Of course I don't.
How could I?'

I took his question as rhetorical.

'Tony, look at me.'

He looked at me.

'Eight hundred-odd pounds, Tony, might be a great help
towards a down payment. On a house . . . or a car.'

He turned on me angrily. 'He didn't steal that money. I've told
you that. So quit going on about it. I came round here because I
thought you would help me. And Andy. If you're going to act like
the bloody police and assume he's guilty before you start, then
. . .' He banged his fist down on the counter.

I held up my hand. 'Now calm down, Tony. I didn't say I
thought Andy was guilty or anything. I was just trying to open up
your mind to every kind of possibility. For neither of us really
know what the truth is. We're reacting by instinct, rather than
reason. We've got to have more to go on than just instinct. You
wouldn't invest money just on instinct, now would you?'

121

He looked across at me, then closed his eyes.

'Had any breakfast?' I asked. I looked at my watch. 'You've just got time to grab some, if I then drop you and your bike down to the school in the car.'

'My bike won't go in your Beetle, will it?'

'I'll take Arabella's Golf.'

'Won't she be using it?'

I shook my head. 'She's upstairs with the flu.'

'Oh, sorry. Yes, I'd love some.'

I shepherded him through into the house.

'Muesli or cornflakes?' I smiled. 'They're both the same price.'

'Cornflakes,' he smiled back and just a little of the old Tony started to return, praise be.

Ten

An hour and a half later, I was seated in the caretaker's tiny sitting-room, having persuaded Gus to look after my shop for the morning. (Having just blown £400 for my own personal satisfaction, I couldn't afford to miss any sales by staying closed.) Arabella was half a degree less feverish, but still too groggy to sit on a hard stool and serve customers with anything but a dose of flu.

Andy Boxall emerged from the minuscule kitchen with a mug of steaming coffee. As he handed it over with shaking hand, he said, 'Very good of you to take the bother, Mr Marklin. Very kind, indeed. Tony really shouldn't have ...'

'Tony is concerned about you, Andy,' I interrupted to save him further embarrassment, 'and anyway, I had nothing special planned for today.'

He sat down on a hard chair opposite me.

'Well, very nice of you, Mr Marklin ...' His voice trailed away and I could see that he was still more than a little shell-shocked from all the questions the police must have fired at him overnight.

I took a first sip of my coffee (Camp, more's the pity), and asked, 'If I'm going to help you Andy, you've got to tell me everything you know. All right?'

He nodded.

I went on, 'Now Tony tells me the police took you in last night because they had a report that you had been seen in a Bournemouth estate agents enquiring about property. Is that correct?'

He nodded again.

'Thinking of buying a house, Andy?'

'No, no,' he sighed. 'How could I think of buying a house? On my wages.'

'Then what were you doing in an estate agents?'

123

He looked across at me. 'I can dream, can't I? There's no law against that.'

I shook my head.

He went on, as if to himself, 'I've always dreamed, Mr Marklin, ever since I was a nipper. Day-dreamed, I suppose you'd call it. You see . . . I've never really had nothing all my life . . . nothing what you'd call worth mentioning.' He tapped his head. 'And I haven't got all that much upstairs, you see. Like brains, I mean. So I've never been able to figure a way to make the odd extra bob or two or even get a proper job that pays well. You know, like pays enough to buy a few little extras beyond your food and lodging. That's why my wife, God rest her soul, had to slave all her poor life. She was still working as a cleaner with the council when she was taken bad.' He closed his eyes, as if to shut out the pain.

After a while, he resumed. 'Still, there we are. I shouldn't bother you with all this, really. I don't mean to. It's just that . . . what was I saying? . . . Ah, yes, day-dreaming. You see, Mr Marklin, that's all I've ever been able to do. Dream. Of all the things I'd like to own. The holidays I'd like to take. All the places I'd like to visit . . . like Africa, with all those animals you see in the zoo, tropical islands with palm trees like in those telly commercials. Ada – that was her name. My wife's – she used to laugh at me, sometimes. She'd say, "Andy, you window-shop your life away." Maybe she was right. Maybe I'll wake up one day and find I'm dead . . . everything over . . . gone . . . for good.'

I put my coffee down. 'It's good to dream, Andy. I do. Tony does. We all do, I guess, in our different ways.'

He nodded to himself.

I went on, 'So you never had any intention of buying a house. You were just looking, dreaming . . . ?'

'That's right, Mr Marklin. Just . . . dreaming.'

I thought for a moment. 'Have you ever done it before, Andy? I mean, go as far as entering an estate agents, as distinct from just gazing at the houses displayed in the window?'

'No . . . no, I don't suppose I have. Normally, I'd just stand outside and look at all the glossy pictures and glossy prices.'

'So what made you go in this time?'

'That's what the police kept asking me, Mr Marklin. It was terrible. They wouldn't leave it alone, especially that Inspector.

124

He kept coming back to it, just when I thought they'd at last let it drop.'

'Inspector Whetstone? Fattish man with a ginger moustache?'

'Right, Mr Marklin. That sounds like him.'

'So go on, Andy. Why *did* you go in this time?'

'I don't know, really. I think I've been getting worse, you see, Mr Marklin, since my wife passed on. My life seems to be nearly all sort of dreaming now I live on my own . . . have nobody to talk to. Except Tony, that is. He's a good boy, Mr Marklin. Ever so kind. Comes here quite often, he does. I look forward to it. I don't know what I'll do in a year or two, when he leaves school. I'll miss him, you know.' He shrugged. 'But then, maybe, I'll be shut away in some prison by then. Plenty of people to talk to in prison, I expect.'

I got up. 'Look, Andy, don't you talk like that. You won't go to prison, if you've done nothing. Anyway, the police released you this morning, didn't they? So they've got nothing on you and know it.'

'They'll be back,' he said hopelessly.

I knelt down in front of his chair. 'Now, Andy, try to forget what happened with the police for a moment and tell me about the nights of the burglary and poor Mr Folland's death.'

His fingers probed a worn line of corduroy in his trousers. 'Nothing to tell. Saw nothing. Heard nothing, I did. Mind you, I had the telly on both nights. But still, you'd have thought I'd have heard something, wouldn't you?'

'Not if someone let themselves in with a key. Or were let in.'

'Or were in already,' he muttered.

'What do you mean?'

'Oh, nothing. There couldn't have been anybody still in the school then, could there? I mean, I always check before I lock up. I know who's staying late and all that. So no . . . I'm just being silly.'

I looked up at him. 'Andy, I have a feeling you are not telling me everything.'

'Yes, I am, Mr Marklin, honest.'

I got up and went back to the settee. 'All right, Andy, I'll ask another question. Who do you think a) carried out the burglary, b) murdered Mr Folland? You must have some theories of your own . . . a day-dreamer like you.'

It took a second or two for him to answer. 'Can't rightly think,

125

Mr Marklin. I've been racking my brains trying to imagine why anybody would want to kill that nice Mr Folland. I know talk goes it was because he had that awful illness, but all the same . . .'

'But what about the burglary, Andy?'

He got up and went over to my still half-full coffee mug.

'Like me to warm you up some more, Mr Marklin? Won't take a jiffy.'

'No thanks, Andy, I'm fine. Now about the . . .'

'Jumble sale money?' he sighed. 'Don't know about that neither. No idea. Could be anyone, couldn't it? Schools are often being broken into, so I read in the paper.'

I didn't like to remind him that caretakers were employed to try to stop that kind of activity.

'Not anybody, no, Andy. Someone with a key or access to a key or access to a person who could let them in. That is, unless the police have turned up some evidence I don't know about. Like a broken window catch or a forced skylight or something.'

He didn't comment. Just subsid-d once more into his unyielding chair.

I persevered just one more time. 'So you've no ideas, Andy?'

'Must have been that bloke Miss Pettican says she saw climbing over the wall, mustn't it?'

I was somewhat surprised by his mistake. 'But that was the night of the murder, Andy, not the burglary.'

He scratched his head. 'Oh, was it? I can't remember. I really can't. I haven't had any sleep, you see, being down at the station all night. My brains are all addled.'

I got up. I could see I was unlikely to get much more out of the caretaker that morning.

'All right, Andy. I'll go and let you get some rest.'

He saw me the few feet to his door. 'I'm sorry I couldn't be more helpful, Mr Marklin.'

'That's all right, Andy.' I gave him my card. 'Now, if you think of anything, or the police come round again, give me a ring at this number.'

He nodded. 'They'll be round again.'

'Why do you say that, Andy? If they were going to arrest you, they would hardly have released you this morning, now would they?'

'Didn't say they were going to arrest me,' he muttered and held the door open for me.

I frowned, but let his remark go. He seemed much too tired to quiz any further. So, with a reassuring pat on the shoulder, I left, lamentably not much wiser than when I had arrived.

I just couldn't get rid of Gus. First, he took an hour to regale me with minute descriptions of not only every single soul who had ventured into my shop, but all those (three of them) who had lingered outside looking in the window. Second, he described how clever he had been in persuading the punters actually to purchase the items they'd apparently hummed and ha'ed over in the shop. And third, (and this last is a winner) how he had persuaded one man, an American, who was lingering over a German Schuco 'Stop and Go' car, complete with tinplate garage – marked £105 together – into believing that this actual toy had originally been bought by Eva Braun in 1938 for an illegitimate child she had borne for the despotic gentleman with the small moustache with whom she was living at the time.

'Only way I could think of, old son, to lift the lucre from his wallet,' he explained.

'Good God, Gus, and he swallowed it?'

'Well, not at first,' he explained. 'Until I showed him the letters scratched on the bottom of the car.'

'Letters?' I began, then suddenly realized what he was talking about. I had bought the car and garage from a man called Brightman, who had been a regular customer until he had been made redundant from his firm. Now his buying days were over. He was a seller now.

'Gus. Those initials stand for Ernest Brightman, not bloody Eva Braun.'

He guffawed. 'He didn't know now, did he? Pleased as punch he was, as he walked out of the shop.'

Hell, I'd never get a visa from the United States embassy ever again.

And then it was quarter past Heineken and so it went on. I ended up swanning into Swanage and getting a Chinese take-away for three, Arabella having decided that something sweet and sour might tempt her into eating a morsel. (I hadn't realized that flu comes second only to pregnancy in producing fancy food fetishes.)

Still, I guess, at best it gave us all a chance to mull over the Manners School mess I now found myself knee-deep in. At worst, it ill prepared me for what followed at precisely four thirty that afternoon – only a couple of minutes after Gus had poured himself back home. I was just about to tackle my mail (neglected since it had arrived that morning), when Tony burst into the shop. And I mean 'burst'. The door banged from its stop and closed itself behind him, all on its own.

'What on earth . . . ?' I began, but he cut in and told me pronto.

'Beamish. It's Beamish. It has to be,' he exclaimed, as he rushed across to the counter.

'Beamish?' I frowned.

'You know,' came the impatient explanation. 'The Head. Beamish. The beak. The mega-cheese. Top Gun. Old Wanko.'

'The Headmaster has to be what?' I rallied.

'The burglar . . . I mean, the robber . . . I mean, the guy who stole the jumble sale loot.'

I held up a calming hand.

'Now, hang on a minute, Tony. What the blazes has happened suddenly to convince you that Beamish is the culprit? Have the police been round again?'

'No, that's the . . .' he began, then hesitated. 'No, they haven't.'

'Then what clue have you unearthed . . . ?'

'Been thinking,' he interrupted. 'Should have thought of it before.'

'Thought of what?' I was getting a trifle on the irritable side by this time. Tony had started with a bang; I suspected he might well end with a whimper.

'Peter, it has to be him, doesn't it?'

'Show me.'

'Well, he's got keys to every part of the school. The safe is in his office. He knows its combination. He didn't bank the money right away. He has admitted to that. It all stacks up.'

'To what? We knew all those facts yonks ago. There's nothing new there.'

He shook his head in exasperation at my seeming thickness.

'Peter, for Christ's sake, I know we did. But we didn't give those facts enough thought. All put together, they're mega-significant.'

I was getting mega-cheesed with 'mega' before every other Tony utterance, but kept cool man, real cool. After all, I remembered my own school days only too well. 'Wizard' had just died a

128

death and 'fab' and 'groovy' had taken its repetitive place. 'Heavy' had yet to come and go. *Plus ça change, plus* whatever the French for etcetera is.

'Tony, when you burst in here SAS style, I thought you were either being chased by that biker on the BMW or had heard that Andy had been carted off to gaol or, looking on the brighter side, had won the pools or something. I really didn't expect you to be blazoning yesterday's news.'

He looked daggers at me. 'So you don't believe me?'

'Tony, if you can give me just the slightest new clue as to why I should. . . I'm not saying it couldn't have been your headmaster, but . . .'

'So you're not going to help?'

'I'm helping, Tony. Andy must have told you I've been round.'

He looked away. I suddenly felt a bit of a rat. Near the tail too.

'Tony, we've got to act sensibly and rationally, if we're going to help Andy.' Then I added, 'That is, if he still needs help.'

It worked. He turned back to me. 'Oh, Peter, he still needs help. I know he does.'

'Why? Because he's got almost as valid reasons for being suspected as you have outlined for Beamish? He's got keys, he's on the premises twenty-four hours a day, he could have got to know the safe combination by spying on the head when he was opening it.'

He slid on to the stool and, elbows on counter, put his head in his hands. 'God, it's such a mess.'

'Mess?' I queried. 'Mystery, yes, but mess?'

'It's not just . . . it's everything.'

I waited for him to continue, which, with a bottomless sigh that only youth is prey to, he did. 'I don't know. Everything's going to pieces. Every bloody thing. It's not just . . . Andy and the . . . money . . . and Mr Folland, it's . . .'

'Winna?'

He looked up at me. 'What have you heard?' I shrugged. 'Nothing. Why?'

He shrugged. 'Nothing. But you're right. She and I don't . . .'

'You told me,' I said quietly.

'I know. But it's got worse. She hardly speaks to me now. Oh, we still go out together, when she has a second off from school work or her gymnastics, but . . . I don't know . . . it's like she's in a

129

dream world, somehow . . . of her own . . . and she won't let me in.'

'She's got her big day coming up very soon, hasn't she? National Championships affect every kind of athlete. Make them retreat into themselves a bit. Only natural. You must make allowances.'

He groaned, in lieu of reply.

'Worried she might be . . . going off you a bit?' I tried.

He gave an almost imperceptible nod.

'I love Winna, Peter. God, I love her. We've always made such a . . . great team. Until the last weeks. Sounds funny, doesn't it? But that's what we were. Are. A team. I don't know . . . I just don't bloody know. And I daren't ask her. And it's got worse since she started to spend more and more time with Delia Pettican.'

Now, I was starting to see his worry.

'You think Miss Pettican is, somehow, influencing her? I can't believe she would really come between you and Winna.'

'Can't you?' He looked at me angrily. 'I saw a play on the box the other night about women like her.'

I racked my memory and came up with a likely drama. I hadn't seen it myself, but I had read a review of it in the *Independent*. It was all about a lesbian who seduces the daughter of the local magistrate and gets murdered by him.

'Tony, if I read you right, you've got it all wrong. I don't think for a minute Miss Pettican is trying to . . .'

'How do you know?' he countered. 'Why else would Winna be wanting to spend time with her?'

'Maybe she just feels she needs an . . . adult friend right now. You know, with the Championships coming up. After all, her father doesn't seem to be exactly the kind of shoulder you can cry on and her mother, I gather, is hardly ever around.'

'I've stopped believing in Santa Claus, you know, Peter,' he sneered.

'I'm not being naive, Tony. I could well be right. And you could well be jumping to all the wrong conclusions.'

I came round to his side of the counter. 'Now, you have never struck me before as a guy who reacts without thinking, makes decisions and takes action before he has sussed everything out carefully, very shrewdly. You've always seemed to know what you were doing.'

'That was before . . .'

'Before what?'

Once more he put his head in his hands. I tapped his shoulder.

'Arabella should be a good deal better tomorrow. Would you like to bring Winna over for the evening, if she's free and perhaps I'll get a video out we would all like to see.'

He took my meaning. 'So Arabella can have a talk with her?'

I nodded. 'Girl to girl stuff.'

His eyes brightened for the first time. 'You'll tell me afterwards what she says?'

'If it's relevant. Promise.'

He got off the stool. 'Thanks. Thanks a lot.' He eyed the shop layout with a critical eye, but made no comment on my changes.

'Sorry to be putting you to all this trouble, Peter. I hope it's not going to interfere with your business too much.'

'Depends how long it takes. So far I'm coping all right.' I looked at him. 'Anyway, people are more important than money, aren't they?'

He looked away.

I went on, 'Tell me one thing. Is your aim right now just to clear your friend Andy or really discover who committed the burglary and the murder?'

'I guess, clear Andy,' he said quietly.

'You realize we may have to track down the real culprit or -prits just to do that?'

I cursed the fact I couldn't see his face.

'Just clear Andy,' he repeated, 'the police can do the rest. That's their job.' He at last looked back at me. 'But remember what I said about old Beamish.'

'You don't like him, do you?'

He shook his head. 'Never have. He pretends to be strong, but really he's mega-weak and I don't go for that. Right now, since Mr Folland's death, he's dead under old Colonel Hawkesworth's thumb. You wouldn't believe the changes the Head's already starting to make to our curriculum. Sailing lessons in school time are already out. PE has become like military drill. All free periods are out. Homework's been increased.' He pointed outside to where he had parked his cycle. 'I've got about three hours' worth in my saddlebag to be done tonight. God knows where it will all stop, with that Colonel Fart pulling old Beamish's strings.'

'What does Miss Pettican say to all this? Do you know?'

He glowered at me. 'Don't talk to me about Miss Pettican any more. In her own way, she may be even worse trouble than old Hawkesworth.'

'You don't know that, Tony. From what little I know of Winna, I can't really believe she would spend so much time with her if she is, as you say.'

He looked at his big, black diver's digital. 'I'd better go, otherwise I'll be doing homework all night.'

I saw him to the door.

'Give me a ring if you and Winna would like to pop over tomorrow night. Or, if Arabella is still a little groggy, we can make it the next night.'

He sighed, then smiled, then winked, then left.

I went back upstairs to Arabella.

'Tony?' she enquired, putting down a Kleenex. 'I thought I heard his voice.'

I nodded.

'That's twice today. What's bothering him now?'

'Oh . . . I guess he's suddenly found out that life doesn't actually go like clockwork, after all.'

She frowned. So I sat on the bed and brought her up to date. She was silent for a moment (save for a monumental sneeze), then said into her Kleenex, 'You dow what I dink?'

'Do,' I grinned. 'Dell me what you dink.'

She pulled a face, which included the putting out of a very white tongue. I deserved it.

'Tony is just throwing suspicion around at anyone, as long as it isn't Andy, in the hope that something will stick somewhere.'

'Could be,' I conceded, 'but still, the way he burst through my door when he first arrived, it was like he suddenly really did believe Beamish has something to do with it all.'

'Do you think he really does?'

I shrugged. 'He's certainly not a strong character – Tony's right about that. And weak people, as they say, tend to be a little more open to corruption. But somehow, I don't see him as even a burglar, let alone a murderer.'

She blew her nose. 'Yet you say you believe Tony was being sincere – not just throwing mud?'

'I did at first. Not so sure by the time he left. Unless, of course, he toned down his attitude after he discovered mine.'

Arabella sat up straighter in bed and I adjusted her pillows to match. She blew a kiss up at me. I caught it and blew it back.

'So what do you think, Mega-mind?' she asked, mischievously.

'Micro-mind would be more appropriate,' I sighed. 'This Manners School affair makes mud seem transparently clear. There are more possible suspects than I've had hot dinners, yet no real leads, as far as I can see . . . except perhaps . . .'

'Except perhaps, what?'

My mental match, that for a split second seemed to burn so bright, flickered and died.

'Oh, I don't know.'

She reached for my hand. Her touch, thank the Lord, was cool at last.

'I have a sneaking suspicion that Tony believes Andy *is* implicated in the whole thing. How, maybe, he has no idea. And, maybe, he doesn't even possess any proof. It would at least help explain why he has been so frantic today, since Andy's overnight police grilling. What's more, it would sort of fit with the reason the police took him in again.'

'Visit to the estate agents?'

I nodded.

'You don't believe his day-dreaming story, then?'

'Oh, I believe he day-dreams. But whether he was doing so on that particular occasion . . . who can say?' I sighed. 'Maybe I'm just getting everything mixed up. What with the caretaker looking at houses and poor Folland, apparently, planning to buy one . . . everyone seems to be house-hunting but me.'

'But, at least, Folland seems to have been expecting a windfall.' She quoted the current comic catchphrase, 'Loadsamoney.'

'Maybe Andy was . . . is . . . loadsamoney,' I mused, then that Swan Vestas struck itself alight again. My eyes must have lit up to match, so to speak, for Arabella asked, 'Inspiration?'

'Don't know,' I replied, 'but I think the next time Tony comes round, I'll have to do a little more than just sympathize.'

Eleven

Little did I know it, but the troubles of that Thursday were not yet over. For just as the dotty titles of the BBC Nine O'clock News were pulsing out, Arabella and I (she had insisted that she was now well enough to don dressing-gown and spend an hour or two downstairs) were seated comfortably, more or less ready for what the world's news-hounds could throw at us, when the doorbell clanged. My first reaction was that it could be Gus, out for an evening spin with yet another weird and wonderful junk-yard refugee – after all, I hadn't seen him for hours – but the face that greeted me at the door was the opposite of stubble and leather. All shiny pink from an evening shave it was, the ginger moustache even more an island set in a sea of flab. Now I'm being unkind. Perhaps if I spent so much time sitting on a chair or in a car or on suspects, I'd put on weight too.

I opened the door and put up my hands. 'All right, Inspector, I'll come quietly.'

He sidled in, with nary a smile. 'Got something to confess, Mr Marklin?'

I wasn't ready for such repartee, so asked lamely, 'Would you like to talk amongst the toys, or come through into the sitting-room?'

'If it's not too much trouble,' he half-replied.

Well, it was, but I didn't tell him. I just asked him to wait a second, whilst I went ahead to warn Arabella that trouble with a capital 'D' was about to size twelve into her life. I gave her the option – to surrender now in her dressing-gown or go upstairs and pack. She opted for the former, but pulled the dressing-gown so tightly around her, I thought it might split.

Digby seemed a might taken aback by her déshabillée appearance and looked round at me, as if he expected my flies to be still undone.

134

'It's all right, Inspector,' I smiled. 'Arabella is recovering from flu, not a bout of me.'

After the greetings and the 'sorry to hear its', he sank into a chair and came out with what I'd been more than half-expecting.

'Been hearing things about you, Mr Marklin. From Colonel Hawkesworth.'

'Ever the flatterer,' I reacted. 'What did he say? That I make a sad substitute for lady reporters?'

'So that was what you were pretending to be at that so-called news conference, was it?'

'I wasn't pretending to be, Digby. I was invited to stand in for Arabella here, when she first got the flu. I was bona fide, a hundred per cent.'

'Who invited you? The *Western Gazette*?'

He'd got me there, so I ignored the question. 'Have you come out here at this time of night, just to spank me for being a naughty boy?'

He readjusted his mass in the chair. 'Well, I was disappointed when I heard the Colonel's news, especially considering our little talk the other day.'

'Peter's not lying to you, Inspector,' Arabella interceded. 'I asked him to cover the event and his report formed the substance of what actually came out in my paper.'

He pursed his lips and his moustache almost disappeared into the gulley. 'So be it, for now. But I don't want to hear of any more reports of . . . shall we say, unilateral action?'

I half-expected him then to get up and go, but instead, he relaxed back and stayed.

'Anything else, Inspector?'

He licked his thin lips. I took the hint and got up. After all, the longer he stayed, the more chance I had probing around for any police progress on the Manners School affair.

'Can I pour you a drink, or are you still on duty?'

He tried to find his watch on his chubby wrist. 'As it's after nine, I guess I could indulge in a small one, thank you.'

We settled on a scotch, straight for him, splashed for me. Arabella declined, with a wry smile playing out the side of her Kleenex. Glass now in hand, he arrived at what I quickly realized was really his main purpose in coming.

'Tell me, Mr Marklin, so far in your . . .' He hunted for a phrase. I handed him his old one, ' . . . unilateral action.'

135

'Thank you,' he twitched, 'have you come to any conclusions about the tragic happenings at Manners School?'

Damn it, now I had a second phrase I'd sooner or later have to hand back to him. I thought for a second, then answered with a question.

'Have you heard Mr Folland was thinking of buying a house?'

He chuckled. 'Yes, Mr Marklin, I have. I have, naturally, talked to quite a few of his acquaintances.'

'What do you make of it?' I said. 'Think Folland was expecting a windfall?'

'He was expecting something, it would seem, wouldn't it?'

I nodded. 'Enough to change him from rather a silent, introspective type to a brighter and breezier fellow altogether, or so a little bird told me.'

'My little birds sing a rather similar song,' Digby said quickly, not to be outdone, ornithologically.

'"Loadsamoney", do you think?'

'Money can sometimes buy happiness, Mr Marklin, whatever they say.'

I smiled to myself. He couldn't hide the philosopher in him, bless his nylon socks.

'Found out where the money might be coming from?' I tried.

He shrugged.

I tried harder. 'Like a Frenchman with a yacht?'

'We have interviewed several Frenchmen. And several yachtsmen, sailors and the like.'

'No success?'

'Oh, yes. Several knew, or knew of, Mr Folland. Quite a . . . nautical boy, he seems to have been in his spare time.' He seemed pleased at his choice of adjective. Wasn't bad, I had to admit. But more for a sit-com, than a sit-trag.

'But no one confesses to offering him any money? I mean "loadsamoney"?'

He shook his head. 'But then they wouldn't, would they, now they know he's been murdered?' He sipped his scotch, then looked across at me. 'If I follow you right, Mr Marklin, you think money is behind this whole affair, do you?'

'Money seems to crop up quite often.'

I knew immediately, I had gone too far. He was in there like a flash.

'Oh? Tell me more. Where else have you heard money rearing its tempting head?'

I thought quickly. 'Same place you did. That's all.'

'Where was that, then? And how did you find out? I haven't seen a fly on the wall of my office for some time.' I didn't blame them. 'That silly estate agent visit.'

'You've been seeing Andy Boxall, then?'

'Yes. Someone had to calm him down after your all-night grilling.'

'We don't relish working twenty-four hours a day, Mr Marklin, whatever the media might hint. We like to go to bed like other people.'

There was no answer to that. Least, no polite one. 'I hope you've cleared the caretaker now,' I ventured.

'In a police investigation, Mr Marklin, no one is cleared until we have discovered the guilty party or parties. Anyway, what makes you think Andy Boxall is pure as the driven snow?'

'No one is pure as the snow, driven or undriven, Inspector, but instinct tells me the caretaker is no murderer and fairly unlikely to be so callous that he'd do Ethiopian children out of charity takings. What's more, I take him at his word about the visit to the estate agents.'

'So what, in your . . . instinctive view . . . happened at Manners School?'

This time I looked at him hard.

'That's why you've come round here, after hours, isn't it, Digby? Not really to tick me off, but to pluck my brains.' I held up a hand. 'Now, don't bother to deny it. I'm not blaming you. In fact, quite the reverse. I'm glad you came. You see, I wanted to pick yours.'

I went on, 'It makes a welcome change from feudin' and fightin' all the time – sitting down and chewing the cud together. The police and we humble members of the public should try it more often. Who knows, a lot more cases might get cleared up that way?'

I finished my drink and got up to take his. 'Drop more cud?' I said. A robot arm extended with the glass.

Whilst I was pouring, Arabella took over. 'Tell me something, Inspector, are you looking for two guilty parties or one?'

I saw him turn to her with his 'you're only a woman' type smile. 'If you mean by that, do I think the robbery and murder are

137

connected, I'll repeat what I've said on radio and television (Get him!), "Coincidence doesn't always imply connection."'

I wondered which police manual quoted that. Maybe 'The Clichéd Man's Guide to Criminality. Part One'.

I passed on the remark and the scotch, 'So you may be looking for two?'

'May.'

'But there is a link, isn't there, Inspector?' she went on between sniffs. 'The means of entry. No break-ins, no noise, no fuss – at least, not enough to rouse anybody.'

'Granted, Miss Trench, but you forget one thing. In the case of murder, Mr Folland was, we believe, already on the premises. So he could, in theory, have known his murderer and let the person in himself. The burglary is somewhat different.'

'Found the famous blunt instrument yet?' I asked and could see Digby's mind trying to decide whether he had traded quite enough for the scant help Arabella and I had proved to be to him.

'No, not yet,' he conceded at last, 'but our forensic boys have at least narrowed down what it was made from.'

'Oh?' I commented enquiringly, but I could now see from his narrowing eyes that a million 'Oh?'s would not elicit the material from him. He fidgeted in his chair, then asked a question I knew was likely to be his last, or thereabouts.

'Your earlier emphasis on money, Mr Marklin – does that mean you think Folland's murder was not what every Tom, Dick and Harry thinks it was about?'

'Aids?' I queried and his mention of Tom, Dick or Harry reminded me of Tony.

'Right.'

'Not necessarily. I just don't know.'

Digby Whetstone let his chair's seat springs return to as near normal as they had ever been. He gave a slight bow in Arabella's direction.

'Hope you're feeling a great deal better tomorrow, Miss Trench.'

He gave me his glass and I saw him to the door. Just as I let the cool, night air in, he turned and asked, 'I have a distinct feeling, Mr Marklin, that you know another reason why money might be at the back of the Manners School mysteries. If you know one, now's the time to tell me.'

138

'Not really, Inspector,' I lied and went on to ask a question of my own. 'But maybe, there's something more you could tell me.'

'Fire away. But there's no guarantee I'll feel it fitting to answer you.'

'The schoolboy, Tony Thorn – the one who was being followed. You know, by the biker on the BMW?'

He frowned. 'Yes, I know him. What about him?'

'Ever find the biker?'

He hesitated, then said, 'No. I can't say we have. But why do you ask? Do you think the biker is important to the school case?'

'Can't say. What do you think?'

He put a freckled hand on my shoulder. 'I go back again to what I've said on TV and radio.'

I mentally raised my eyebrows. Inspector Terry Wogan went on, 'Coincidence doesn't always imply connection. Just recently, the Bournemouth area has seen quite an increase in cases of child molesting.' He held his hands about two feet apart. 'I have a dossier this thick. So . . .'

'. . . you think the biker is just one of those? Nothing to do with the murder or burglary?'

'Why should he be connected? Just because this boy, Tony Thorn, attends the same school?'

He had a point. Then he rather startled me with, 'That is, if the biker actually exists, Mr Marklin.'

I pulled a face. 'You think he doesn't?'

'Who knows?' he shrugged and made to leave, but I stopped him.

'Come on, Digby, you can't just come out with a thing like that and then leave. Remember . . . the cud?'

He sighed. 'All right. Here's something for you to chew over. You know this boy Tony quite well, I believe. Well, don't you think he is a bit hyper-imaginative?'

And with that, he was gone to his Granada, shining in the lamplight, white as the driven snow. Except for the blood-red slash, that is.

Next morning, Arabella insisted on taking the last vestiges of her flu to work, despite my doctorly advice. But at least the day was bright and clear, which was more than my mind felt.

After she had gone, I decided, before more ado, I had better actually talk to the one man in the Manners School affair I had so

139

far missed out meeting face to face – the mega-cheese, as Tony had put it. What's more, the last mentioned, after his last visit, would at least expect me to have taken some action in his direction. So I reached for the phone and rang the school, spinning a garbled story about being a parent who wanted to send his son to the school, but was concerned about all the recent publicity. The school secretary, after enquiries, informed me briskly that if I came right away, the Headmaster could spare me quarter of an hour, but no more. I went right away – but via Gus's cottage. He seemed quite chuffed to be C-in-C of my Toy Emporium for one more morning, though I must say, I blanched at what he might get up to in his manic bid to be Dorset's salesperson of the year.

Once at Manners School, I was not kept waiting. The lisle-stockinged secretary bustled me into the Headmaster's office, as if I was express stamped.

Henry Beamish extended a rather clammy hand and bade me sit down. He seemed smaller than when I had seen him at the Colonel's conference, but there, I guess, he had been elevated by the school stage to a height he couldn't sustain on the level.

'So, Mr Marklin, I gather you have a son who . . . ?' he began, but I had to cut in.

'I'm afraid I'm here under false pretences, Mr Beamish. I haven't got a son.'

'A daughter, perhaps. As you know, we're co-educational.'

'No. I have no children.'

He looked bemused. I didn't blame him.

'You see, I thought that if I told the truth over the phone, you wouldn't have seen me.'

Podgy fingers stroked a podgy hand. 'And what would the truth be then, Mr Marklin?'

'I want to talk to you about the burglary and the murder.'

I watched his eyes flicker at my deliberately bald statement. He did not reply immediately, but his beetroot complexion bled a little more. Eventually, he cleared his throat.

'May I ask what your interest can possibly be in my school or its affairs, if you are not a prospective parent?'

I was prepared for that one. 'I'm acting on behalf of a party who does have connections with your school, but who wishes to remain anonymous.'

He shook his head and rose from behind his desk. 'I suppose I should have guessed that this would happen.' His beady eyes

140

sought mine. 'Some over-zealous parent, no doubt, not satisfied with the pace of the police progress.'

I didn't comment. But I was relieved at his assumption.

'You are a private investigator?' he then asked.

'A friend,' I smiled. 'Just a friend.'

'Your full name is?'

'Peter Marklin.'

'Where do you live?'

'Locally. Up the road at Studland.'

He turned back to his desk and made a note on a pad with a pen with a gilt complex. Soon, I guessed, my name would be British Telecoming its way to dear old Digby's earpiece.

'Are you willing to help me?' I said briskly, 'or shall I report back . . . ?'

He hesitated, then patting his bay-fronted stomach, sat rather primly back in his chair. Parent power had worked.

'You have ten minutes, Mr Marklin, until my Scripture period.'

I wasted no time pussyfooting. 'I won't keep you long. I'll start with the burglary.' I pointed to an old-fashioned safe which I'd spotted in a corner behind his desk. 'The proceeds from the jumble sale were in that safe, there, I believe?'

He gave a bored nod.

'Why didn't you bank the money right away, instead of keeping it around so long?'

He bristled and the beetroot bled again. But he kept what little cool he had, thank the Lord.

'I was still expecting more money to roll in.' He tried a smile. 'Bit like a Telethon, you know. Pledges were still being converted. Still, I naturally regret the delay now.'

I moved on speedily. 'The safe was not tampered with, I gather. In other words, someone else knew the combination.'

'Only the school secretary, Miss Prism, and myself knew the combination, as far as I know.'

'Did anyone ever watch you taking things out of the safe?'

'Could have, I suppose. Occasionally, someone forgets the courtesy of knocking. Usually impetuous members of the school corporate, I'm afraid to say.'

'So someone could have watched you?'

'I suppose so, yes.'

'Have you any idea, Headmaster (I thought he'd like my using his title. I was right. The beetroot stopped bleeding), how either the burglar or the murderer got in? I gather, rather like the safe, nothing was forced.'

He shook his head and his chins Jelloed. 'That's what I – and the police – would dearly like to discover.'

'So you have no idea?'

'Only that they must have used a key. They must, mustn't they, unless someone let them in?'

'Have you ever lost your keys?'

'No. Not that I can recall. No.'

I was temporarily out of intermediate questions, so went straight on to my planned pièce de résistance.

'What happened yesterday, Mr Beamish?' (Note my switch from his title to his name for this one.)

His podgy fingers stopped playing pork sausages with each other.

'Er ... yesterday?'

Hell, I hoped I'd been reading Tony right.

'Yes, yesterday, Mr Beamish. I have been given the impression that something new or rather significant may have occurred yesterday.'

'I don't know what you can be referring to – who gave you this impression?'

'It's not my role to say. Sorry,' I replied rather curtly. (If I didn't actually hate being beastly to people, I could at times see its attraction.)

I went on. 'Are you saying nothing untoward happened yesterday?'

'Er ... well ... the police came round again, if that's what you mean?'

He was now starting to look as uncomfortable as his weight should normally make him feel.

'That's not what I mean?'

'Then what ...?'

'You tell me, Mr Beamish.' Raymond Chandler would have been proud of me.

He suddenly got up from his chair. 'Look, Mr Marklin, I was prepared to answer a few polite questions, but your tone ... really ... is becoming quite insufferable.'

I could see beads of sweat on the beetroot now and I had a feeling they weren't just springing from anger.

142

'So you're not going to tell me about what happened yesterday?'

He came round to me and extended an arm towards the door. 'Nothing happened yesterday, Mr Marklin, beyond yet another police visit to inform me about their interview with my caretaker. And, of course, the usual curriculum of the school.'

'The *new* curriculum of the school,' I corrected him.

He blustered.

I went on, 'Haven't you changed course now, Mr Beamish, since the Colonel appointed himself your commander-in-chief?'

'The door is that way, Mr Marklin.' By now, it wasn't just his hands that were shaking.

I rose from my tapestry chair. 'My bringing up yesterday bugs you, doesn't it? Why, Mr Beamish?'

'Goodbye, Mr Marklin, and don't come back. I'll be giving my secretary strict instructions not to . . .'

'. . . mention yesterday.' I grinned. As I reached the door, I said, 'Was it to do with the burglary or the murder? At least, you could have told me that. We're not playing Cluedo, you know.'

Five pork sausages gave my pullover a push and the door closed behind me with quite a bang.

As I strode up the corridor, with a medium pleased smile on my face, Miss Prism stuck her head out of her office. 'He'll be just in time for the Scriptures,' she beamed. 'We're doing the Commandments.'

'All ten of them,' I said, 'or just eight?'

'Pardon?'

I waved my hand and left. It wasn't really fair to involve Miss Prism in my tangled and wild thoughts about 'Thou shalt not steal' and ditto re kill.

All the way home, I kept my mental replay button down on my quizzing of the 'mega-cheese'. I was relieved that by the time the Toy Emporium hove into view, I still had the feeling that Beamish's manner betrayed that something untoward had indeed occurred on the previous day; and not just another visit by the police, either. What that something might be, I couldn't fathom. But I was pretty certain that Tony had cottoned on to it somehow and that his Beak was rattled by my knowledge of some occurrence. By the time I had parked my car in the loose assembly of rotting timbers laughingly called a garage, I had decided a full

143

frontal question to Tony was the only chance I had of finding out what it might be. And Tony was at school all day. I just prayed he and Winna would contact me late afternoon to say they would love to come and video gaze that evening. (In any case, Arabella was scheduled to pick up a tape of *Wall Street* on her way back from Bournemouth. I thought Winna might go for Michael Douglas and he for the financial skulduggery and Daryl Hannah, strictly in that order. Me? I'm easier to please. The last mentioned, I reckoned, would do nicely.)

Gus was in full flight with a customer when I went through to the shop. I was just going to stand back and listen to his Super Salesman of the Year spiel, when, to my horror, I saw what lay on the counter between his hairy sweater and the bald and goggle-eyed customer, who, after eyeing me, said, 'How would you like it? You can have a banker's draft in the morning or, I suppose, if you prefer cash, I might be able to come back with it later this afternoon.'

'Cash,' Gus beamed. 'It's Toy Emporium policy with large amounts.'

It was at this point, I had to interrupt. 'Excuse me, Gus, where exactly did you find this box?'

He frowned at my interruption and said, obliviously, 'We'd prefer cash, wouldn't we?'

As I was getting nowhere with Gus, surprise, surprise, I turned to old goggle-eyes. 'I'm sorry to disappoint you, sir, but these items are not for sale.'

His goggle boggled. 'But your colleague here said . . .'

I sighed. 'My colleague here obviously did not realize that this set of aircraft is not part of my shop stock.'

Gus looked daggers at me and shook his head. 'But we've already agreed a price, old lad. Wait and listen to the price.'

'And if necessary,' Baldy beamed, 'I'm willing to pay some-what more than the fifteen hundred pounds.'

Gus nudged me in the ribs. I was to feel it for three days. 'One thousand five hundred pounds,' he stage whispered.

I quickly picked up the French Dinky aircraft set and held on to it tightly.

'I'm sorry, but these items are part of my personal collection and not for sale.' Then I added for Gus, 'That is why they were not in the shop, but in my sitting-room.'

'Oh, I'm really sorry,' Baldy sighed. 'Still, it's probably my fault. I asked your colleague if you had any Dinky aircraft other than those on display and he said he thought you might have some stashed away in the house.'

'See?' Gus hissed at me through clenched stumps.

'Well, apologies for the mistake,' I nodded. 'If there's anything else you would like . . . ?'

'No, no, really. I'd better be going. I'm on my way to Torquay. Said I'd be there by lunch.'

He smiled awkwardly and left. Immediately the door closed behind him, Gus started. 'Look what you've done. Fifteen hundred bloody nicker, maybe more, gone out of the window. Have you gone crazy?'

'No, Gus, I haven't.'

'Then what are you passing up thousands for, then? They're only tiny lumps of lead, after all.'

'They are not tiny lumps of lead. For a start, they are made of Mazak and secondly, Gus, they are quite wonderful and thirdly, not everything in life is for sale.'

He threw his arms up in the air, with a long, drawn-out, 'Gorrrr . . .'

I turned on him. 'Look, Gus, what the hell's gone wrong with everybody suddenly? Everywhere I seem to turn, people, young and old, are obsessed with money. Loads of people, loadsamoney. At least, I thought you, Gus, would be the last bastion of . . .' I hesitated. I wanted to say things like 'sanity', 'reason', 'common sense', but none of them seemed to fit Gus – at least not literally, or like a glove. I suddenly realized, there wasn't a word in the English language that quite describes old Gus. Now, in retrospect, I guess the nearest anyone can ever get to describing Gus is to use the name of a weather-beaten, primeval and craggy outcrop in the Mediterranean. Gibraltar.

'You calling me a bastion?' Gus asked, his fists at the ready.

'No, Gus, I'm not. A bastion doesn't mean what you think it does. It's actually a compliment.'

I was relieved when the tinkle of the phone put paid to this ridiculous exchange. I went through into the house and answered it.

'Mr Marklin?'

I recognized the gravelly voice immediately.

'Speaking, Miss Pettican.'

'Oh, good. Right, well . . . er . . . I'm really ringing to see if you could come over and see me.'

My mental eyebrows went up. 'See you? Yes, fine, yes.'

'You couldn't make this morning, could you? I know it's not long to lunch-time, but I've got an appointment in Dorchester this afternoon and something has just come up you see.'

'Something to do with . . . Manners School?'

'Yes. Yes. That's right. I'd rather not talk on the phone.'

'All right, Miss Pettican, I'll come over. If you can give me some directions to your house?'

'Oh no, Mr Marklin. I'm not in my house, this morning. I have to collect fossils for my talk in Dorchester this afternoon. You know, to prove that anyone can find fossils any day. All they've got to do is look. I'm speaking from a call box right now. In Charmouth.'

'Is that where you want me to meet you? In Charmouth?'

'Yes. If you don't mind. Luckily, the day's dry.'

'Where will you be?'

'Still on the beach, I expect.'

'Which end?'

'Golden Cap end.'

'I'll see you in around . . . twenty minutes, half an hour. Beneath Golden Cap.'

'I'd be very grateful.' Then I heard the click of the receiver.

I stayed by the phone for a minute or two, trying to figure why Delia Pettican should want to see me and, what's more, see me so rapidly. When I found I couldn't answer myself, I ambled back into the shop.

'Gus,' I began, but by then, he was half-way to the door.

'I'm off, old son. Can't seem to do no good sticking around 'ere. Bad for me 'ealth.'

'Gus. That was Delia Pettican. She wants me to go over and see her in Charmouth right away.'

'So, off with you then,' he grunted. 'I'm not keeping you.'

I felt dreadful, as Gus was intending.

'Gus, I was wondering if . . .'

'I'm not staying to look after your shop again, if that's what you're on about.'

'Why not, Gus? I'm sorry about the aircraft business, but they're pretty rare. I'll never find another set like that in a month of Sundays.' .

'Sorry, old lad, this time you'll have to shut up shop. I'm not ruddy staying.'

'Oh, come on, Gus. Why not?'

'I'm not. That's why not.'

'I didn't mean to offend you. Really. I'm sorry if . . .'

'Too late to be sorry, old lad. You'll have to shut up shop. I'm not staying and that's that.'

'Just give me a decent "why not".'

His face suddenly broke into a giant grin. 'Because I'm ruddy coming with you, old lad, that's why. You've done enough ruddy Ercool Parroting without me.'

Twelve

Charmouth lies just east of its famous neighbour, Lyme Regis, and is as different from that small harbour town as could ever be. Though approached via the steep incline of Chideock, Charmouth's main street, if you can even call it that, climbs gently away from the village garage and cluster of old-fashioned shops at quarter the angle of its equivalent in Lyme.

Going west, there is an inconspicuous turning to the left off that main street that leads to Charmouth's greatest asset, its sand and shingle beach. It stretches quietly, even at the height of the tourist season, towards the crowning glory of Golden Cap, so called from the sandy yellow glow the sun kisses on to the cliff's crown, whenever one wants romance to enter (re-enter?) one's life.

It was down that turning that Gus and I sped in my Beetle that midday, the former, as ever, grumbling about 'it not being natural for the phutting of an engine to come from behind'.

We parked in the car-park, which was deserted save for Miss Pettican's old MG Midget, and walked down to the beach. Though the sun was indeed shining, the fresh autumn breeze was turning its rays down to Regulo 1. For once, I envied Gus the extra heaviness of his old sweater.

Luckily, we did not need to take many paces along the shingle before we saw what we took to be Miss Pettican: a distant glimmer of white that seemed to be bent double over something. But quite a few paces were needed before we actually saw a head – or, to be more accurate, a seemingly grey and shapeless hat. Something just below the hat eventually started to wave in our direction and I felt a surge of relief. It was then I suddenly realized what I must, subconsciously, have been dreading – that I might not find life amongst the fossils. Such was the tension, drat it, that the Manners School affair was now generating.

We quickened our pace and soon were within hailing distance.

'I'll . . . er . . .' Gus began and his voice faded away.

'You'll, er, what, Gus? On the side of caution?' I asked, but quite deservedly, got a frown.

'I'll . . . er . . . keep in the background.'

I stopped in my tracks. 'Gus, a three-mile-long totally deserted beach doesn't provide any background. Just foreground.'

'Well, anyway, I'll wait around here. You go on.'

'I thought you wanted to be involved? Do a bit of "Ercool Parroting"? Don't leave me out, you said.'

He scuffed his foot in the sand and lost at least fifty-five of his years in the action.

'Well . . . er . . . didn't you say she was a bit, you know, a bit . . . strong?'

'So I did, Gus. But so are you. A bit strong.' I chuckled. 'Especially in that sweater.' I took his arm. 'Come on. She won't mind.'

He eventually sloped after me and, no doubt, would have mewled and puked some more, had she not been in earshot.

I was soon grasped by strong fingers and greeted with a hearty, 'So good of you to come, Mr Marklin, and at such short notice, too.' Her eyes flicked to Gus and then flickered. She'd obviously not been expecting one short of a crowd.

'Ah, this is Mr Tribble, Gus Tribble. He's an old friend of mine – I mean a friend of mine from way back.'

She extended a hand which Gus shook. I could see, grip for grip, she realized she had met her match.

'Well . . . er . . .' she began hesitantly. I helped her out.

'I assure you, Miss Pettican, anything you can say to me, you can say to Gus.'

She looked both of us up and down for a moment, then looked away at the cliff face and then upwards at its golden cap, as if for some form of fossilized or God-given guidance.

'Er . . . well . . . I suppose it will be . . . all right. I . . . er . . .'

Gus made to go, but I stayed him.

'Mr Tribble has been invaluable to me in the past in helping out in cases like . . . well, the kind of problems you're having at Manners School.'

She looked back at us. Especially at Gus. I guess she felt he looked as far from Basil Rathbone's Sherlock Holmes and Peter Ustinov's Hercule Poirot, as made all the difference.

149

'But if you would rather just speak to me . . .' I proffered, half-heartedly.

She shook her head vigorously. 'No, no. Wouldn't think of it, Mr Marklin. I'm sure . . . everything . . . will be all right.'

She moved a little away from the cliff edge and sat on a fallen boulder. She indicated two other large stones fairly near for Gus and myself. Both of us braved piles and sank down on to the ice-chill, unforgiving and irregular surfaces. (If God had intended man stroke woman to sit on rocks, He'd have given us dimpled behinds like giant golf balls. I guess, by the time we went, we'd both got them.)

'So, Miss Pettican, what did you want to see me about?'

Instead of answering, she reached for a stout leather carry-all that was lying nearby and brought from it a lump of rock which she handed to me.

'Isn't that wonderful, Mr Marklin? I found it further up the beach a little before you arrived.'

I turned it over and saw the reason for her enthusiasm. Fossils aren't really my game, but even I could see this was a perfect specimen.

'It's a humble ammonite. From the Jurassic period. That's around a hundred and fifty million years ago. Makes one feel very unimportant in the scheme of things, don't you think? We all live for a mere split second and then' – she pointed to the cliff – 'most of us crumble away to dust, leaving not even a tiny print on the pages of time. This ammonite was lucky. We will always now know of its brief fragile existence.'

I handed the fossil to Gus, who almost immediately handed it back to its finder. (Tact is hardly Gus's strongest suit. He's the Ace, King and Jack of its reverse, however. Quite a card.)

She put the rock back in her bag, which I could now see contained gardener's type rubber gloves and two small dust-covered picks – the tools of her trade.

'Sorry, Mr Marklin. I shouldn't really be taking up your valuable time in rabbiting on about my hobby. Forgive me.'

'Forgiven,' I smiled. 'My mother used to live in Charmouth and she has often told me stories of the fossils that have been found around here. Had quite a few herself.'

She rubbed her strong, sinewy fingers together to rid them of the rock's dust. 'Now, back to why I wanted to see you, Mr

150

Marklin. It's all because of a fine young girl who attends our Manners School. Ella Eames.'

'Winna?'

She smiled, deep-etching the lines in the leathery tan of her skin. 'Yes, I believe she calls herself that sometimes. Certainly, her young friend, Tony Thorn, does.'

'What about Ella Eames?' I asked. 'Is she in some kind of trouble now?'

She shook her head vigorously.

'No, no, no, Mr Marklin. Nothing like that. I only mention her name because she has told me a bit about you and how you are trying to help her boyfriend, Tony, and poor Andy Boxall, our school caretaker. It is most generous of you, both to care and to spare the time.'

'I'd just like to see your school get back to normal as soon as possible, that's all. It must be very disturbing, right now, for all concerned.'

'I can't tell you – and Mr Tribble – what a terrible tragedy this whole affair has been for Manners.' She shook her head. 'No words can describe the effect it's all having. On everyone. Teachers and pupils alike. Much more of this and the school, I'm afraid, may lose the confidence of parents, and then . . .'

'It hasn't happened yet,' I smiled sympathetically.

'You don't know how near it's getting, Mr Marklin.'

I decided to switch from the morbid to the positive. 'So you rang me because something new has happened or you've thought of some new way I might be of assistance?'

'The former,' she replied gravely.

'Tell me.'

She rose from the rock and started to pace up and down in front of us. 'I think I'm being followed.'

It could almost have been a replay of Tony's statement of days before.

'Followed? Are you sure?'

She nodded. 'I wasn't at first, but now I am.'

'When did all this start?'

'Soon after I had told the police about seeing a dark figure on the school wall the night of the murder.'

Her constant pacing was not exactly helping my wits. I was a trifle slow with my next question. 'Have you told the police about your suspicions?'

'No.'

'You should, you know.'

'I thought I ought to speak to you first.'

'Me? Why? It's really a police matter, if you think you are being followed. After all, you could well be in danger, Miss Pettican, and I can't. . . .'

She stopped pacing and looked down at me.

'I know you can't protect me like the police, maybe, can. But if I tell them my suspicions, then the whole thing may stop. It did after Tony Thorn told them about the man on the motor cycle. He hasn't been seen at all since that day, it would seem.'

'But isn't that what you want to happen? The following to stop?'

'Not really. If it stops, we may never discover the culprit. And I feel he might well be the key to solving all our problems. Do you see . . . ?'

Her logic was a bit twisted, but I sort of saw.

'It's a risk you must take, Miss Pettican. The risk you can't take is what your follower may end up doing . . . to you. By the way, you said "he" just now. Does that mean you have seen the person close enough to be sure it's a man?'

'Yes. I'm sure it's not a woman.'

'When have you seen him? How many times?'

'About five times. Once, I found him hovering around my front gates, when I came home early from a lecture. He ran off immediately. The second time was here, on this beach. I was conscious of a figure watching me from a distance the whole time I was chipping away at a rock. It was a showery day and the beach was otherwise deserted.'

She resumed pacing. 'Third and fourth times were both when I was shopping. I noticed him once in that big new supermarket in Weymouth. Another time, hanging about opposite that fossil shop in Lyme Regis.'

'And the last time?'

'This morning. Here. On the beach. That's why I went up and rang you from the call-box in the village.'

'How do you know it's always the same man?' Gus asked, taking the words right out of my mouth.

'Same build. Tallish. Same kind of clothes. Sort of buff trench-coat, as far as I could see. And a flat cap pulled low over his eyes.

Oh – and big sunglasses. That's why I've never really been able to see his features. That and the fact he's always kept his distance.'

'Any feelings about his likely age? I mean, did he come over as young or old?'

'He seemed about in the middle,' she smiled. 'A bit like me. He certainly wasn't young. You can always spot a young person by the way they move. They always look as if they're on the way somewhere. Older people tend to move as if they're on the way back.'

I liked her spot-on description.

I rose from my rock to ease the pain. 'Any idea why anyone should be keeping tabs on you?'

'I thought you were the sleuth, Mr Marklin. You tell me.'

I thought for a moment. 'Tony was followed. Now you are being followed. It could be the same person. Yet there might be no connection at all. Inspector Whetstone inferred to me the other day that he thought the guy on the BMW might well be not connected with the case.'

'Child molester?'

I held my hands wide apart. 'He says he's got a dossier that thick.'

'Seen this bloke's car or anything?' Gus asked quite rightly. 'He can't be walking everywhere after you, can he?'

'I don't take much notice of cars or things like that, Mr Tribble. I certainly haven't spotted how he gets around.'

She suddenly stopped pacing again, then dusted her hands together in rather a 'Well, that's enough of that' way.

'So, Mr Marklin, I just thought I would tell you, that's all. In case it helps in any way. Or gives you any new ideas.'

Gus took the hint and rose, groaning, from his rock of pain.

'Ought to tell the police, you should. Never know what can happen with weirdos like that.'

'Gus is right, Miss Pettican. You should tell the police right away. He may well be after you because he read in the papers that you are the only witness to the figure clambering over the wall.'

'You're starting to convince me,' she smiled, then proffered a hand. 'Thanks so much for bothering to come. And you, Mr Tribble.'

'S'right,' Gus waved a hand and shuffled back up the beach. Always the gent.

As I too turned to leave, Delia Pettican delayed me with, 'By the way, Mr Marklin, I believe Ella Eames is coming over to you tonight.'

'Is she?' I said. 'Oh, good. We did invite her and Tony.'

'When she comes, don't mention our little conversation this morning, will you? You see, she might get worried about me and it could put her off concentrating on her gymnastics. Her big day is very near now.'

I put my finger to my lips. 'Not a word. Promise.'

And with that, I moved on up the shingle after dear old Gus, who was now some way ahead. But I hadn't covered more than about twenty yards or so, when I heard a noise behind me. A slipping, sliding stony cacophony that grew into a whooshing climax.

I spun round instantly and looked back towards where Miss Pettican had been. But all I could see now was a billowing cloud of dust. I looked up at the cliff face, my eyes ascending whilst the last stones and rocks did the reverse. And up further to the cliff top, where, to my horror, I saw a dark figure. As my focus improved, I saw that the figure seemed to match exactly Delia Pettican's description of her follower – right down to his trench-coat and up to his flat cap and sunglasses. I say 'seemed', because the dust cloud, swirling upwards in the thermals, eclipsed the figure from sight in next to no time.

I shouted after Gus, but he was already on his way over to me at a rate of knots belying his age. I started to run towards the high pile of rocks that now pyramided the spot where we had all sat only moments before, but not really in the hope of trying to save Delia Pettican, who, I reckoned, would have been killed by the fall.

Then half-way to the spot, a ghostly figure started to materialize through the clouds of dust, rather like Hamlet's father in the famous Olivier film. Where colour had been in clothes and skin, white now reigned, but the figure still moved with a determination and stride that could only have belonged to the school governor we had come to see.

She waved weakly, then shouted, 'I'm all right. Don't bother with me.'

I ignored her and raced on, but she pointed to the cliff top. 'Did you see who it was? Did you?'

I reached her, but she shook off my supporting arm.

'No. I'm fine, I tell you. But did you manage to see who started it? A rock fall like this just couldn't have happened on its own.'

'I saw a figure. Yes.'

'Like I described?'

I nodded.

By then, Gus was by my side. I turned to him. 'Look, Gus, you stay here with Miss Pettican.'

To my amazement, she now seemed only too willing for someone to help her and directly his massive arm was around her waist, she nestled against his hairy sweater. They would have looked like long-time lovers on a second honeymoon, had she not been dressed overall in a thick film of yellowy white dust.

'Why? Where are you going?' Gus mumbled.

'I know it's probably far too late, but I'm going after the bastard who started all this.'

And I pelted back up the beach to where I knew from my childhood, there was a path that wound its way up to the top of Golden Cap.

Before I started the long ascent up the grassy slope, I glanced back at the car-park. But there were still only two cars; Miss Pettican's Midget and my Beetle. So I reckoned the would-be murderer must have parked his car somewhere in the main village or on the sea road, some way back from the beach. It made sense. Cars identify people almost as easily as finger and genetic printing. And you don't need their owners there to do it.

As I climbed, I continually scanned the horizon, but there was not a soul to be seen. And I knew that, in reality, I had little chance of catching up with flat cap and sunglasses. However, I had forgotten one important physical fact of life. The higher you get, the further you can see.

So that by the time I was, breathlessly, half-way up the ever-steepening grass side of the Cap, my eyes could see a fair old distance in all directions. I flopped to a stop, because I knew that if the figure had descended the further, eastern side of the cliff, I would have no chance in hell of getting near enough to make out his appearance, let alone catch him up. So my only hope lay in using my present high vantage point to scan the fields that led back towards both the village proper and the sea lane.

Cursing the fact that God hadn't seen fit to give me zoom lens oculars and sun filtration to boot, hand on forehead I squinted out across the browny green of the autumn pastures. At first, the only things I could see moving were four-legged things with udders and black hides patched with white, but then, bingo, I thought for a second I had got him, as a human figure moved out from behind a hedge. But, a moment later, it was joined by another figure who seemed to be adjusting something below her waist. Being a true gent, I assumed it must be her skirt.

More squinting seemed to reveal nothing – except a dog, who had obviously decided to try to get the herd of cows to play 'He', or should it be, in this case, 'She'? I could hear their lowing and no-ing from where I was standing. I was about to give up and go back and save Miss Pettican from Gus and take her to the police, when, way over to the right, I saw a flash of light. It seemed to come from the base of what looked like a large wizened oak. I watched intently and soon was rewarded with another flash of light.

I didn't wait for my bewildered brain to try to work out what could be its cause, but immediately started to run inland, across and down the slope towards the tree. Downhill running gave me well over double the pace of my uphill variety and I had to concentrate on where my Pegasus winged feet were landing, so as not to go wotsit over tip. As a consequence, I couldn't keep my eyes riveted on the tree and what was worse, once I was back on the level, I had lost my vantage-point view.

Needless to say, between me and the flashing oak lay two lines of hedges – the old-fashioned thick and wild kind, a million brambles per foot, so loved now by birds and conservationists, and me, for that matter, in normal circumstances. But when you have to fight your way through them, you tend to prefer the skinny, pestified and poisoned variety, as recommended by today's cost-conscious agricultural marketeers.

I had lost valuable seconds by the time I emerged through the last barbed-bramble entanglement, bloody and a trifle bowed and the tree, that was now only some fifty yards away, looked as innocent of flashes and flashers as could possibly be. After a sepulchral sigh and a curse, I ran on regardless and was soon standing in the gnarled network of its root system. A three hundred and sixty degree scan around me produced zilch. Whatever or whoever had caused the flashing was still a mystery and, maybe, I realized, a completely bum steer, which could have taken my attention off the real route of my quarry. I was just about to curse again, then make my way wearily back to the beach, when my foot crunched against something that gave. I bent down and saw that I had been standing on some glass. I carefully picked up the pieces and it wasn't hard to see that it had been a pocket mirror of some kind. But the small, square variety, not the round type more favoured by the fairer sex.

I stared at my reflection in the largest of the jagged pieces, as I tried to work out whether some animal might have disturbed a piece of the mirror and thus, accidentally, caused the flash, or whether some person had actually been holding it, either to check on his or her appearance or, wild thought, to attract my attention. Unable to come to a conclusion worth a damn, I gingerly put the pieces in the back flap of my battered wallet, then took a last look around. As I did so, I heard a car start up not so very far away. Instantly, I started to run in the direction I thought the sound was coming from. But now the noise was of a car accelerating swiftly away. And a powerful car at that.

I could see nothing, because another, even higher, conservationist's dream totally barred my view and way, and by the time I had got down to the gate I could see at the end of the field, the car's engine note was no longer discernible above the general drone of traffic on the Charmouth road.

The only reward for my labours – beyond perhaps the mirror – was to find where I guessed the car had been parked. In a gateway at the end of a short gravelled track that led back to the main road. And being gravel, damn it, there weren't any tyre tracks worth a damn. But the particular noise the car's engine had made had certainly rung my bell. For you hear it quite a few times a day, if you live in an area where farms are big enough to crop acres of money. It's a burble. It's a V8 roar. It's Super Farmer on his way to the bank. With his obedient four-wheeled friend who answers to Range Rover.

Thirteen

By the time I had retraced my steps to the start of the main incline, I could see the two figures standing by our cars in the car-park. I swung to the right, away from the beach, and joined them.

They saw in my face the result of my chase.

'Got away?' Gus asked needlessly.

'Yes, damn it, ' I sighed. 'Away, but not necessarily clean away.'

Delia Pettican, whose face, if not her clothes, was now a mite less like a messy flour worker's, looked at me expectantly. 'You've discovered something, Mr Marklin?'

'I don't know, really.' I took out my wallet and withdrew a jagged remnant of the mirror. 'I saw something flashing by a tree, over towards the Chideock road, and found this.'

Miss Pettican took the fragment from me with the academic care she would, no doubt, have shown with a dinosaur tooth.

'A mirror. Or a bit of one. Quite clean too. Do you think it might have belonged to *my* man?'

I was somewhat amazed at a would-be murderer being regarded as anybody's property. 'Can't say. But something made it flash. Could have been an animal, I suppose.'

'Animals don't use bloody mirrors,' Gus observed. 'One thing in their favour.'

'I mean an animal may have disturbed it, scurrying about.'

Gus made a face. 'Pull the other leg, old lad.'

'Anything else, Mr Marklin?' She handed me back the fragment.

'I heard a car start up and pull away. Not far from the tree. But I was too late to see it. Now it could have been some farmer or courting couple or somebody else, but it also might just have been *your* man.'

'But you didn't see it, so you don't know what kind of car it was,' she asked.

'No. But I heard it right enough. And as Dennis Norden says, "Sounds familiar".'

She looked rather surprised. 'You can tell the make of a car by its sound, Mr Marklin? Amazing. But then, I remember, my late lamented brother, when he was still at school during the war, could tell a German aircraft from an Allied one just by the sound of its engines.'

Gus winked at me. 'All right then, old love, was it a German car or an Allied one?' (Gus's other reason for hating my Beetle is that he has a bee under his own bonnet that Hitler actually designed it himself. No amount of chat about Ferdinand Porsche will convince him otherwise.)

'Allied,' I said. 'British chassis and coachwork with V8 engine from an old American Buick. Commonly known as a Range Rover.'

'Are you sure, Mr Marklin?'

'Well, some of the old Rover saloons used the same engine but have a different exhaust note. Why? Do you know anyone with a Range Rover?'

She thought for a moment. 'Well, yes, more than one person, actually. There's the secretary of the Flora and Fauna Society, a Mr Edmund Whittaker. He's away, though, at the moment in the Himalayas. And Mrs Swinburn, who lives over Osmington way. She owns the Star and Garter Hotel. And then, of course, there's . . .' She suddenly stopped and patted some dust out of her long skirt.

'There's who?' I asked rather impatiently.

She would not look at me. 'It can't be him. No, it can't be him.'

'Can't be who, Miss Pettican? It's important you tell me.'

She looked up. 'Well, Colonel Hawkesworth has a Range Rover, though he usually uses his Jaguar.'

'Hawkesworth,' I repeated, mainly for my own benefit, as I tried to mentally photo-fit the figure I had seen on the cliff with my memories of the Colonel. 'More or less the right height,' I went on. 'And you reckoned, Miss Pettican, that the figure you've seen following you is likely to be middle aged.'

She waved her hand in dismissal at the idea. 'No. But it couldn't be. Not the Colonel. Much as I dislike the man and he, no doubt, me, I doubt very much if he would ever contemplate such a violent and heinous act as my murder. And anyway, he has very little motive now that he seems to have got the head-master more or less under his thumb since poor Mr Folland's death. No, no, no, Mr Marklin. It's much more likely to be some poor crazed individual, perhaps someone none of us knows or has even heard of, who is after me because I'm the only witness to the figure on the school wall on the night of the murder. Much more likely it's that French friend of Mr Folland's, don't you think?'

'Supposing that figure was, indeed, Colonel Hawkesworth? It's possible.'

She rested back against the boot of the Midget. 'It's possible, I suppose, that there was no figure and I actually did the murder, when you come to think about it. But it's not probable.' She forced a smile. 'It's all right. There was someone on that wall. And I did not kill Mr Folland. And nor, I think, did the Colonel. There are many, many, other Range Rovers around here and what's more, I know there's a place in Weymouth where you can even hire one. So . . . that Frenchman . . .'

I took her arm. 'So . . . we should go to the police. Like right now.'

She grimaced. 'Do you think we must? Maybe I'm wrong. Maybe the rock fall was accidental.'

'But just now, you said it couldn't have been.'

'Couldn't have been,' Gus grunted. 'Had a good look after you'd gone, I did. That slide wasn't ruddy natural. Rest of the cliff is sound as 'ouses. Someone has been hacking about at it. I reckon if we went right up there, we might find enough evidence to hang him.'

'Well, the police will, no doubt, save us the bother.' I went round and opened the MG's door. 'Feel fit enough to drive, Miss Pettican?'

She shook herself, like a dog raring to go. A cloud of dust haloed around her, some settling on her car, making it look even more matt.

'It takes more than that to stop me, young man,' she grinned. 'I'm tough as old boot leather.'

And so we left in convoy. Half-way back along the sea lane, Gus suddenly broke into guffaws.

'What the hell's amusing, Gus? We have just witnessed what may be an attempted murder and you laugh like a drain.'

'It's her,' he grinned.

'Miss Pettican?' I frowned. 'What about her?'

'Yea. Her calling you "young man". That's the biggest laugh in years, ain't it?'

I didn't comment. Thirty-nine-year-olds don't comment on things like that, even when their minds aren't full of murder and mayhem. They're too ... youthfully mature, or is it maturely youthful?

Gus and I did not leave Digby Whetstone's filing-cabinet-grey and anonymous office until six thirty; by which time I was well and truly knackered. Surprisingly, Gus still looked as fresh as a ... well, hardly daisy, I suppose. Try something heftier. A tree would do.

Not that we were chez Whetstone all that time. Far from it. Most of the day was spent back in Charmouth or in radio-controlled Rovers in transit there and back. Gus loved the luxury of the latter and actually asked what the police did with the cars when they had finished with them. I think he fancied himself in such a literally flashy vehicle and imagined he could buy one for a sea shanty. He was soon disillusioned.

I must say the police were thorough. I've heard of beach-combing, but this was ridiculous. Ten boys in blue (soon turning to dust grey) combed every pebble, rock and seashell in the area of the rock fall, whilst around ten more went over every blade of grass at the top of the cliffs. Their professional conclusions matched our amateur ones. Marks on the grass and on the face of the cliff made it apparent that someone had chipped away at the surface to loosen it, probably with a pick, and made a pile of the loose rocks on the grass edge, so that one last blow and a shove could cause a rock slide more than sufficient to bury someone working on the beach close to the cliff face. If Delia Pettican had not reacted as quickly to the first sounds of the slide, she would undoubtedly have been buried alive.

My fragments of mirror and estimate as to the make of vehicle that I had heard drive away were treated somewhat with contempt by dear Digby, if not by his side- and under-kicks.

'The mirror could have been lost days ago, Mr Marklin,' he had observed. 'Didn't you say you saw a courting couple around here this morning? Well, I dare say these fields attract them like flies. My men even found three used condoms on the incline up to

161

Golden Cap. Anyway, a would-be murderer would hardly bother about his appearance, when he's on the run from the scene of the crime, now would he? Unless he was very . . . shall we say . . . camp?'

He had a point. Not the inevitable tilt at homosexuals bit, but the rest.

'And as for your hearing a vehicle driving off, it could have been anybody, now couldn't it? A farmer, a late tourist, a courting couple again, a person breaking his or her journey, the possibilities are endless. And as for it actually being a Range Rover, well – ' he chuckled, 'I'd love to hear that bit of evidence being dissected by a defence lawyer in court. Make my day.'

There was no point in arguing, so I changed the subject.

'Tell me, Inspector, do you think this attack on Miss Pettican is connected with Folland's murder?'

He sat back in his chair and tried to look wordly wise. 'Well, it would be foolish to ignore a connection, wouldn't it? But we won't really know until we can establish some kind of motive for this morning's attack.'

'Isn't that fairly obvious? I mean, Delia Pettican is the only person who may have actually seen the murderer the night Folland was killed. You know, the dark figure on the wall. And all the media reported her sighting.'

'But she only caught a brief glimpse, a flash of movement. That was reported too.'

'The murderer may reckon that's just a police bluff to fool him. Been done before, as you should know better than anyone.'

He pulled the next best thing to a smile. 'You amateurs read far too many thrillers. You don't want to believe everything you read in their ludicrously over-dramatic pages.'

He abruptly sat forward at his desk and fixed me with his beady eyes. 'Now, that reminds me, Mr Marklin. How come Miss Pettican rang you this morning and asked you to come over? I don't go for her story about you wanting to know about fossils. You're hardly the fossil type. And certainly Mr Tribble is not.'

I laughed. 'You mean I'm not bald with a goatee beard. Come, Inspector, I'm surprised you weren't warned about stereotyping at police academy. Anyone can be interested in fossils, you know. And, for your information, Mr Tribble was just along for the ride.'

'And babies are found under gooseberry bushes and tooth fairies . . . Really, Mr Marklin, you must think I was only born yesterday. You're still up to your old larks, aren't you, of butting into matters that are solely the province of the police. I have told you a thousand times that . . .'

'Funny timing, wasn't it?' I butted in, anxious to avoid the need for a response.

'What timing?'

'The attempt on Miss Pettican's life.'

'Go on.'

'You would have thought he would have waited until some time after Gus and I had left the beach, wouldn't you? Not try it in full view of witnesses.'

'The same thought had naturally occurred to me. But there could be quite a few reasons why he felt that it was unsafe to delay it longer. Don't forget, he may have been about to commit it when you and Mr Tribble suddenly appeared out of the blue. Secondly, he may have been worried about his car being noticed if he hung around too long. Or his alibi may depend on his not being away on the cliffs too long. Lastly, he knew, anyway, that the cliff was far too high for him to be positively recognized from the beach and that by the time anyone could get up onto the cliffs, he'd have had plenty of time to make his getaway. Which is what happened.'

I was quite impressed by Digby's reasoning, but still retained the sneaking suspicion I had nurtured all day that the actual timing was somewhat eccentric; nay, surprising. I had discussed it originally in the car with Gus on our way to the police and he'd just grunted that if I'd been right about the Range Rover and it had been the colonel's, he was such a pompous show-off, from all accounts, that he might well enjoy the thought of an audience for his rock festival. And there was something in that, too. That was the cursed trouble with the whole Manners School affair – there seemed to be something in almost everything.

Anyway, Gus and I did eventually get away from that bleak Bournemouth station, but not until both of us, separately and together, had been warned yet again about our hasty and dangerous habit of turning up where only Whetstone's angels should dare to tread. And, as I say, Gus seemed the better for the day's wear and tear. I put it down to his feeling really involved with the case for the very first time. My problem now was how to keep him down on the funny farm, now he'd seen Poirot's Paree.

When we at last arrived back, there was no sign of Arabella. But a note had been thrust through the shop door. It was from Tony, saying he and Winna would love to come round after doing their homework and to expect them about eight thirty. Arabella soon rang, however, saying she'd be late, because she had only just got back to the office from Charmouth and had to write up 'guess what?'. She asked, to save time, if Gus and I could give her some quotes over the phone. This we did, although I had to rather censor Gus's offerings. I ended by asking her if she had managed to get the tape of *Wall Street*. She said she hadn't and suggested I might pop into Swanage and get it, as she might be late.

By the time I had replaced the receiver, Gus had thrust a Heineken into my hand. (We had bought a six-pack on the way back from Bournemouth, just in case. I was positive the case would come up.)

'Will we be in the papers?' he gleamed.

'Looks like it,' I replied flatly. 'And it may not end there.'

'What d'you mean?'

'Well, the local radio and TV people will be on to us soon, I expect.'

Gus instantly put down the Heineken. 'Well, old son, I'd better go home and put on my best bib and tucker, then.'

And before I could stop him, he'd gone. Still, I couldn't remember ever having seen Gus in anything but a sweater and corduroy trousers, so at least his concept of posher duds might hold some intrigue. And the hiatus did give a little time to gather my thoughts.

Quite a short mental scan made me realize it was now high time Peter Marklin did the very reverse of Digby's strict cautions and started to throw a few wild dice of his own into the game. That very evening would do nicely indeed for the first toss – but only if the media would let me.

I got out the phone book and looked up the numbers of the local commercial and BBC radio stations and our dear old BBC South and Southern Television. Many calls, pints of perspiration and hanks of hair later, I collapsed into a chair with at least the knowledge that I'd done my level creative best in trying to stop them all contacting me or Gus or arriving on our doorstep with mountains of equipment and invasions of crew. For no one in any of these organizations seemed willing to accept that anyone in this wide world would insist on passing up a chance to be broadcast or televised. Not even when I added the threat that Mr

Tribble and I might even go as far as to take them to court for trespass if they dared to ignore our wishes. Calls over, I Beetled down into Swanage and picked up the *Wall Street* tape as I'd been bidden.

I did feel a bit of a rat, when, soon after, Gus bounced back in his best bib and tucker. I almost didn't recognize him at first. It wasn't just the half gallon of Brylcreem slicking down the last of his hair, or the aftershave that made him smell like a Tunisian brothel, or the closeness of his shave that revealed the true contours of his face for the first time. And it wasn't just the suit or rather, it wasn't *all* the suit. Some it had to be, when you remember it looked as if the last person to wear it was Al Capone, all wide shoulders, wide lapels and a stripe bold enough to draw blood on the cloth. No, it was the change all this tarting up brought about in Gus's manner. Instead of downright grumpy, he was now upright cheeky. There was bounce in his step. Brightness in his red rims. Smiles had moved in where frowns used to live. Indeed, the media seemed to have done for Gus all the things that petfood manufacturers promise for dogs. Even down to the glossy coat. For Al Capone, before he departed, had certainly shone that suit up at elbow and knee, not to mention the derrière.

'Well,' he said, picking up his Heineken, as if he'd never put it down, 'when are they coming?'

'They're not, Gus. Least, I don't think they'll dare risk it.'

To say his crest fell is the understatement of any year.

'Not coming? Why bloody not, old son?' He stabbed at the air with his thick, but now unusually clean, finger. 'We were *there*. We *saw* it. In front of our very eyes, it sodding happened.'

I put my hand on his shoulder pad. It crackled.

'I know, Gus, I know. I'm afraid it's all my fault. I've rung them and . . . put them off, you see.'

It took the next ten minutes and another Heineken to convince Gus that I wasn't just being a spoilsport or radio and camera shy, but it meant coming clean to him about my suspicions and my plan for the evening. But whilst I had quelled his anger, I'm afraid I could never make up for his disappointment. However, he did seem to cheer up a smidgin at the idea of being privy to the hatching of a plot, though he voiced his doubts about my theories.

165

'Bit wild, old son. Sure you haven't been watching too much Dallas or that other one.'

'Dysentery?' I offered.

'Yea. That's it. Dysentery,' he accepted as gospel. 'You should be writing for that Carbolic, you should, with ideas like you come up with.'

(I had never heard him refer to soaps as 'Carbolics' before. I loved it so much, I've always referred to the genre since as 'Carbolicals'.)

I drained the last of my lager and got up. 'Well, we'll see what happens tonight.'

Gus crackled up out of his chair. I think the interlining of his old suit must have dried to a crisp over the years. 'Well, old son, I'd better leave you to it.' He made for the door.

'You're welcome to stay.'

'That's all right, young man,' he winked. 'Your company is going to be a bit youthful for me tonight.'Sides, I want to get out of me Sunday best. Got things to do. Like me clothes 'orse collapsed last night. Still, teach me to put a wet mattress over it.'

'Wet mattress?' I blanched.

'Dirty sod,' he guffawed. 'Spilt me ruddy cocoa over it, didn't I?'

I delayed putting *Wall Street* on for as long as I could in the hope that Arabella might get home. But at nine, I just had to press the 'Play' button. I sat back and watched. Not so much the wheelings and dealings of Michael Douglas as he clawed his way up the Big Money Tree, or even the startling sensuality of Darryl Hannah, but the couple on the sofa. Tony was certainly riveted. Winna less so, but then the macho machinations of megalomaniacs were probably not up her particular street. Besides she had obviously been far more shocked by the attack on her friend, Delia Pettican, than Tony had been. His main reaction seemed to be surprise, not so much at the public way the murder attempt was mounted, but that it had happened at all. Even when I expounded a possible motive for its commission, that it would, at a rock slide, get rid of the only witness to someone climbing the school wall that fatal night, he didn't seem impressed and rapidly turned to an array of questions as to how my sleuthing was going otherwise – the clearance of Andy Boxall still being his main preoccupation. I was quite glad when I could delay *Wall Street* no longer.

166

Arabella returned about quarter of an hour into the film. I excused myself when I heard her car pull in and went to greet her. After the usual billings and cooings, I explained my plan. She listened with her already big eyes growing bigger every second.

When I had finished, she said, 'Do you really believe that's what's been happening?'

'Could be, couldn't it? Would explain a few of the things that don't add up at the moment, wouldn't it?'

She didn't disagree. 'So you're going to stop the film around half-way through. Suggest a sandwich and drinks break. You want me to take Winna into the kitchen and drop the odd question, whilst you take Tony into the shop?'

'Right, Miss Vane.'

'Stick to Miss Trench, Mr Marklin.'

I saluted and went back to *Wall Street*. As I walked in, I was amused to see Tony's arm slide out from around Winna's ridiculously small waist.

After about an hour of the film, I coughed to get the couple's attention.

'How about a little refreshment?' I offered and got up. They both nodded. I pressed the 'Stop' button on the recorder before anyone could object.

Arabella rose and went over to the settee. 'Come on, Winna. You can help me cut the odd sandwich, If you would.'

Good girl. So far it was going to plan. I looked down at Tony.

'Rather glad they're gone,' I said, 'because I have something in the shop I think might interest you.'

Tony got up and followed me through.

'You've rearranged the traffic flow again?' he asked.

'Nope.'

'Got more special offers?'

'Not for customers, no.'

I stopped by the counter.

He frowned. 'What do you mean, Peter? Offers are always for customers, aren't they?'

I reached under the counter and produced a parcel wrapped in brown paper. 'No. This one is specially for you ... a friend.'

He blushed. 'For me?'

I nodded. 'I thought you might be interested. I know you're not into toys, but you do appreciate a good investment, don't you?'

He watched me undo the sellotape and carefully draw the object out of its wrappings.

'Wow!' was his first comment, followed by, 'Man, that looks really old.'

'It is,' I said. 'Circa 1938. Made by a German firm called Märklin, would you believe. They made a range of cars you could screw together yourself. This is the only military one they made.'

He picked it up gingerly and swivelled the turret. 'Armoured car?'

'That's right.'

He traced his finger along the swirls of its orange, green and yellow camouflage.

'Funny finish. It looks a bit like when you roll different colours of plasticine together.'

I smiled. 'I guess they thought it would attract kids more than drab Wermacht grey and brown. Less menacing, anyway.'

'Looks in beautiful condition.'

'Mint, as we say in the trade. Only one thing wrong with it. The clockwork motor is broken. Won't wind up.'

Tony smiled across at me. 'No problem. Dad could no doubt fix that in a jiffy.' The smile turned into a frown. 'But why are you showing me this, Peter?'

'Thought you might like it. It's a sure fire investment at the price I got it for a month or so ago.' I took the armoured car from him. 'At Sotheby's, with its clockwork mended, this might fetch anything up to fifteen hundred pounds. Maybe more.'

He whistled. 'And what did you pay for it, if it's not a rude question?'

'Two hundred pounds. And I'm willing to sell it to you at that price.'

Tony thought for a second, then enquired, 'But why not just make the profit yourself? That's mega-money you're talking.'

'A little token for all the marketing ideas you will no doubt go on giving me about my shop,' I smiled. 'And anyway, I thought you could do with a little cheering up right now.'

'Are you really serious, Peter? I mean about selling me this for only two hundred pounds.'

'Yep.' I turned away. 'But of course, like all special offers, this must be for a limited period only. The next Sotheby's sale is only six weeks or so off. And if you don't want it or can't raise the money . . .'

He thought for a moment, then said: ''Course I want it. But two hundred is quite a bundle to raise.' He looked up and smiled. 'But hold on. What Tony wants, Tony usually gets – somehow.'

I put my hand on his shoulder. 'Tony. The car is yours. But only on one condition.'

'What's that?'

I led him round to the stool opposite my counter and sat him down on it. 'You tell me how you plan to get that kind of money that quickly. Or isn't it the truth that you've already got it?'

His eyes gave the game away. 'What do you mean ...? he began, but I cut him off.

'Come on, Tony, you know what I mean. The jumble sale money. You took it, didn't you?'

He shook his head so vigorously, he almost fell off the stool.

'No, no, no, Peter. I'd never do a thing like that. The money from the jumble sale is all there . . .' He stopped and hid his face in his hands.

'Where, Tony?'

He took a deep breath. 'In the headmaster's safe.'

'It *was* in the headmaster's safe. It's not now. You know that.'

He shook his head again. 'No, no. It's back there. At least, it should be.'

'Back there?' I came round to his side of the counter and put my hand on his shoulder.

'You had better tell me everything, Tony, hadn't you?'

He slowly lifted his head from his hands and looked up at me, moisture now glistening in the corners of his eyes.

'I guess, I had,' he said, in a voice now scarcely above a whisper.

Fourteen

They didn't leave until well after eleven thirty. In fact I felt I had to ring their respective parents to apologize for having kept them up so late, during term time. Needless to say, Mr Eames was the least charming about it all. 'Bugger term time. What about Ella getting enough rest before her big gymnastics challenge?' I could hardly tell him the real reason for a lot of the lateness, so I mumbled an extra 'Sorry' and left it at that.

Tony and I didn't dare look at each other during the rest of *Wall Street*. But I peered round at Arabella occasionally to try to guess from her expression what success, if any, she might have had with Winna. But the one time she caught me at it, her return look was as inscrutable as Charlie Chan's. So it availed me not a whit. I was madly impatient for the tape to end and the departures to be made.

We both came out with the same sentence simultaneously, the second the bicycle rear lights twinkled out of view.

'Did it work?'

'Did it work?'

I nodded. She nodded. And we both rushed back into the sitting-room, ensconced ourselves, goggle eyed and eared, for the respective revelations.

'You first,' I said.

She wrinkled up her nose. 'Must I?'

'You'd better,' I said. 'Mine may take up quite a bit of time.'

'Mine won't,' she sighed. 'Still, I'll tell you what there is of it. It's mostly about Delia Pettican.'

'The attack on her this morning?'

'No. I was quite surprised. She hardly mentioned it.'

'Still too shocked, I expect.'

'Maybe. Anyway, the sum of it is, I began asking her about how she was feeling about her chances in the Championships.

170

Who she regarded as her main rivals, how much training she had put in, that kind of thing. I won't bore you with all the literal answers, but it became plain as punch that she is a bundle of nerves about it all. Somehow, I think she would give it all up, even now, if it wasn't for her father. I don't reckon her own heart's in it now, even if it was once.'

'Daughter living out father's ambitions. Not the first time that's been known in this crazy world.'

'It doesn't make it any better though, does it?'

I shook my head. 'Funny, isn't it? There's Tony, brimful of his own ambition and rather self-conscious of his father clearly having none – not the type or scale that Tony reckons. And there's Winna . . .'

'. . . with few ambitions of her own,' Arabella went on, 'but a million she has to adopt to placate the pater familias. Yes. I know. Topsy-turvy, isn't it? And she seems as if she would be such a quiet, pleasant and happy girl, if she had a different influence in the home. I really like her, Peter. I only wish we could help her in some way. Even during my brief chat with her in the kitchen, she seemed so near to . . . I don't know . . . breaking down and crying, I suppose.'

'Anyway, back to Miss Pettican. Did she say anything that might give a clue as to why she and dear Delia seem to be so close right now – or has Tony really got the wrong end of the stick?'

Arabella came over and joined me on the settee. 'Yes, that's what she ended up talking about mainly. And it's more or less what we guessed. Delia Pettican is her shoulder to cry on – well, not literally, perhaps, but you know what I mean. She says she doesn't know what she'd have done without her over the last few weeks. And that Delia Pettican has been kindness itself in all sorts of ways.'

'No sign of . . . ?'

She shook her head. 'No sign of . . . not that I can see. Tony's imagination, I think, must be working overtime. Or he's just getting jealous, because Winna seems to need Delia right now more than she seems to need him.'

Arabella lifted her head from my shoulder and looked up at me. 'Talking of Tony, I'm dying to hear how you got on with him in the shop. Your conversation produce anything, or is your imagination as wild as Tony's seems to be about Winna?'

I sighed. 'I wish it were.'

171

She turned to face me. 'You don't mean . . . ?'

''Fraid so.'

She whistled her amazement. 'So it was Tony who pinched the jumble sale takings. I'd never have believed it possible. I thought you would be bound to find your stab in the dark was mis-aimed.'

'Right on target, damn it. But don't look so shattered, darling. Tony is not a thief in the strictest sense of the word. Otherwise, I would hardly have spent the rest of the evening watching a ruddy video with him.'

'If he took the money, he's a thief. What else can he be?'

'A borrower.'

'Borrower? I don't understand.'

'He just borrowed the money for a bit, then put it all back again in the Headmaster's safe. Every penny, he claims.'

'And you believe him?'

'Yes, I do.'

She rearranged herself, cross-legged, on the settee.

'Now, come on, Peter, you've got a lot more explaining than that to do. One, how did he get into the school to take the money? Two, how did he break into the safe? Three, why did he borrow the money? Four, how did he get it back again? And five, if he did put it back, how is it the whole world doesn't now know it's been found? And I guess, six, does this mean the whole burglary thing has nothing to do with Folland's death, after all?'

'Whew!' I smiled. 'I should have taken notes of all that.'

She smiled back. 'I'll help you, featherbrain. Firstly, how did Tony get into the school?'

'He didn't. He was already in the school. Some months ago, he had been in the Headmaster's study, when a master had come in and asked for something from the safe. He memorized the combination the Headmaster used and remembered it ever since. So it was only the work of a moment to get into the study just before school ended that day, open the safe, take the cash and stow it in the "executive briefcase" he carries his school books in. Then, on his way out, he handed the money over to Andy Boxall.'

'The caretaker? What on earth for? And how did Tony know the money was still there? Wasn't the Headmaster a day late banking it?'

'The answer to your second question is that he overheard the Headmaster telling his secretary not to bank the money the next morning, as he was still expecting more to roll in. Otherwise,

Tony had intended to carry out his plan the night of the jumble sale day. By the way, I'm a bit suspicious of the Headmaster's delay in banking the money, but I'll tell you about that in a minute.'

'So, back to my first question. Why did Tony give the money to the caretaker? Because he was afraid his parents might discover the loot if he took it home?'

'No. Nothing like that. Tony was using Andy Boxall, you see.'

'Using him? What for?'

'To buy shares that Tony reckoned would net him a hundred per cent profit within a week.'

'Shares? Like stocks and shares, you mean?'

I nodded. 'Remember all the fuss in the media over the last few days about the takeover of Jones Industries?'

'That old clock company that's now hit it big with electronic gadgetry and instrumentation?'

'Right, my darling. Well, Tony's father, being a clock buff, has a friend, apparently, who has been with Jones Industries since it started as a clock and watch company in the nineteen thirties. Tony heard his father talking about a tip he'd had from the American electronics giant, Claymore-Burgess. Tony tried to get his father to buy shares instantly, but his Dad just laughed and said only fools play the stock market. So Tony decided if his father wouldn't try to make a killing, he would. He has no friends or relations, apparently, with that kind of money, and had no time for protracted negotiations for a loan – even if he could get one, at his age.'

'So he used an adult – Andy – to buy the shares on his behalf, presumably for a cut.'

'Right again. Tony chose the stockbrokers – a firm in Bournemouth. Andy did the actual buying, under Tony's strict instructions. Now you see why I used the word "borrowed", rather than stole. Tony always had every intention of replacing the whole of the jumble sale takings the instant he had made his profit on selling the shares, which he did on take-over day. He made almost exactly one hundred per cent. He's no fool, is our Tony, even if his methods are dubious, to say the very least.'

'Illegal. Not dubious,' Arabella sighed. 'He'll end up in prison, if he goes on like that. Taking other people's money to make profits for himself.'

I laughed and took her hand. 'Industrialists and successful entrepreneurs are often knighted by the Queen after a lifetime of doing just that, my love. And worse. The trick, if you're doing it illegally, is to be successful and thus not be found out – or, at least, not by the media.'

She was silent for a moment, digesting this rather unpalatable fact of life. 'Hell, Peter, what are we going to do? I mean, about Tony?'

I shook my head. 'It's not so much Tony I'm worried about now. It's what you asked at the end of your mega-long list of questions.'

She swung her lovely legs to the floor and stood up. 'My God, yes. About if the money's now been replaced in the safe, why hasn't the Headmaster . . . ?'

'Why hasn't the Headmaster,' I said in unison, 'told the world about it – or at least the police?'

She looked down at me. 'So why hasn't he?'

'Remember I said earlier that I had come back to my worry about the Headmaster's decision to postpone banking the money?'

She nodded.

'Well, I reckon the Headmaster planned to use that jumble sale money for some purpose of his own.'

'Rather like Tony?' she interrupted.

'I don't know. I doubt it. I think old Beamish might have been planning to steal it – period. Like he may well have done now it's been mysteriously replaced. It must have seemed like manna from heaven, when he opened his safe and found the money returned. What a chance for him. Who would ever suspect that the stolen money would turn up again?'

'The person who replaced it.'

'Yes, sure. But I guess, if I'm right and Beamish is that desperate for money, then that's a detail he would have to ignore. After all, he could always swear that the money had never reappeared and headmasters, as a genre, tend to have a certain degree of credibility in society – more than thieves who return their loot, anyway.'

She tried to smile, but no go. Then she queried, 'Are you sure Tony is telling the truth? I mean, I know he's a yuppy puppy with a manic drive to coin it in, so it all fits, but even so . . .'

'I believe him.'

'Even down to the replacement of what he stole. Sorry, borrowed. Key isn't it? In many more ways than one.'

'It's key. And I believe him.'

'Millions wouldn't.'

'I'm not millions. Are you?'

'I'm unique.'

'Well then.'

'Well then, what? What? What? What? You're up a gum-tree, Marklin, old boy, you know that?'

'Mega-gum-tree.' I forced a smile. 'If I go to the police about the money being returned – as I guess I should – then they will want to know immediately how I know. And bingo, Tony is . . .'

'Up a gum-tree.'

'I can't see any way round it. If I'm right in believing Tony, then someone has to try to get at the Headmaster to winkle out the truth. After all, it could all have a bearing on Folland's death, too.'

'Like Folland might have found out what the Headmaster was up to, you mean. So Beamish killed him.'

'Could be, couldn't it?'

'Well, I suppose so. But it still leaves a lot of questions unanswered. Like the guy on the motor cycle who was after Tony, the figure in the flat cap and sunglasses who's after Miss Pettican's blood, Folland's expectations of money . . . etcetera, etcetera, et-bloomin'-cetera.'

'But we do at least now know where Andy's expectations of money came from. Why he changed from windowshopper to actually daring to go into an estate agents to enquire about houses. Tony told me he was livid with Andy about that little visit. Told him he'd blow all their plans for future investments, if he wasn't careful.'

'Future investments?'

'Yes. Tony informed me that he and Andy have already reinvested five hundred pounds of their eight hundred or so and expect another killing any day. The other three hundred, he divided two hundred to himself and a hundred to the caretaker. So he already has enough in cash for the Marklin armoured car.'

'No wonder Tony got so fussed every time the police took Andy away for questioning. He must have been worried sick that Andy would confess everything, if only to get himself cleared of the worse charge of murder.'

'And it explains why Tony burst in that afternoon with his unexpected switch of suspicions to Beamish. For by then, he had replaced the money, when the Beak was out of his office, so he

175

knew the Headmaster had some nefarious reason for not announcing to the world that it was back. Also fits in with Beamish's discomfiture at my repeated question about what had happened that day.'

Arabella climbed back on to the settee and knelt beside me.

'Does Winna know about all this; what Tony's done and is still doing?'

'I asked him that. He says no. She knows nothing.'

'Thank God,' she sighed. 'She's got enough problems right now without that. So, my darling, how did you leave it with Tony? What is he expecting you to do?'

'Firstly, keep mum about him. And Andy.'

'You may not be able to do that for ever. And secondly?'

'Check out old Beamish again. He's desperately anxious that I discover for myself actual confirmation that the money was replaced, even if it's no longer in the safe now.'

'How the blazes are you going to do that, my love?'

I leaned forward and kissed her lightly on the lips. 'I haven't the foggiest idea, my darling. Not the foggiest.'

She took my hand and urged me off the settee. 'Let's sleep on it,' she said.

We did just that.

When I woke up, of course, it was Saturday. Schools tend to award their aspiring pupils and perspiring staff two days' freedom from the fight over weekends. So I had a wee problem if I was to get at Manners School's headmaster. I didn't have his address and I soon discovered he was ex-directory, for which I didn't blame him.

So, after some Snap, Crackle and Pop and a slice of rather burnt toast (I hadn't noticed the heat control on the toaster had slid itself to one notch down from 'max'), I excused myself from Arabella and her muesli and Bing and his Whiskas and went to ring Delia Pettican. Luckily 1), she was in. Luckily 2), she knew Beamish's address and telephone number, which she gave me, but only after enquiring why I wanted them. I obviously couldn't tell her the truth, so I concocted a story about a friend of mine who was only down for the weekend and wanted to check out schools, as he was thinking of moving to the area. She seemed quite pleased that I was willing to recommend Manners School to anyone after all the 'goings-on'. 'You can always tell who your

176

real friends are, Mr Marklin, when disaster strikes . . .' I didn't disagree.

'Get them?' Arabella asked, as she downed the last muesel. ('Muesli' has to be a plural, doesn't it?)

I nodded and bent down and stroked Bing.

'Going to ring first or just turn up on his doorstep?'

I looked into Bing's big, blue eyes. He narrowed them into somnulent slits. I took his hint.

'I think I'll play it very cool,' I replied, narrowing my own brown ones. 'After all, why warn him?'

'So you'll just roll up his drive, if he's got one and say . . . what, Mr Cool?'

She had me there. 'Don't know yet, love of my life.'

'Full frontal? I mean like, "Information has been laid at my door by an impeccable source that you have just robbed your school of eight hundred smackeroos."'

I smiled. 'I don't think I can generate enough sauce of my own to go that far.'

'So?'

I took my car keys from a hook on the dresser.

'So . . . I'll try and dream up something on the way over.'

She got up from the table and put a hand on my arm. 'Be careful, my darling, for Christ's sake. Remember, Beamish might not just be a thief, but a murderer. Once you've committed one, as they say, the second and subsequent ones come that much easier.'

I kissed her on the forehead. 'I'll be careful.'

She saw me out to the car. As the Beetle phutted into life, she gave me a long and lingering kiss. As our lips parted, she began, 'Sure you don't . . . ?' Then she stopped suddenly.

'Don't what?' I asked.

She shrugged. 'Oh, nothing. Just be ultra careful, that's all. And hurry back.'

I tipped my forelock and reversed out of my over-leaning lean-to. For a split second, the cold engine faltered, then picked up. It had caught my mood exactly.

The day was grey and brisk to a fault, south-westerlies piling up the clouds ready for the evening downpours that the weatherman had promised us. So I kept the top up and switched the heater on. But I found the fug just fogged my mind, so I switched it off again. Not that the chill did much for me, I must admit. For, by the time I pulled into the cul-de-sac where Beamish lived, just on the northern limits of Swanage, I still hadn't formed a master plan worthy of a Clouseau, let alone a Poirot.

I pulled to a stop, two houses or so down from his, and looked round. The blind street was more Sidcup than Swanage, suburban rather than seaside. Each neat mock Tudor house was mirror image to its neighbour, which seemed to defeat the architect's purpose and make the houses look even more like peas from a pod.

Still, the cul-de-sac was a haven of tranquillity that Saturday morning. Not one Volvo was being washed, nor hedge trimmed, nor border dug for the spring. I guessed everyone was still indoors, finishing their *Daily Express*es and *Mail*s over a last cup of decaffeinated coffee. Keeping up with the Joneses, obviously, didn't kick off until after ten o'clock.

I, for one, cursed the quiet. Bustle would have suited me better. After all, would a cry for help be heard over the clarion call of the *Daily Express* and the slurping of Café Hag? I spotted one of the small Rovers parked in the drive next to Beamish's. I prayed the owner would decide to come out and polish it, before I had to knock on the headmaster's door.

I waited as long as I could, but the powers that be obviously didn't hear my prayer. At last, with a sigh, I opened my door to get out. The second I did so, I saw the oak door to Beamish's house open also and my quarry emerge. This rather threw me. I closed my car door as silently as I could and watched. Beamish took a key from his pocket and opened up his garage to reveal an old model Vauxhall Carlton Estate. A moment later and he was reversing down his drive at a rate of knots.

I hid my face in my hands and waited until I heard his car swoosh past mine. Then I started up, turned in the first drive-way and sped off after him in 'hot pursuit', as they used to say in 'Dukes of Hazzard'.

He was simple enough to track. The roads were well-nigh deserted, until we reached what Arabella laughingly calls 'Downtown Swanage', where there were just enough people out weekend shopping to keep the shopkeepers from calling it a day. But Beamish did not make for the High Street or harbour, but went on to the sea-front, where he turned right, then parked just up from the public shelter. I instantly pulled in, so that there was a parked car between me and his Carlton – just in case he had noticed my hardly anonymous bright yellow Beetle in his cul-de-sac.

He did not get out right away and I began wondering if he had only taken the trip to get some lungfuls of bracing briny air. But after a couple of minutes, he emerged, locked his car and started to walk towards the now dead amusement arcades that led on to the traffic lights, where the sea-front joins the High Street. I followed on the other side of the road, about seventy-five yards behind.

Once in the High Street, however, I crossed the road and quickened my pace, as there were now enough shoppers around on the pavements to give me good cover and I didn't want to risk him suddenly ducking into some shop or café and losing me. As it was, I only just spotted him going into a greengrocer's. I hovered outside a jeweller's two shops down and waited for him to emerge. My anticipation and excitement were ebbing fast, as I realized the sole fruit of my morning's sleuthing could be just that. Beamish had been sent out to get the fruit or vegetables his wife had forgotten on her Friday shopping trip. And lo and behold, guess what he was clutching when he came out. A bunch of bananas, and a cauliflower in a paper bag that was already splitting at the seams.

I looked back quickly at the rows of glitzy Sekonda and Rotary watches in the jeweller's window, as I caught his eyes scanning the High Street. When I thought it was safe, I looked round again. But to my horror, there was now no sign of him – in either direction. I had seen this kind of vanishing trick happen in 'Cagney and Lacey' and cops and robber movies from way back. But Swanage High Street doesn't exactly sport a million alleys, fire escapes, parking lots or 'Knock twice and ask for Nellie' type doorways, with peep-holes the size of pin heads. So, at first, I didn't really believe my eyes and stood in the gutter, swinging my gaze from left to right and back again, like a spectator at a Becker-Lendl match.

But reason did at last prevail. After all, people don't just vanish. Especially headmasters. (In my tender youth, I'd tried to make quite a few disappear, with not a soupçon of success.) I stopped peering up and down the High Street and switched my attention to the shops in the immediate vicinity of the greengrocer's. To its left was a toy shop, and quite a decent book shop. To its right, a small café of the 'Chips with everything', including the crockery, variety, and a ships' chandler and sports shop. I started at the toy shop and cautiously peered in the windows and doorways of all of them. But no chubby shapes of headmasters were to be seen. I then went back to the café and waited outside a moment or two, in case Beamish might have been in the boys' room in the back. But no go. So I had no alternative but to widen my search. Hazarding a guess that he hadn't passed right by me at the jeweller's, I walked on up the High Street. And there, three doors up from the ships' chandler, I found him, or rather, he found me. I might have guessed it really. Certainly, a Lord Peter Whimsey or a Marlowe would have made straight for the place in the very first instance, bless their little, respectively, silk and cotton socks.

He didn't look too pleased to see me. But then, maybe, no one likes to be spotted emerging from the jet-black glass of a betting shop.

His eyes gave the game away immediately.

'Er, excuse me,' he said, as we almost collided, then turned to walk off back towards his car. I reached forward and restrained him by the arm, thus almost making him drop his bananas et al.

'What do you need excusing for, Mr Beamish?' I nodded towards the betting shop. 'Or can I guess?'

He tried to brush my hand away, but it was difficult with the fruit and veg. 'Look, I'm in a hurry. I have to go. Really.'

'To get back to your cosy cul-de-sac or get away from me?'

He suddenly whipped round ninety degrees and I lost my grip on his arm. A second later and he was off down the street with strides that would have done credit to a three-times marathon winner. I made off after him, as the bananas started to rain from his now disintegrating paper bag. Thank God they weren't peeled.

I caught up with him again just before the traffic lights.

'Look, Mr Beamish,' I mouthed above the drone of the traffic. 'Wouldn't it be better for you and me to talk privately some-where, rather than let the whole of Swanage know about . . .' I at last caught his eye, 'Your Ethiopian race-horses?'

Now I've said he was a fat man and I've seen tons of them in my time, as have we all. But I have certainly never seen one deflate

180

like a pricked balloon before. And it wasn't just the bulk that seemed to evaporate, but the colour as well.

This time, I didn't restrain his arm. I took it to prevent him keeling over under a bus.

The little circular public shelter on the more or less empty promenade could have been purpose built for what I had to do, divided as it was into sections, partly to promote privacy and partly to defeat the keen sea breezes. We sat down side by side, facing the white and grey rollers that were punishing the beach and occasionally spraying our faces with a fine mist.

I sat him down. But his eyes now flashed some fight.

'What's all this about? Why are you following me?'

'You know why, Mr Beamish. It's too late to play innocent now.'

'Now look here,' he began, stabbing at me with a podgy finger.

'No, you look here, Mr Beamish,' I snapped. 'And don't prod me with that thieving finger of yours.'

'Thieving?'

'Yes. Thieving.'

He turned away. 'I didn't steal that money.'

'Not first time you didn't, maybe.'

'What are you talking about?'

'I'm talking about what you did when you discovered the money had been returned.'

'Returned?'

'Yes, returned, Mr Beamish.'

'What cock and bull rubbish . . . ?'

I cut in with a lie, before his confidence had time to reflate. 'Someone saw you take the money from the safe, and I'm willing to produce the witness in court if I have to.'

Silence.

I went on: 'But it needn't come to that if . . .'

Suddenly he put his head on his hands, and I could almost hear the last of the air escape.

After a while, he said, in barely above a whisper: 'It all got too much for me . . . all of it.'

'All of what?'

He turned to me. 'Are you married, Mr . . . er . . . ?'

'Marklin. Peter Marklin. No, I'm not married. Why?'

His head sank back into his hands and his words were hard to hear over the crashing of the breakers. 'Oh . . . maybe it's not marriage . . . maybe it's just Margaret . . . just Margaret.'

'That your wife?'

'I should have known before I married her. Her mother is the same.'

'Same as what?'

'Greedy, I suppose. Everything they clap eyes on, they want to own. Her mother bankrupted her father . . . killed him in the end . . . she made him feel so inadequate.'

'Was your wife bankrupting you? Is that what you are saying?'

He nodded, looked up and stared at the sea, his eyes now moist from more than its spray. 'In the end, I took to gambling to try to bridge the gap between what I have and what she wanted.'

'And the horses, surprise, surprise, didn't match their form?'

'It wasn't just horses. I could have coped with that, maybe. But I was a fool. A damned fool. I joined a gambling club in Bournemouth. It's called the Lucky Rabbit.'

I had just about heard of it. But in my innocence, I had thought it was simply a night club.

'And the croupiers were about as obliging as the horses?'

He squeezed his eyes tight shut. 'God. I hated it . . . all of it . . . and not just the losing . . . I was always terrified of being recognized, you see, and the people who hang out in these places . . . their faces all screwed up with their greed and their eyes slits of red from cigar smoke and vanishing chips.'

'Did your wife know what you were doing?'

'No. I always made up some story to cover why I'd be out so late. Like having to see a worried parent or attend a meeting of local headmasters. It got more and more difficult to think up a new one.'

'Instead of a big win, you ended up with a big debt?'

He didn't need to reply.

I went on. 'And the Ethiopian jumble sale came at just the right, or maybe wrong, moment?'

Again no reply needed.

'You planned to steal it right from the start, didn't you? That's why you didn't bank the money that first day.'

He suddenly looked round at me. 'I didn't steal it then, I swear. The robbery was real. I was shattered.'

'I can imagine. But you stole the money, when it was returned, didn't you?'

He nodded. 'But I could have sworn there were no witnesses . . . Who was it? Tell me.'

I shook my head and kept silent.

'You've been following me before, haven't you? That's how you knew I gambled. I've been dreading someone seeing me in these places and putting two and two together.'

I left him with his assumption intact and cut in, 'Is it too late to get the money back?'

He rested his head back against the wooden slats of the shelter. 'It's too late for everything now, isn't it, Mr Marklin?'

This time it was I who didn't need to reply. The wind gusted sea-spray into our faces sufficient for me to reach for a handkerchief. Beamish just sat immobile and the droplets started to descend his cheeks like salty tears.

'Someone did find out about your gambling, before me, though, Mr Beamish,' I tried.

He looked around sharply, fear now added to the death in his eyes. 'Who? What do you mean? Who found out?'

'Mr Folland. Didn't he discover what you were up to? And you panicked and killed him?'

He made a sudden move with his arm and I thought he was going to hit me. But all he wanted was a wrist to grab tight, while he cried out in a voice shot through with pain. 'Christ, you can't believe that. I'm not a murderer. You must believe me. You must.'

'It's not really me you have to convince, Mr Beamish. It's the police.'

He collapsed back against the boards of the shelter, his podgy face glistening with both spray and tears. 'You're going to tell them . . . what you think?'

'I'm not going to tell them anything.'

He turned his head wearily towards me.

I went on, 'I'm going to leave it to you.'

'Why . . . ?' he began, but I cut in, 'Because as it happens, I think there's a helluva difference between a thief and a murderer. And I'm not sure that you bridge that gap any more than your horses and "Lucky Rabbit" bridged that ruddy great hole between your income and your wife's demands.'

'So, what do you plan to do, Mr Marklin?'

'Leave it all to you. You must have enough assets you can sell or mortgage to raise that eight hundred pounds or so, even if it means your money-grabbing wife and mother-in-law knowing the truth. And the police and courts will look far more kindly on a man who has tried to make amends, than one who hasn't.'

He closed his eyes tight and gave my wrist a last squeeze. 'I don't know why you're being so kind to me. I don't deserve it. What I've done is totally despicable . . . a betrayal of every kind of trust so many people have placed in me.'

I turned to him. 'Now, forget the self-pity. Try to make some kind of amends. It won't save you, but, at least, it'll leave you with a modicum of self-respect.'

I offered him my handkerchief. He shook his head and wiped his eyes with the Harris tweed of his sleeve. I got up to go, but he still held on to my wrist.

'I didn't kill Mr Folland. You have to believe me.'

'If you didn't, have you any idea who did? The police are bound to jump to the same conclusion I did. And unlike me, they have professional reputations and track records at stake. They love to close a file with the big word "Solved" on it. So they'll go on harbouring their suspicions about you until the real murderer turns up. That is, if you are telling the truth and aren't the real McCoy yourself.'

'I am telling the truth, Mr Marklin. You have to get them to believe me.'

I shrugged off his grip. 'I don't have to do anything, Mr Beamish. Or have you been a headmaster so long you think everyone should jump to your every command like a school kid?'

His head fell back against the boards with a crack. I could hardly hear his next words against the wind and the waves.

'I'm sorry . . . I'm sorry . . . I'm sorry.'

I tried one last time. 'So you have no idea who might have killed Folland?'

His eyes slowly lifted to meet mine and I saw bitterness now added to despair.

'Maybe the same person who replaced the money, Mr Marklin . . .'

I turned away.

'. . . have you ever thought of that?'

A seagull screamed as it rode a thermal above my head. With one last look at the grey and spitting sea, I walked slowly away, up the promenade to my car.

I shivered as I got in behind the wheel and the windscreen was now sticky with salt. I switched on the wipers but they smeared more than cleared. And it took me a little time to recognize the car that had just pulled in and parked ahead of me.

Fifteen

'What the blazes are you doing here?'

She smiled through my open window. 'What d'you think?'

'Seeing a little boy doesn't get into too much trouble?'

She nodded. 'You passed me, when you first started tearing after Beamish.'

'And you were tailing me all the time I was tailing him?'

She saluted. 'You didn't see a thing, did you?'

I had to confess I hadn't. I guess a tail looks ahead, rather than behind, if you see what I mean.

'How did it go?' she asked. I looked behind me through the rear window, but there was no sign of movement from the shelter.

'He is the burglar,' I sighed.

'And the murderer?' asked her big beautiful eyes.

'I don't know yet. I think if he is capable of killing, he would have murdered his wife, not Folland. But I'll tell you all about it later. Right now, you'd better get back in your car and lie low.'

She looked miffed. 'Why, what are you going to do?'

'Hang around and see what Beamish does now.'

'What do you think he will do?'

'God knows. He may just go straight to the police and confess all. On the other hand, there's just a chance he may know more about the murder than he is confessing, panic and run off and lead us to . . .' I shrugged.

'Mr Blunt Instrument?'

'Possibly.'

'Is that why you didn't turn him in now?'

'Not on its own. It's not my job to make arrests. I'm not a vigilante. Anyway, I think he is intelligent enough both to get the message that it's all up and, perhaps, to have a conscience.' I smiled. 'But I must admit, I'm hoping he might just panic.'

186

Arabella suddenly ducked down and hissed. 'Watch out, he's coming.' And then she was gone.

I instantly pulled a map from the glove locker and then slid my frame down as far as it would go beneath the steering wheel, unfolding aforesaid map around me. To a passerby, it must have looked as if Dorset had sprouted knees.

I heard footsteps approach then pass my car. As they receded, I peeped out round the side of the map. I could just see Beamish unlocking his Carlton. A moment later, he had performed a ragged U-turn and accelerated back past me. As I prepared to do likewise (least, the first bit), Arabella beat me to it in her Golf. And now my quarry had two tails, but I doubt, had he known, he'd have been as chuffed with them as that old proverbial dog.

It quickly became obvious that Beamish was not driving to the nearest police station. For he continued along the road out of Swanage and thus, I immediately assumed he was making his way back home, maybe to bid an unfond farewell to his wife and mother-in-law before ringing the police. But wrong again, Marklin. His Carlton did not slow an iota before the cul-de-sac turning, but sped on towards the lovely grey village of Corfe.

By the time we arrived in convoy around the base of the hill upon which the ruins of Corfe Castle stand, the jagged tips of its fortifications seemed about to pierce the weatherman's now blackening clouds. And as we raced across the flats that lead into Wareham, their pricking had obviously done the dirty trick, for raindrops as big as peas bubbled on to my windshield and pattered on the Beetle's soon-to-leak top.

The deluge that followed hardly helped an amateur tailing. For there's an old unwritten rule in Britain, that rain on the highway cuts the traffic speed in half. Now that would have been acceptable, if someone had told Beamish about it. As a result, he was the last person to squeeze by a giant container lorry the size of a Zeppelin, before the oncoming lane suddenly filled with more vehicles than I've had hot dinners. Result? We trailed the Zeppelin, instead of Beamish. By the time both Arabella and I made a daring dash past it, the Vauxhall Carlton was nowhere to be seen.

Cursing the weatherman in a thunderstorm of expletives, I honked Arabella (so to speak) and we both pulled up just past the lights in the centre of Wareham's quietly attractive (out of season) High Street. Holding the all-purpose map I had previously hidden behind, above my head, I ducked across the rapidly growing puddles to Arabella's Golf.

'What do we do now?' she shouted above the rain.

I leaned my head through her window, for the map was now wetter than the sea printed on it and was as limp as a ... well, limp.

'Take a flier,' I shouted. 'All we can do.'

'Flier to where?'

'To the Colonel's. He's the only person round here I can imagine that Beamish might run to.'

'Good thinking, Poirot,' she nodded sagely.'I'll lead you to his house, if I can remember the way.'

And that's just what she did.

Luckily, Hawkesworth's mansion was visible from the road. Just. Its long gravel drive curved up to the house, so that we could see what was parked in its forecourt.

We both parked behind some tonsured hedges that bordered what was obviously the main gates to the property and I joined Arabella in the dryness of her Golf.

'Well, you were right. He fled to the Colonel.'

'Yea,' I said, none too brightly and adjusted my damp frame on the Golf's seat, so that at least parts of my now soaked trousers had a chance to get some air. 'Know a way to change us both into flies, oh wizard lady?'

'Yea,' she copy-catted. 'See what you mean. We know where he is, but we don't know what he's doing or saying.'

'And if we knock on the portals, we won't know either, will we? They'll both deny everything and come out with some claptrap or other to cover themselves.'

'It might be worse than that. I wouldn't like to see Hawkesworth when his dander's up.'

'Don't go for him when it's down,' I grinned, as a raindrop took a shallow dive off my nose. 'I'm afraid all we can do, my love, is wait out here for a bit and see what happens.'

Arabella frowned. 'Nothing can happen, can it? I mean nothing that can really tell us anything.'

I shrugged, setting off various other raindrops.

'Well, Beamish has to leave sometime.'

'So?'

'Directly he does, I'm going to sashay up old Hawkesworth's drive and confront him.'

She looked horrified. 'You *what*? You're mad. If Hawkesworth really is the murderer, then he'll have you for breakfast.'

I looked at my watch. 'Lunch,' I smiled, then was confronted by a wagging finger.

'Look, Peter Marklin, if you're going to beard old Hawkesworth, then you're not doing it alone. I'm coming with you.'

I wagged my head. 'No, you're not. Because you will be busy.'

'Busy?'

'Following Beamish. Remember, that's how all this started?'

She swore. She doesn't often. But she did, then went on, 'You're crazy, you know that? God, what I wouldn't give for old Gus right now. I thought of picking him up, when I set off after you. But I thought it might waste too much time.'

She'd hit a nerve. I could have done with old Gus too. As I've said, he can be a Rock of Gibraltar on those rare occasions when he forgets to be a pain in the arse.

'Well, it's too late now. We can't ring him, as he's not on the phone. And the lady next door to him is as deaf as a dozen telegraph poles and wouldn't hear hers ring, until Hawkesworth had died of old age. Anyway, there isn't a call box round here.'

'Great.'

'Great.'

'You're crazy as a jay bird.'

She saw my frown. 'Thurber,' she explained.

'Oh,' I nodded. 'Didn't he do that cartoon of a woman looking at her dog and saying, "Why don't you go out and trace something"?'

'Right.'

'Well, when Beamish drives out, that's what I want you to do. Trace where he goes. Even if it's only home.'

'But I'll be crazy with worry.'

'Don't be. I've just thought of a little story that I can trot out if the Colonel gets nasty.'

'Which is?'

'That I've told you to ring the police if I'm not out in twenty minutes.'

'Make it two. Correction. One minute.'

'Twenty. I need time to work on him.'

She threw her eyes up to the roof. I caught them on the way down.

'Crazy. Plumb crazy,' she sighed.

'This jay bird will fly away, don't worry.'

We switched our eye-to-eye contact to one for lips.

'Oh hell, Peter,' she murmured.

'Is other people,' I murmured back and anticipated her frown. 'Sartre,' I smiled.

'Oh, her,' she winked.

Ten minutes later and she was off down the road after Beamish, whilst I beetled up the long drive, sitting on my now underwater seat.

I was a trifle startled when the Colonel answered the door himself. For it was the kind of mansion that one usually associated with hot and cold running retainers. Maybe he thought Beamish had forgotten something – like confessing to the police.

'*You*,' was the only greeting I got.

'Right first time.' I attempted a jauntily confident grin, but I think it must have come out like a berk's smirk. Still, he did look a little rattled.

'What the hell are you doing here?'

I put my foot in the door, foolish me. Toes don't stand a chance as an oak sandwich.

'More to the point, what was Mr Beamish doing here?'

That seemed to faze him a little. At least enough to enable the rest of my body to join my foot in the baronial-type hall.

'That's none of your business. I've told you many times before that the affairs of Manners School are no concern of yours.'

'Even when its headmaster confesses to stealing eight hundred smackeroos from the old school safe?'

His eyes flickered for a second, then he extended his arm. 'You had better come through.'

'Yes, I thought I'd better,' I rejoined and our footsteps echoed across the acres of polished parquet as we made our way to a vast drawing-room that was British gentility at its Hollywood best. I almost expected Joan Fontaine to be sitting amongst the chintz reading *Rebecca*.

He did not offer me a chair, either because he thought me unworthy of such a gesture, or because he was a rude sod, or he didn't want his upholstery to suffer from descending damp. My pride made me settle for the last two.

'Make it snappy, Mr Marklin. I have things to do.'

'Like ringing Inspector Whetstone to tell him Beamish is his own burglar? You're not going to try to deny all that, are you, because it's too late now, Colonel?' Then I added a lie to add force to my argument. 'I tape-recorded our whole conversation on Swanage front.'

He looked me up and down, as if I was on some military parade. 'You're a pretty nasty piece of work. The Inspector warned me several times of your propensity to interfere in other people's private business, but obviously I did not take you seriously enough.'

I looked him up and down. Two can play at that game.

'Headmasters are public business, once they put their hands in the till, Colonel. Now tell me why Beamish ran to you the minute after I had exposed him.'

He looked away to the French windows, through whose raindrops one could just discern tonsured lawns and ornamental hedges that seemed to stretch for ever.

'I am a governor of the school, Mr Marklin. He came to confess his surprising misdeed and to hand in his resignation.'

I cursed not being able to see his face.

'Is that all, Colonel? Are you sure there's nothing else?'

'What is this "else" that is flitting through your tiny mind?'

My tiny mind could not conjure up anything specific right then, so I tried, 'Did you discuss who might have been responsible for the burglary the police are currently investigating?'

He turned back to me, curiosity now glinting in the coldness of his eyes.

'I take it you mean the identity of the thief who had second thoughts and apparently, returned the money?'

'So you two did discuss it?'

'We did.'

'Come to any conclusions?'

He smiled patronizingly. 'You are the so-called sleuth, Mr Marklin. We are not in your league at jumping to conclusions, I'm sure.'

I notched up one for Tony Thorn. For it looked as if he might be safe from suspicion – at least for the moment.

191

I instantly changed the subject and began, 'Now tell me, Colonel . . .' but he cut in.

'Now let me tell you, Mr Marklin, I've had enough of you this morning. And not only this morning, but for ever. The instant I shut the door on you, which will be any minute now, I'm ringing Inspector Whetstone. Not to tell him about Mr Beamish's unfortunate lapse, but to inform him that you are still sticking your nose in where it's not bloody wanted.'

He made a move towards me, but I stuck my ground with, 'It was you on the cliff, wasn't it?'

He stopped in mid-stride. 'What on earth . . . ?'

This time it was my interruption. 'Earth was only a small part of it. The main mass was rocks. Lots of them. All aimed at poor Miss Pettican, your beloved school co-governor.'

He made neither move nor comment. I went on, throwing in the odd exaggeration. 'How do I know it was you? I heard your Range Rover – and was just in time to see you driving away.'

At last, he reacted with a slow blink and a smile.

'Really, Mr Marklin, you're letting your hyperactive imagination run right away with you.'

I slow blinked back and continued, 'That you might want to do away with the only voice of common sense at Manners School, I can understand. But it's the timing of your attempt that niggles me. Why should anyone let off a lethal rock fall whilst there were still two potential witnesses on the beach?'

Again that sickening smile. 'You must ask that "anyone". Not me. When I heard about that lamentable attempt on poor Delia's life, I too was . . . "niggled", as you so quaintly put it, about its timing. But murderers, you know, don't seem to follow the same rules of rationality as the rest of us.'

'I wouldn't know, Colonel. But my guess is that rock fall was very deliberately timed to occur in front of witnesses. Why, I'm not quite sure yet, but I'm certain there is a reason.'

'Are you trying to say the whole attempt on dear Delia was just a front?'

I shrugged. 'No. The aim might well have been to kill Miss Pettican. But with a couple of people around to confirm it happened.'

'Maybe this "someone" is a bit of an extrovert. Likes an audience. Except when he's climbing over the school wall, that is.'

I tried to read his eyes, but they might as well have been written in Sanskrit or Minoan B.

'So you're sticking to the story that the man on the cliff was the man Miss Pettican saw on the school wall the night Mr Folland was murdered?'

He made a show of looking at his Omega.

'Time's up, Mr Marklin. Off you go.' He 'shooshed' with his hands. 'Back to whatever hole you climbed out from. What that lovely girl from the paper, Arabella Trench, sees in you, I just can't imagine.'

'Just as well,' I said, 'and stop shooshing me. I will only go when I'm good and ready. I have a load more questions yet.'

His broken nose twitched, then he suddenly strode across the room and picked up a cordless phone from one of the window-sills.

'One last chance, Mr Marklin, before I ring the Inspector to get you evicted.'

Just at that second, to my intense relief and delight, the phone in his hand started to ring. He looked at me as if it were my fault, then pushed the talk switch and held the phone to his ear.

'Yes . . . Who? . . . Say it again. Augustus . . . Augustus who? . . . Trickle? . . . No, you'd better spell it . . . Ah, Tribble. Now, what do you want, Mr Tribble? I don't know you and . . .'

I smiled broadly, as dear old Gus then proceeded to give him an earful. It was at least two minutes before the Colonel turned back to me.

'Seems it's a friend of yours. I can hardly make out what he's saying. Has an accent you can cut with a knife.'

'But only one as big as Crocodile Dundee's,' I grinned and took the proffered phone.

I'll cut the next bit short. Apparently, Gus had become worried that no one had been around the Toy Emporium all morning and he had noticed both cars gone, which is never the case at weekends. He'd put two and two together and made sixteen and reckoned we might have run into mega- (sorry!) trouble investigating the Manners School affair. So he had gone to his deaf neighbour's, borrowed the phone and started to ring up everyone connected with Manners School whose numbers were not ex-directory. Delia Pettican was his first call and she had advised him to try the Colonel next, if he was really concerned, because there was just a chance we might be there. And so it came to pass . . .

It took me at least three minutes to convince Gus that I wasn't hanging naked from a meat hook in Hawkesworth's cellar, surrounded by a sea of snakes, rats and scorpions, writhing, scurrying and whatever scorpions do, about on the dank, dark floor. (He had recently seen an *Indiana Jones* movie on television and hadn't really recovered.)

'Well, that's you ruddy accounted for,' he grunted. 'Now what about your Arabella?'

I looked up at the Colonel. 'Do you know where Beamish was going after he left here?'

He nodded. 'Direct to Swanage police station. Apparently, he couldn't face going home first.'

I didn't blame him. 'She should be back any time now, Gus. Tell her I'm all right and will be leaving here shortly.' Before I could say any more, the Colonel snatched the phone from my hand and switched it off.

'Not shortly, Mr Marklin. Now.' He advanced on me. This time I retreated. For I reckoned Gus's phone call had, unwittingly, given Hawkesworth too much of a breathing space in which to recover from my accusations.

'All right, Colonel. *I* will go. But my questions won't go away. Nor my suspicions. You are up to your epaulets in something pretty horrendous, even if it isn't murder. But two can contact Inspector Whetstone, you know.'

He extended the aerial on the phone, switched on the talk button and started to dial.

'But only one,' he smiled, 'will be able to get to him first.'

All the way back home, I felt as lugubrious as the weather. For the bombshells I had blown the Colonel's way had hardly dented his armour, let alone destroyed it. What's more, I couldn't help counting the ways I could have improved upon my performance – and then, damn it, I lost count.

About the only thing I had learnt for certain, as far as I could see, (besides that Hawkesworth's hide was as thick as the armour plate on a 'Chieftain',) was that the Colonel had something more serious on his mind than the light fingers of his dice-throwing Headmaster. For he had not seemed as concerned over Beamish, or at least, his confession, as I had expected. Now that could

194

obviously be for more than one reason – for those who are already in the know are hardly surprised when they're put in the know. But somehow, however low my opinion of Hawkesworth, I couldn't see him condoning the stealing of charity funds, especially to repay gambling debts and debts and, what's more, run up by a man for whom I doubted he had much respect. For bullies tend not to look up to lackeys, any more than they would to doormats. Besides, I reckoned mine charming host would only plunder or murder for some tub-thumping cause or other and not just for personal gain. (NB. I don't think Hitler left a great deal of money.) So I would just have to hope that Beamish, in his confessions to the police, would reveal rather more than he had to me.

My spirits were not to be lifted when I pulled in at the Toy Emporium. First, there was no sign of Arabella's Golf. Second, Gus was still around, huddled under the lean-to, trying to dodge the drips.

'She's not back, old love,' he sniffed. 'Thought I'd better wait.'

I patted his shoulder and we went indoors into the dry.

'Thanks, Gus, for ringing.'

He smiled sheepishly. (Not that I've ever seen a sheep smile.)

'S'all right. Thought I'd better, just in case you and her'd been kidnapped or something.'

I went through to the phone. 'I think I'd better ring Swanage police station.'

He frowned. 'You don't think she's . . . ?' He didn't finish. He didn't need to.

'I'll explain later, Gus.'

So I rang through. It was some time before I could get any sense into or out of anybody. But at last a Sergeant Musgrave came on.

'I gather you are enquiring after a Mr Beamish of Manners School.'

'Yes,' I confirmed irritably. 'And a girl called Arabella Trench.'

There was a buzz of assorted voices and noises in the background and he was hard to hear. 'Well, Mr er . . .'

'Marklin. Peter Marklin.'

'Well, Mr Marklin, I think it might be wiser if you came in to the station.'

My heart sank a billion fathoms.

'My God, why? Has something happened to Arab-, Miss Trench?'

'No, sir.'

'Why should I have to come in then? Can't you tell me what's happened over the phone? For Christ's sake, don't pull some bureaucratic blather about . . .'

'I'm not pulling anything, I assure you, sir,' he interrupted in a monotone. 'It's just that . . .'

'Just *that*, what?' My temper was now well and truly up the spout.

I heard a short muffled exchange in the background and then a totally different voice snapped back. 'Marklin, this is Whetstone. If you don't get your arse over here double quick, Sir, I'll send one of my boys over to fetch you.'

Now, who could decline such a charming invitation?

Sixteen

I quickly explained everything to Gus, then left him in charge of the Toy Emporium, with strict instructions to adhere to the prices on my sticky labels, and not invent more Eva Braun-type stories to wheedle out an extra buck. He saluted, and I beetled off down to the police station.

I guess Digby Whetstone's already irate mood was hardly improved by my warm embrace of Arabella, but then, voyeurs can't be choosers. By the time we unstuck, his rage registered at least nine on the Richter scale.

'Well, Mr Marklin, what have you got to say for yourself? From what I gather from your Miss Trench here . . .'

'She's not my Miss Trench. She's her own Miss Trench,' I elucidated. This late-twentieth-century update didn't help either, seemingly.

'. . . you have not only been putting your amateur nose yet again into affairs that should be the sole province of us professionals, but have also been quite willing to risk the life and limb of this young lady into the bargain. Really, your conduct this time has gone beyond all bounds and I must . . .'

Arabella put a slender hand against his gesturing, raincoated arm. 'Inspector, I think it only fair that you let me explain to Peter what happened, before you go any further.' She turned to me. 'I was never in any danger, Peter, honestly. I just followed Beamish, expecting him to go straight into Swanage. But, instead, he doubled back into Wareham, then took the Dorchester road. I had a hard job keeping up with him in the rain and spray. Then at Warmwell roundabout, he branched off towards Weymouth. Then, to my surprise, just before Osmington, he swung left to Osmington Mills. I followed, as I told the Inspector, expecting him to stop at one of the houses in the village or the pub, but instead he crashed through a fence and tore across a wide expanse of grass that leads to the cliff edge.'

'I tried to cut him off but my wheels wouldn't grip on the wet grass. Then, thank God, his car suddenly stopped, only a few feet from the edge. And Beamish got out, and started running . . .'

'Towards the edge?' I asked.

She shook her head. 'No, across the fields. By the time I'd got my car going again, he'd disappeared. I searched for quite a while but there was no sign of him.'

'So, Miss Trench, quite rightly, came straight on to us,' Digby glowered at me. 'Better late than never, Mr Marklin.'

I held my hand up. 'All right, I get the message.'

Digby threw up his arms. 'Good God, don't tell me the penny's at last dropping . . .'

I turned to Arabella. 'Has Beamish been located yet?'

She shook her head. 'They're still looking for him. Sorry, Peter. I didn't quite know what to do when I lost him. I was so worried he'd kill himself, in one way or another.'

'He probably intended to, but got cold feet as he got near the cliff edge.'

Digby suddenly slammed his fist down on the desk. 'Now look here, Marklin, I didn't get you down here so that you could hobnob away with Miss Trench. From what little I have been able to glean from your over-loyal friend here, you are the root cause of the disappearance, or maybe even death, of a key figure in the Manners School case – a man who may well be able to provide us with further valuable information as our investigation progresses.'

'Come on, Inspector, it's his own terrible sense of guilt that's made him run.' I glanced at Arabella. 'I take it you have told him that much.'

She nodded, then added, to reassure me, 'He knows you found out about the Headmaster's penchant for gambling, then deduced he might have stolen the Ethiopian funds himself to pay back some gambling debts.'

Bright girl. No mention of another burglar, thank the Lord. I held up my hands.

'So, Inspector, all I did this morning was tackle him with my discovery and my guess at his self-burglary. He confessed almost at once. I wish I'd had a tape-recorder running – especially after all that's happened since.'

Digby stood in front of me. 'Do you realize that if you had come to us with your suspicions, Mr Beamish would not now be roaming about the countryside probably hell-bent on his own destruction.'

I had to admit he had a point and I felt as guilty as hell about it. 'I'm sorry. I guess you're right.'

'Bit late to be sorry, I must say.' He turned to Arabella. 'Now you say, Miss Trench, that you followed the Headmaster because Mr Marklin was with Colonel Hawkesworth.' He glanced back at me. 'May I ask what little game you were up to with him? I can't see you and the Colonel as Saturday morning buddies, or any other day of the week.'

'We're not,' I said, then went on to describe as near verbatim as damn it, my talk with Hawkesworth and my reasons for the visit in the first place.

When I had finished, he resumed his seat with a sigh. 'We discussed all that, you and I, when it happened, Mr Marklin. Your suspicions about the timing of the rock slide and why didn't the culprit wait until the beach was deserted. And as I remember, I recounted quite a few reasons why it might have occurred that way. Your trouble is you won't listen, won't take advice, won't even do what you're told by an officer of the law. What do I have to do to keep you from constantly fouling up on our professional investigations – lock you up?'

I leaned forward in my chair. 'Look, Inspector, I've said I'm sorry if I've muddied your water, but at least I've now solved one of the Manners School mysteries for you. The question of the stolen money.'

Now it was his turn to lean forward. 'You think I should thank you? Do you realize that Mr Beamish . . .' He stopped suddenly and I guessed what he was going to say and why he couldn't say it.

'. . . could also have murdered Mr Folland? Okay, I understand why you have to keep mum about your suspicions, until something is proven. But if it's any consolation, I don't think Beamish did kill Folland.'

He smiled a mocking smile. 'Oh? Why not, pray?'

'One, because I doubt if anybody would kill to stop someone blabbing about gambling. Two, there's no evidence that Folland had found out who stole the money. (Here I was treading on treacherous ground.) And he seems to have been an honest Joe

199

and there was time between the burglary and his murder for him to have voiced his suspicions to somebody, surely. Thirdly, and this is key, Beamish doesn't strike me as resolute or cold blooded enough to commit murder for any reason under the sun. If he had been, his simplest action would have been to kill his wife – the Mrs Money Grabber who seems to have been the root cause of all his troubles. After all, I'm sure someone with a headmaster's qualifications could think up a way of getting rid of his wife that would seem an accident.'

Digby did not reply at once, his only reaction being a massaging of his freckled fingers.

'Sound reasonable?' I prompted.

The said finger was aimed at me. 'So, Mr Super Sleuth, may I ask where all this leaves you? If Beamish did not kill Folland, then who did? From your antics this morning, it would look as if you want to pin it on the Colonel. Let me guess at your reasoning. The Colonel is well known for his anti-homosexual views. He has a set of keys to the school. He somehow arranges for Folland to be in the gym, lets himself in and murders him. The final trigger – the news that Folland has Aids.'

He smiled across at me. 'Shall I go on?'

'Oh, please do. I love to hear a professional.'

He double-took, then continued, 'But Delia Pettican sees him either leaving or entering the school over the wall. Reason for this unorthodox means of entry for a man who has keys to the main gates? Lord knows. Maybe because they're metal and clang together or have rusty and thus noisy hinges, which might rouse the caretaker. Anyway, Delia Pettican sees this figure. The Colonel's anxiety mounts and mounts as the days go by, in case his co-governor suddenly remembers who the figure reminds her of. So he decides to rid the world of the only witness who could condemn him. Knowing her love of collecting fossils from the cliffs, it was simple for him to arrange that she should join her fossil friends in the rocks through rigging a landslide. But Miss Pettican is more nimble than he thought and manages to dodge death by inches. Etcetera, etcetera, etcetera.'

He gave a theatrical yawn and sat back in his chair. 'Makes as much sense, Mr Marklin, as a script of "Murder She Wrote".'

'Right,' I said. 'I agree.'

He frowned. 'You agree?'

200

'Yep. You see, the scenario you outlined for me isn't actually mine.'

'So where does yours differ, pray?'

'I don't think Hawkesworth killed Folland. I'm not sure yet who did, but I doubt if it was the Colonel.'

'Yet you accused him of attempted murder this morning?'

'Yes, I did. I wanted to get a reaction because I'm pretty certain he was the figure I saw on the cliff. Even more sure since I saw him again this morning. He holds himself in a different way from most people. Upright. Stiff as a poker. Military bearing, I suppose. That's how the figure stood on the cliff.'

I saw Digby's eyes float to the ceiling. I went on, 'So, in my current book, he caused the rockslide that could have killed the woman he blames for all the troubles at Manners School.'

'But it didn't,' Digby rightly observed. 'Not much military precision there.'

I took up his point. 'And that worries me too. I can't see the Colonel failing at anything he really sets out to do. So, either he just intended to give Delia Pettican a helluva scare, or . . .'

It was saying that 'or' that suddenly switched on a thousand-watt light bulb and I shut up like a clam. For the glow was far too dazzling as yet, for me to see straight.

'Or what, Mr Marklin?'

I instantly put a substitute 'or' in. 'Or the Colonel set off the rockslide prematurely, by mistake.'

'Oh, that all?'

''Fraid so.'

Digby rose wearily from his chair and went over to Arabella. 'I'm sorry, Miss Trench, but I'll have to ask you – and Mr Marklin – to make a full statement of what happened this morning.' He moved towards the door. 'Whilst you two are doing that, I'll be doing a little damage containment – tracking down the hare you scared this morning, in the hope we get to him before he does too much damage to himself.' And with a last glower, he was gone.

And that's how Gus came to be lord of my Heineken and Toy store for quite a spell. The score? Down by a six-pack, up by an incredible eight hundred and twenty five smackeroos from four apparently contented Dinky Toy, Tootsietoy and clockwork customers.

Gus said he wanted to repair some of his fishing gear, soon after we got back and trundled off home, after he had milked us of our talk with Digby. Then, just as I was about to expand on my thousand-watt light bulb theory – a skinny outline of which I had given Arabella in the car on the way back – the boy wonder burst into the shop with a 'Mega-shock, horror, Peter. Heard the radio? Old Beamish's car has been found abandoned at Osmington cliffs. And the police are searching for him everywhere. Hey, think he could have committed suicide, because he was really the murderer?'

I quietened him down, and explained what had happened at some length, ending on a firm assurance that I had kept Tony's name and part in the burglary strictly under wraps. But my response to his question, which was along the lines I'd offered Digby, disappointed him.

'Hell, Peter, when I heard the news of old Beamish's disappearance, I sort of hoped he'd left a note or something, confessing all – you know, robbery and murder.'

I shook my head. 'No luck, Tony. I'm afraid your caretaker friend isn't in the clear yet. Not until the police find the real culprit.'

'Maybe they never will. And then they'll try to nail it on poor Andy just to write closed on their ruddy file.'

I sat him down on the stool by the counter. 'Look, Tony, I'd like to see Andy again myself.'

'Why . . . what . . .?' he stammered in alarm.

'Now calm down. I just want to check a few things with him, that's all.'

'What things? Why?'

I put a hand on his arm. 'Tony, I can't tell you right now. I wish I could, but I can't.'

'Why? Oh, Peter, can't you even tell me why?'

I shook my head. 'No, sorry. You must just trust me. No harm will come to Andy. I won't get him into trouble.'

He looked uncertain.

'Oh, come on, Tony. Have I let you down over what you confessed to me the other night?'

'No . . .'

'Well then, trust me now. By the way, does he know I know about you and him?'

'No, and please don't tell him.'

'I won't.'

His eyes brightened. 'You've got a theory, haven't you?'

'Not really. Not until I've discovered even the merest trifle to back it up.'

'A germ of a theory?'

'A germ. Microscopic.'

'Germs multiply.' But he saw from my expression that no amount of probing would break my resolve. He changed the subject and tried, 'I suppose what you told the Inspector about our Headmaster's confession puts *me* in the clear.'

'Might do. Depends upon everybody keeping their mouths shut, doesn't it?'

'You mean Andy?'

'And you.'

'Me?'

'Yes, you. One day you might feel like bragging about how you started making money or want to offload your guilt by confessing.'

'Guilt?'

'Yes, guilt, Tony. You stole other people's money for your own ends. Beamish's confession doesn't whitewash that. Nothing can.' I looked him in the eye. 'Success in life isn't just measured in what you can get away with, you know, whatever reports in the City Pages and on Money Programmes may have misled you into believing.'

He fast blinked. 'I know.'

'All right. End of lecture.'

We were both silent for a moment, then he said, 'I told Andy to sell those new shares we bought.'

'Make a second killing?'

'No. Quite a loss. You see, I sold them the day after my chat with you. I thought you would want me to.'

I smiled. 'Any money left?'

'A little.'

'What are you going to do with that?'

'Done it.'

'What?'

'Sent it to the Ethiopian fund direct. Their headquarters are in London.'

I took his hand. 'Like a drink? I could do with one.'

He nodded. 'Thanks,' he said quietly. 'And not just for the scotch.'

As I followed him through to the sitting-room, I wondered how much of his new high-flying morality would survive when he met the pressures of Adultland and Big City life.

Andy Boxall looked somewhat rattled when he saw who was at the door.

'It's okay, Andy. I'm not the police.'

He smirked and led me through to his postage-stamp living area.

'What's the trouble, then, Mr Marklin? Tony hasn't been . . .?' He stopped and shuffled towards his primitive cooker.

'No, Tony hasn't been anything. I'm only here to ask you a few questions, that's all.'

He looked back at me, lips pursed. 'Like a coffee?'

I remembered his previous Camp offering only too well. 'No, thanks.'

He leaned against the wall. 'Well, how can I help you, Mr Marklin? I don't know anything more than I've told everybody time and time again.'

I held up my hand. 'No, I'm sure you don't, Andy. I'm just checking on a few things that's all. Don't worry.'

'What kind of things?'

'Well, about how Mr Folland's murderer got into the school, really.'

'Must have had keys or been let in. Stands to reason. Otherwise, I'd have heard something, wouldn't I?'

'Maybe. Maybe not. Your annexe is a bit away from the gym, isn't it? And you had the TV on.'

'All right. So what would you like to know?'

I sat on the arm of the one easy chair. Its venerable stuffing gave beneath me and I held on to the back for support.

'Well, basically, can you think of any other way someone could have got into the school? I mean, are there skylights or man-hole covers or coal-holes to basements. You know the kind of thing.'

'The police asked me all that when they first came round. I took 'em all over the school. They probed and prodded and checked every ruddy thing you can think of – even the drains. And came up with nothing . . . nothing anybody could get through, anyway. Why are you asking?'

'I'm just intrigued with how the murderer gained entry, that's all.'

'I told you. They must have had keys or been let in. Mr Folland might well have known his killer, mightn't he? Would have done if he turns out to be that French yachting friend of his that the police are looking for. You know, the one who wouldn't take no for an answer, Miss Pettican told us about. He'd be bound to let the likes of him in, now wouldn't he?'

I didn't comment, but got up from the semi-collapsed arm. 'Andy, I know it's getting dark, but would it be too much trouble for you to show me round the school? I won't keep you long. Promise.'

He chewed his already well-chewed lip. 'Well . . . er . . .'

'I won't tell anyone else. Another promise.'

With a sigh, he turned to a small cupboard by the window and got out a bulky bunch of keys.

'Where would you like to start, Mr Marklin?'

I'm afraid I broke my first promise. But I didn't regret it. There was more to the buildings than I expected, as over the years the school had grown like Topsy (and a bit like Turvy), and extra classrooms, annexes and additions had sprouted seemingly without plan in every direction. As a result, I had to explore more nooks and crannies than a hungry house mouse. By the time we had gone almost full circle and were back in the gym area, it was over an hour later and Andy had gone back to fetch a torch.

Whilst he was away, I walked around the two exterior walls of the gym in the dim light, but could see no way whatsoever where someone could gain or force an entry, for the windows were barred on both sides, presumably to prevent the glass being broken from volley balls inside and errant playground balls outside.

By now somewhat gloomy and frustrated, I moved back to where I could see the beam from Andy's torch and my sweater brushed against some ivy that badly needed cutting back. I picked a dead leaf from my shoulder, as Andy handed over the torch.

'Yea . . . well, with all the kerfuffle and that, I haven't had time to do me usual clipping and weeding and stuff. This ivy is nothing to what the hedges round the front look like. Poor Mr Beamish – you've heard about him, of course?'

I nodded.

'Well, he was only saying yesterday that I must get down to me gardening jobs . . . Oh, terrible, isn't it, him disappearing and all.'

I nodded once more, but didn't want to get into the subject of his headmaster right then, in case I revealed more than was healthy – for me, *or* him. I swung the torch up over the ivy, but could see nothing but a brownish, dead-looking patch about twenty feet up, just to the right of the roof of a low extension, that looked as if it was used for coal or a generator or such.

'Wonder why that's dead,' Andy grunted. 'Usual reason ivy goes brown is dog's pee. But no dog pees that height, now does it?' He grinned for the first time.

I looked back at the roof of the extension. 'Not unless he climbed up that drain pipe and on to the roof of that thing, no, Andy.' And with that, I turned away.

'S'pose it must be fumes or something killing it.'

I flashed the torch back at the brown patch. 'Fumes? What do you mean fumes?'

He shook his head. 'No, you're right. It can't be. The big boiler was taken out nearly ten years ago now.'

'What do you mean, Andy? Is there an old chimney or something up there?'

He saw the glint in my eyes and smiled. 'Now, calm down, Mr Marklin. I told the police about it the first time they came round. One of the constables had a look – maybe he killed the ivy. And he looked the other end.'

'What other end?'

'Where the boiler used to be at the back of the gym. Covered with a grating now. You see, it wasn't no chimney. Sort of ventilation shaft, I suppose. Before my time, though.'

'How wide is the shaft?'

He shook his head. 'No width at all, really. But that's not important, as the police pointed out, when they went up on to the roof and saw all the ruddy corners and kinks it's got in it. Nobody could crawl round those, even if they could force their shoulders through the opening. They'd get stuck in no time, they would. Like those potholers you hear about on telly. No, you can forget this old shaft, Mr Marklin, I'm afraid.'

I flashed the torch one last time over the brown patch of ivy and behind it, in the shadows, could now just discern the likely width of the opening. Andy had been right. It looked minuscule and a major obstacle for anybody, irrespective of the kinks and corners of the actual shaft.

I looked back at Andy. 'Well, I guess, that's it. I'll let you get back to your evening.'

I handed him the torch and he led me back to his annexe.

'I'm sorry I haven't been much help, Mr Marklin.'

I patted his shoulder reassuringly. 'Not to worry, Andy. Thanks all the same. And at least I'll keep my second promise and keep mum about your showing me over.'

He gave me a nervous glance. 'Sure there's nothing else you want to know?'

I smiled, for I knew what prompted the question – a fear that Tony might have split on their Stock Exchange gambles.

I went to the door. 'No, that's it, Andy.'

As I let myself out, he asked, 'Think the murderer will ever be found and brought to justice now, Mr Marklin?'

I hesitated, then said quietly, 'Found, maybe. Brought to justice? That I'm not sure we can ever know.'

Soon after reaching home and updating Arabella, a most unholy racket shattered Studland's autumn quietude. It began as a car horn, progressed through squealing tyres to a grand climax composed of horn, tortured rubber and ricocheting gravel. I rushed to the window, just in time to see the rear of an old Avenger disappear round towards my shop entrance. A second later, a new instrument took up the rhythm – my doorbell.

Arabella, laughingly, handed me a poker from the grate, as I marched into the shop. The nine o'clock shadow outside the glass door had 'Gus' written in every lumpy outline.

I opened up. 'What the hell have you done now, Gus? I thought you said you were going to muck about with your nets or your boat or something.'

'Fooled you, didn't I?' he grinned and padded into the shop. I peered out at the old Avenger.

'That the same ruddy car I warned you off the other day?'

'Right.'

'Eames's banger?'

'Right.'

'You been and bought it now, you silly bugger?'

'Nope.'

God. Gus in his monosyllabic mood is as rewarding as a dripping tap.

'Well, what the hell have you got it again for?'

''Nother trial.'

'Gus, SHIT is still SHIT the second time you step in it.'

He wagged his finger. 'Tut, tut, tut.'

I was losing my patience now. I needed tomfoolery from Gus right then like a second hole in the head.

'Look, King Tut, either tell me why you've driven round like a maniac to ruin my evening or . . .'

'Know who tried to kill Miss Pettican, I do,' he cut in.

I cupped my ear. 'Pardon?'

'That prick Eames has got a ruddy Range Rover on his forecourt. Passed it when I was getting some new tackle.'

'Hold on a minute, Gus. Are you telling me you took the Avenger out again as a pretext for snooping round his place or something?'

'Or something,' he grinned. 'Talked to his mechanic just before he knocked off, I did. Seems Eames took that Range Rover in part exchange the day before the rock fall. And he was out in it, so the mechanic told me, all the next morning. So it could have been his Range Rover you heard drive away, now couldn't it?'

I couldn't deny it, though I was still pretty sure it was the stiff upper-blimp figure of the Colonel on the cliff top and not that of a burly Mr Universe.

'Thought you ought to know, old son. Like right away.'

'Thanks, Gus. Appreciate it.'

He screwed up his face (even more, that is). 'Not convinced, are you? I can tell.'

'I don't know what to think at the moment, Gus, to be honest.' That last bit slipped out; the bit about honesty. Because I did know what to think and what I thought right then, I just didn't like, that's all.

'Want a quick beer?' I said. I mentioned 'quick' because I had a phone call I was about to make when Gus skidded and honked his way round. And I had no wish to postpone it too long.

'You having one?' he beamed.

'Maybe. Just the one.'

'Only got two beers left, then?'

'Got more. But got some things to do this evening.' I pointed back out to his junkyard special. 'When are you taking that back, then? Won't Eames raise the ruddy roof when you say you're not buying it a second time, either?'

'Doubt it,' he winked. 'Mechanic tells me he's got plenty else to raise the roof about right now.'

'Oh?'

'Yea. Seems that daughter of his, whatshername?'

'Winna. I mean Ella. Anyway, I know who you mean. What about her?'

'Seems she had this big championship event coming up this Wednesday.'

'What do you mean "had"? She still has.'

'No, she doesn't, old lad.'

'Why, is it cancelled?'

'No, *it's* not cancelled. Mechanic says it's she who's bloody cancelled. Pulled out. Scrubbed. Won't do it. Touch it with a barge pole.'

I looked at him aghast. 'You're not serious?'

He crossed himself. Wrong way round, admittedly, but the last time Gus saw the inside of a church, was when he was having his hair washed in the font by the vicar.

'And hope to die,' he finished.

'When did all this happen?'

''Bout ten minutes, quarter of an hour before I pulled in, so the mechanic said. Caused an explosion he reckoned could be heard as far away as Bournemouth. Wonder you didn't hear him ranting and raving.'

I collapsed onto my counter stool. 'Did you hear him?'

'No. She'd scarpered off somewhere by then. And Eames had gone tearing off to see his wife down in Weymouth. See if she could bring her daughter to her senses.'

'To her father's senses,' I muttered with a sigh. 'From all accounts, she's at last come to hers.'

'Eh?' Gus emitted graciously.

'Never mind,' I said quickly. 'Come on in. You know where the beer is or Arabella will get you one.'

He frowned. 'Not joining me? Thought you said ...'

'In a minute,' I said. 'There's someone I've got to ring. It's very important.'

'More important than a Heineken?'

209

'More important than a Heineken.' And I refrained from adding that now that call was probably more important than the whole of the sodding brewing industry.

Seventeen

Quite a few 'drings' went by before the receiver was lifted.

'Hello.'

Her voice sounded peremptory, even on one-word evidence.

'Hello. This is Peter Marklin.'

'Oh . . . er . . . hello, Mr Marklin. Er . . . what can I do for you?'

'Hopefully, a couple of things, Miss Pettican. First, you don't happen to have Ella Eames with you, do you? I'm a bit worried about her, that's all.'

There was a slight hesitation, then, 'Yes, Mr Marklin, Ella is here.'

'And she's all right?'

'She's as well as can be expected.'

'You mean after pulling out of Wednesday's championship?'

'Yes, Mr Marklin,' she replied firmly. 'I *do* mean that. But I'm rather surprised you know about it all so quickly. How did you hear?'

'A friend of mine was at her father's garage this evening. That's all.'

'Mr Tribble?'

'Mr Tribble.'

'So what was the second thing, Mr Marklin – '

Her tone remained cool and spartanly direct, quite unlike her normal rather warm and chatty self.

'Well, this may sound daft, but you don't happen to possess any architectural plans of Manners School, do you?'

'Plans of the school? Why on earth would you need those?'

'I . . . er . . . want to check on one or two things, especially the course of an air duct that I believe once fed the old school boiler.'

Another hesitation and quite protracted, this one. 'Air duct? I've never heard of any air duct.'

'Oh, it's still there, Miss Pettican, I assure you.'

211

'Well, there or not, Mr Marklin, I can't see what it has to do with you or with anything. And what's more, I don't possess any plans of the school of any kind. The one or two I did have, I gave to our present architects the other day – you see, we are considering the need to make further extensions to the property fairly shortly. So, I'm sorry but I can't help you.'

'You sound annoyed with me, Miss Pettican. Why? I'm only trying to help solve the mystery of your teacher's death. The other day, you seemed to welcome my intervention.'

'That was the other day. I've changed my mind now. I think things are better left to the police. Especially after . . .' She stopped suddenly.

I tried to restart her. 'My part in Mr Beamish's disappearance? Is that what you were going to say, Miss Pettican? Or are you closing up on me for some other reason?'

'Well, you've said it yourself now, Mr Marklin, so I won't be hurting your feelings so much. Now, I must ask you to . . .'

'Just one more thing, before I ring off. Has Colonel Hawkesworth contacted you since this morning?'

'Of course, Mr Marklin. He has not only contacted me, but we have had a meeting. As governors of the school, we naturally had a lot to discuss after Mr Beamish's car was discovered.'

'No, I didn't really mean that. Of course, you had to discuss the future of the school together. I meant, did the Colonel contact you about me?'

'*You*? I assure you we have plenty on our minds right now, without worrying specifically about you. Why do you ask?'

'Oh . . . only that I accused him of being the guy on Golden Cap who tried to fossilize you in the rock fall. I thought he might have mentioned it.'

That set her waffling. 'Well . . . er . . . I suppose he might have mentioned it, I can't remember quite. I was so shaken by the news about Mr Beamish that anything else could well have gone in one ear and out the other. I'm not young, like you are, Mr Marklin (boy, would Gus have loved that comment), and we older people can only really handle one thing at a time.'

'Just thought I'd ask,' I said, noting her lack of comment or surprise at my accusation.

'Well, thank you for calling about poor Ella. It was a kind thought. Once I've calmed her down a bit, I'll get her back to her

212

father. I've rung him several times, but he doesn't seem to be there.'

'He's in Weymouth, apparently, trying to contact her mother.'

'Oh. Quite likely. She has a sister living over there, I believe. I really must get back to Ella now, Mr Marklin. You understand?'

'I understand.'

And that was that. I'd sown the seeds. Now all I had to do was sit around and pray that I was right and that they would grow.

Tony, curiously, did not contact us that evening, as we'd been expecting. We learned later that he didn't hear of Winna's gymnastic defection until quite late the next morning.

That night, I just couldn't sleep. And it wasn't only because of the tension of waiting, as Arabella (insomnia is one of the most contagious afflictions to beset lovers) soon pointed out.

'You're crackling,' she observed with a yawn.

'You're pretty good, yourself,' I countered, then had to clear my throat.

She turned over to face me. I saw the glint of an eyeball in the moonlight filtering through a gap in the curtains.

'No, idiot. Your breathing is crackling. Don't tell me you're getting a cold.'

I swallowed and it hurt. 'All right, so I won't tell you.'

Her hand went to my forehead. 'You feel a bit hot. Maybe you're getting my old flu.'

'Drat. And I ordered brand new flu.'

I felt my own forehead. Externally it did seem hot and, come to think of it, internally it didn't feel so hot. (If you see what I mean.)

'Shall I get you a Lemsip or Night Nurse or something?'

'Prefer a Night Nurse,' I said. 'Around eighteen, and thirty-six, twenty-one, thirty-six.'

'I have a feeling they don't make Night Nurse anymore.'

'So I'm not likely to make one tonight, either, then.'

Neither of us laughed. Not because the joke was so diabolical, but because of what we both feared the morning might bring.

'Sorry my crackling woke you,' I added.

'Didn't. I *was* awake, anyway.'

'Miss Pettican?'

'Miss Pettican.' She snuggled up to me, as if she wanted her old flu back. She was welcome to it. 'Let's hope you're wrong.'

'Yea,' I sighed, 'let's hope so.'

Here followed at least an hour and a half's intermission, where we both tried to get to sleep. Then she asked out of the black, as if we had never stopped talking, 'What are you going to do if you're right?'

'God knows,' I said.

'You'll have to tell Digby, you know.'

I didn't reply. And not just because a sneeze intervened.

'Poirot always told the police. So did Lord Peter,' she whispered.

'Marlowe didn't always.'

'But Digby is not the Bay City boys. And you're already keeping Tony's little escapade to yourself.'

I pulled my knees up into the womb position. 'Maybe I've got it all wrong.'

'Yea.'

'Good night,' I coughed.

But she had already sidled out of the bed covers on her way to the packet marked Lemsip.

Sunday dawned cold, but dry as a bone. Quite unlike my head and nose, the latter by then runny as the proverbial tap. Every time I sniffed, Bing looked up at me, his blue Siamese eyes kind of warning me not to pass the sniffles on to him.

I had breakfast in bed, at the insistence of Miss Lemsip, although I was really too nervous to appreciate the luxury or the extra rest. So by the time the *Sunday Times* plopped on to the doormat, all chewed at the edges as always from the narrowness of the letter-box, I was up and dressed and tapping my fingers on anything or anyone who came to trembling hand. Silly really, in retrospect, as my seeds could well have taken a day or two to germinate, even if they were to do so at all.

As the morning progressed, I was tempted several times to ring the Colonel or Delia Pettican, or even dear Digby Whetstone to see if any of the green shoots had shown above ground, but I knew that if I did, it could well be tantamount to a dose of weedkiller or a number twelve boot on anything that might be there. Besides, I didn't really dare ring Digby, until he'd found Beamish, which according to the radio, he still had not. I couldn't even go and see Gus, because I knew, right then, he was taking the 'Illman H'Avenger back to Eames, or rather back to the forecourt to exchange for his own Ford Unpopular.

214

So Arabella and I sat at the kitchen table and drank enough coffee to make Nescafé's shares hit the Stock Exchange roof come the morrow's trading. We divided up the *Sunday Times*, but whilst our eyes scanned the print, our brains took in little, so full were they with dread and anticipation.

But our watched pot didn't show any signs of boiling, until well after twelve, when I heard a car draw up outside, followed by the old ding-dong. I knew it couldn't be Gus, as the car had neither squealed, shrieked nor banged. And the exhaust note sounded too civilized for Delia Pettican's MG. So I reckoned it was either the Colonel or . . . It turned out to be the 'or'.

'Well, well, well,' he beamed, his ginger moustache thinning into the creases of his smile.

'Well?' I asked, letting him into the shop. 'What brings you here, Digby? Found Beamish?'

He shook his head. 'Now, now, now, Mr Marklin. (Hello, hello, hello, do policemen always have to talk in triplicate?) For once I'm not here to berate you.'

'You're not?'

We sat down each side of the counter and, as ever, he began by casting a jaundiced eye across my stock. 'Still making money, Mr Marklin? Old toys, I mean.'

'Keeps me in bread and milk.'

'That all?'

'I'm not in them for the money.'

'I thought these days everyone was in everything for the money.'

'That why you're a policeman?' I asked, pulling as innocent an expression as I could muster, commensurate with the onset of a sneeze.

'Caught a cold, Mr Marklin? Thought perhaps something must be wrong with you.'

I blew my nose. 'And what made you think that?'

'I was most surprised not to find you at the scene of the crime this morning. In the murder mysteries I've read, the amateur sleuth always seems to happen by at the exact moment skulduggery is afoot.'

Stifling back the next of a long series of sneezes, I snapped impatiently, 'What crime, for Christ's sake?' although I was pretty certain I knew the kind of answer he would give.

'Someone broke into Miss Pettican's home during the night and tried to murder her.'

I thought for a moment. 'She's all right, I hope?'

'Yes. But only by the skin of her teeth, or rather, the string of her bow.'

'Bow?'

'Yes, she's a much travelled lady, as you probably can imagine. And after one of her fossil-hunting trips in Africa, she brought back what you might call a native bow and arrow set. Masai tribe, or something like that. Keeps them hanging on the wall of her study as a form of decoration.'

'Tell me more, Inspector.'

He put his elbows on the counter and squinted across at me. 'Aren't you a bit surprised I've come all this way to tell you anything? Don't you wonder why?'

It would have been downright cruel not to humour him. 'Enlighten me.'

'Got it right in one, Mr Marklin. I've come to enlighten you. To bring you up to date with the Manners School case, so that you can keep your sticky fingers out of it from now on.'

I smiled. 'You're trying to let me down lightly about not needing me any more, aren't you?'

'Just so.'

'Found the murderer, then?'

He blinked, as I knew he would.

'Not exactly. But this latest attack on Miss Pettican contains pretty clear evidence that the finding of said murderer will be entirely out of your parochial court.'

His rather upstage lingo amused me.

'Why is that?'

He rubbed his hands together. 'You got a direct line to Interpol?'

'No. Would I need one?'

'There are now clear signs you would. That is why I came round. To show you that the Manners School affair has now moved firmly outside the confines of your ... talent. So you can relax now, Mr Marklin, and leave it all to the professionals – as you should have done from the beginning.'

I couldn't resist it. I asked, 'Found a beret and a squeeze-box at Miss Pettican's, then? Perhaps an Aznavour record or an Yves Montand video-tape? Or Maigret's pipe?'

'Don't be facetious, just because you are miffed at finding yourself right out of your depth.'

'All right, Inspector, but it's only fair to ask what you found that makes it a case for Interpol.'

He pursed his lips, then obviously decided I might not lie down unless he patted me further. 'Miss Pettican had an intruder at about two thirty this morning. He broke a small panel of glass in the leaded glass of the dining-room window, opened the catch and climbed over the sill. In doing so, he left clear imprints of his footwear in the flower bed below the window. We have identified these as belonging to a type of boot only available on the Continent.'

'Anyone could have bought a pair on a trip abroad.'

He held up a hand like a . . . policeman.

'Hold on. There's more, Mr Marklin.'

I held on.

'Miss Pettican, luckily, was woken by the noise of the glass splinters falling on to the parquet floor and immediately got up. She went down the back stairs to try to get to the phone, but the intruder was too quick and grabbed her in the hall, as she was about to lift the receiver.'

'What did he look like?' I tried.

'He had a stocking over his face.'

'French stocking?'

'Mr Marklin, either you want to hear about all this or you don't. In which case, I might as well leave.'

I gave a Red Indian peace sign, or what I reckoned was one. 'I want to hear.'

But he had to repeat his next few words, as I drowned them in yet another sneeze, which did nothing for my sore throat.

He resumed: 'Otherwise, Miss Pettican says he was dressed completely in black leather and reminded her immediately of the figure she had seen on the wall the night of Mr Folland's murder. What's more, he apparently spoke with a fairly thick accent, which she is quite certain was French.'

'What did he say in this thick French accent?'

'He said that if she didn't withdraw her statement about seeing a figure on the wall and Folland having a French friend of whom he was afraid, he'd have to kill her. She refused point blank and as he was reaching into his pocket for what Miss Pettican assumed was a gun, she managed to break free from him and lock

217

herself in the study. He then tried to force the door – the marks are quite evident – but the house is old and the main doors are of oak and secured by both mortice locks and thick sliding bolts.'

'So then he just packed up and went home . . . to France, of course?'

Digby got up from his stool in exasperation. 'Really, Mr Marklin, I regret bothering to come, now.'

'Sit down, Inspector, and finish your story. I'll be good, I promise.'

By now, anyway, I wanted our little exchange to end as soon as possible. One, I had heard enough for my purposes. Two, there were hammers in my hot head that were now definitely beating out a flu tattoo.

'One more interruption . . .' he warned.

I nodded.

'In answer to your question, the intruder did not give up right then. He went outside and stood by the library window. Again his footprints bear out Miss Pettican's story. But now he could see that she too was armed, having taken the bow and arrows off the wall.'

'Couldn't he have still shot her through the window, though?' I couldn't stop myself asking.

Digby frowned. 'I'll forgive you for interrupting this time, Mr Marklin, as the same question went through my mind. So I put it to Miss Pettican. She said that firstly, she didn't actually see a gun at any time and secondly, right then a police or ambulance siren sounded in the distance. We've checked. There was a serious motor accident around that time about half a mile from her house. Anyway, he took fright and went. Miss Pettican waited about an hour to make sure he had gone before she ventured into the hall and telephoned us.' He slapped the counter. 'So now you know as much as we do.'

'Right,' I sniffed. 'Thanks.'

He started to move his bulk towards the door. 'And this incident, Mr Marklin, fits in with our latest information from our counterparts across the Channel.'

'Which is?'

'They are on to at least two French friends of Mr Folland's, who make regular trips to England and who have unsavoury reputations for violent behaviour.'

'Criminal records?'

He gave a 'holier than thou' smile. 'Not quite. You are sophisticated enough, I think, Mr Marklin, to be able to guess what a certain kind of homosexual gets up to as an extra night-time entertainment. Wearing black leather is only the start, if you get my meaning.'

'Beats straight sex?' I tried limply.

'With the emphasis on the beats,' he added, with the smug, self-satisfaction of those who never appreciate the witticisms of others.

'So let me guess your scenario now, Inspector, like you did mine the other day.'

'Go ahead.'

'In a nutshell, Mr Folland was murdered by a whip- and chain-loving gay friend from France – motive, that Folland might well have given him Aids.'

'Not bad. Not bad,' Digby smiled.

'And this same gay Frog has tried to get the only witness, Miss Pettican, to croak on two separate occasions. But failed both times.'

He opened the shop door. 'I have postponed a million things by coming to you, Mr Marklin. I really must go and catch up now.'

'Well, anyway, kind of you to bring me up to date.'

He grinned. 'Kindness doesn't come into it one whit, don't kid yourself. It's purely self-interest to prove you are now well and truly out of your depth. So unless your old toys are making you so much money you can afford countless trips to France . . .'

'Goodbye, Inspector.'

He nodded his farewell, like a character out of 'Dallas'.

I watched him squeeze into his brand new Rover 800, then I went back to Arabella and brought her up to date. She wasn't surprised.

'Do you think old Digby really believes all that?' she asked.

'Don't know. He might, although he could well be just spinning me all that to get me out of his hair or to put me off the scent, so that he can get all the kudos of solving the case.' I took her hand. 'It doesn't alter things though, does it?'

She shook her head, then looked up at me.

'You look dreadful, Peter. Is the flu getting worse or is it the prospect ahead of us?'

'Ahead of me,' I corrected her.

'Us,' she reaffirmed. 'You're not going alone. Especially feeling ill.'

There followed an argument my health could well have done without, especially as I lost it. But, at least, I got her to take out Third Party Insurance, if she was coming. In the form of one Gus Tribble.

Gus, of course, pretended he wouldn't play, until we had fed him some lunch and at least a couple of Heineken. So we had to indulge his pretence before we left, though we both knew he was actually tickled pink to be involved with our mission.

I have to admit I didn't tell him the truth. Not at this stage. For I could still have sussed it all wrong and prayed that I had. After all, try as I and Arabella might, neither of us could come up with any motive that would add vital rationality to my theory and without that, it was all wild surmise. So all Gus knew was that we were going to see Miss Pettican to check out her story of the night intruder, which, I suppose, was not wholly untrue.

As always when dreading arrival, our destination seemed to heave into view in no time at all. I asked Arabella to first drive past the long, low thatched house, so that we could make certain there were no cars in her drive, beyond perhaps her own MG. To our relief, there were none. And we could see her matt MG tucked safely away in a small barn alongside the drive.

We parked under some trees about a hundred feet from the house and Arabella and I got out. I wagged a warning finger at Gus, who was already clambering from the rear seat into the front.

'Now, Gus, remember what I said. Stay in the car and act as a look-out for any person or vehicle approaching the house. If you see anything suspicious . . .'

'Sound the horn six times. S'all right, old love, my memory's not a ruddy sieve, you know.'

He was right. For his age, his memory was, I suppose, ace. But it was its selectivity that always worried the living daylights out of me.

As we approached the house, we could see the garden was still marked out with stakes and lines of white ribbon, presumably to keep people from trampling all over the evidence of the reported night intruder. And a piece of cardboard covered part of one of the front windows.

I looked at Arabella. She looked at me. I rang the doorbell with crossed fingers and waited. And waited.

'Better try again,' Arabella urged.

I did so. And this time, almost immediately, heard movement from inside the house, followed by Miss Pettican's face at the small triangular window in the oak door. She unbolted in no time.

'Oh, Mr Marklin . . . *and* Miss Trench.'

She seemed somehow relieved I was not alone.

'Can we come in?' I smiled.

She hesitated. 'Er . . . if you're calling to ask about poor Ella Eames, she's back at home. Her mother came to pick her up just after eleven last night.'

'No, not really. We would just like a word or two with you, that's all.'

'About last night? You've heard about this awful man breaking in and threatening to kill me?'

'Yes, we've heard,' I nodded.

She looked at me. Then at Arabella.

'Well . . . er . . . you'd better come in, I suppose. Mind your head on the beams, though.'

The house was warm and shot with shadows and shafts of light from the small mullioned windows. And smelt of fresh flowers and generations of wax polish. She led us through into what was obviously the sitting-room, dominated by a splendid inglenook fireplace, still complete with bread oven.

'Do sit down and tell me how I can help you.'

Her voice betrayed her apprehension. We both remained standing. I cleared my clogged throat and began.

'We have come to get the truth, Miss Pettican.'

She looked away. 'The truth? Truth about what? I've told the police all I know.'

'You've told the police what you want them to know, yes. But it's not the truth, is it, Miss Pettican?'

She went over to the window, her back to us.

'I don't know what you mean. I have told you, Mr Marklin, that I don't want you interfering any more in our affairs, however honourable your motives may be.'

'I'm afraid I have to. And I suspect it's much better for you, Miss Pettican, that I'm the first to discover the truth, rather than Inspector Whetstone.'

221

She didn't reply, so I went on, 'You see, when I rang you last night about the plans of the school and the air duct to the boiler, I was pretty certain you would respond by inventing another attack on yourself.'

She turned round to us. 'Invent?' She pointed back to the window. 'Are those footprints invented? The broken window? The mud he left all over the . . . ?'

'No, I admit they exist. But I suggest you arranged all the evidence yourself to give credibility to your intruder story.'

'And I arranged for a rock fall to almost kill me too, I suppose? Really, Mr Marklin, you were there. You witnessed that attempt on my life yourself.'

'I witnessed a rock slide, yes. But not an attempt on your life. You used me, Miss Pettican, to add credibility to your story of some mystery killer.'

'Oh, this is all so much rubbish, Mr Marklin. You haven't a shred of evidence for what you're saying.' She turned to Arabella. 'You don't believe him, surely, Miss Trench? I mean, what possible motive could I have for manufacturing attempts on my life?'

'Easy, Miss Pettican,' I replied quietly. 'To protect the real killer. For you've always known, or suspected, who that is, haven't you?'

She came back towards us, her eyes not so much fearful as resolute, and her voice firm. 'And who, then, is your crazed imagination saying killed poor Mr Folland?'

Arabella came to my rescue and put a hand on Delia Pettican's arm.

'Forgive us, if we're wrong, but we think you are protecting . . . Ella. Ella Eames.'

She shrugged off Arabella's touch. 'Ella? A child? Are you mad? What on earth made you think of such an absurd idea? And what possible motive could a child have for murdering Mr Folland?'

'I don't know the motive yet. That's what's been bothering me ever since I had the first inkling you might be protecting her.'

'And when was that, pray?'

'When I was talking to the Inspector yesterday. I was saying to him that I had become more and more convinced that the figure on the cliff had been that of Colonel Hawkesworth and I was

222

worried about the timing of the rock fall. For I couldn't see the Colonel ever failing at anything he really set out to do.'

'So?'

'So I then went on to run through why the Colonel, if it was him, did fail. Either he intended just to give you a scare, but it seemed to me a bloody dangerous way of scaring you, or . . . and the alternative I didn't divulge to the Inspector, for its implications immediately hit me like a bombshell . . . you and the Colonel were in league together. So you actually knew the rock fall was coming and could take the necessary avoiding action in time.'

'Why should the Colonel and I be in collusion, Mr Marklin? You are well aware there's no love lost between us.'

'There could only be one reason. To protect someone you both knew, whose reputation must be preserved for the good of the whole of Manners School and its future. For the school actually unites you both, rather more than it divides you, doesn't it, Miss Pettican? You both love it, but for different reasons. He, as a proud ex-pupil and governor; you, as the grand-daughter of the founder. And you both show your love in dramatically different ways. What's more, I suspect you felt a certain guilt for forcing the appointment of Mr Folland as a teacher and thus, unwittingly, setting in train a course of events that has led to not only appalling personal tragedies, but which has put at risk the whole future of the school.'

I looked her in the eyes. 'God, I've prayed that, when I came here, you could prove me wrong, but I don't think you can, can you, Miss Pettican?'

She slowly moved away from us and subsided into a chair.

'Do you want me to go on?'

She shook her head. 'There's no need,' she said, barely above a whisper. 'You see, that night, I instantly recognized her little figure on the school wall. It was unmistakable. I kept it to myself for some time, but then one day when she came to tea with me, I told her very gently that I knew. You see, that's why she's been spending so much time with me recently. She needs so much comfort, reassurance that someone understands . . .'

Arabella went over and put her arm around her shoulder.

Miss Pettican went on, 'I invented the story of the violent French friend of Mr Folland's, not just to keep suspicion off dear Ella, but also poor Andy Boxall and anyone else who might come under police investigation. But the Inspector seemed to go off the idea, somehow, so I had to find a way of giving it some substance. It was then . . .'

Suddenly there was a violent crash. I looked up in alarm. The sitting-room door had been thrown open and in the doorway was a shotgun aimed at my vitals. And the strong hands that were holding it belonged to Colonel Hawkesworth.

'It was then she rang *me*, Mr Marklin,' he growled.

When I'd pushed my heart down out of my mouth, I moved with the speed of light to stand between the twin muzzles and Arabella. The muzzles followed me.

'Come away, Delia. I've got them covered.'

Shaking now, she glanced at us, then got up and moved towards the doorway. The Colonel went on,

'I must say, Mr Marklin, you've got more intelligence than I gave you credit for. Especially for working out what might unite two sworn enemies. A common goal, my dear fellow. A common cause, if it's grand enough, can make allies of the most unlikely people. At least, temporarily. Like Churchill and Stalin during the war and before that, the Nazis and Russia over Poland.'

History lessons was all I needed right then. I turned to his current unlikely ally. 'Can't you get him to put that gun down, Miss Pettican? It's not the war now.'

She hesitated, then put her hand on the shotgun's barrel. '*They're* not our enemies, Colonel.'

He lowered the muzzles towards the floor, but kept his finger on the first trigger. 'I can't see their car, Delia. The police might be . . .'

I cut in. 'We came alone. The car is just up the road.' I omitted to say it wasn't empty. 'But where's yours, Colonel? We didn't see it in the drive when we came in. And I didn't hear you drive up.'

'It's at the back of the barn. You see, we had a feeling you might turn up, Mr Marklin. I've been outside the door all the time, listening to every word you've said.'

'Were you the night intruder too?' I enquired, somewhat wearily, my head now burning hot and muzzing my mind.

'No. I told Delia what to do and say, gave her some boots I'd bought in the Dordogne . . .' He sighed and now looked about as tired as I felt.

'. . . and the rest is history,' I helped him.

'What are you going to do now, Mr Marklin?' Delia Pettican asked, pleadingly. 'And you, Miss Trench? We can't turn poor Ella Eames in to the police. We can't. We mustn't. It wasn't her fault.'

I pointed at the gun and sneezed. 'I think more clearly, when I'm not about to be peppered with lead.'

To my amazement, she managed to take the gun from the Colonel and prop it up against the door jamb. Arabella immediately went to Delia Pettican's side. 'Why did Ella kill Mr Folland?' she asked, very quietly.

There was a long silence, before Miss Pettican replied, almost as if in a trance. 'They fell in love, you see. Deeply in love. During the long hours he helped her with her gymnastics.'

'But I thought he was . . .'

She stilled me with a slight wave of her hand. 'She told me he was unbelievably and wildly happy when he at last realized his feelings for her. He wanted the whole world to know. Yes, I know, Mr Folland was a homosexual. But obviously he had emotions and physical needs even he didn't know about until he met Ella. Maybe it was her boyish figure that started it all, I don't know. All I do know is that something magical sparked between them. Poor Ella didn't dare let him tell anyone else until she had, at least, taken part in her championship finals, or even, perhaps, finished with school altogether. For her father would have killed her, had he known. At the least, she felt her family would disown her.'

'Is that why Mr Folland was talking of buying a house?'

'Yes. They arranged that he was to go ahead and buy a modest house away from this area, where they could go and live when the time eventually came to bring their relationship out into the open.'

I kicked myself. Or rather, Tony Thorn and even Gus recently, and the Loadsofmoney merchants, City journalists and yuppy lifestyles that had masked my mind to all forms of expectations other than financial ones. The change of life to which the antique dealer from Dorchester had reported Folland alluding, had been, after all, love for an innocent called Ella, a living breathing being, not lust for inanimate loads of watermarked paper.

'Why did she kill him? Or can I guess?' I asked. 'You needn't tell me how. Your reaction to my mention of the old air duct told me that.'

'That was clever of you, too, Mr Marklin,' she replied and closed her eyes. 'The police, thank the Lord, never suspected any human being could crawl through that tunnel and get around those bends. But then, I dare say, they've never really studied a gymnast. It's almost as if they were shaped, built and trained to do the impossible, isn't it? Tiny. Lithe. Like India rubber.'

'How did she know of the duct in the first place?'

'She had noticed the architects inspecting it when they went over the school some weeks ago.'

'Why did she need to use it at all, when Folland would have opened any door in the world to her, if he'd known she was there?'

She opened her eyes, now red rimmed, and looked at me. 'Do I need to tell you that?'

I thought for a second. 'She couldn't face killing him, if he saw her?'

She nodded. 'She knew he would be in the gym that evening. He had told her he would be working out there for a bit – he was very particular about keeping fit. Apparently, he was kneeling down tying his shoes, when she hit him with that hammer.'

'Hammer?'

'Yes, she'd taken one from the tool kit of her father's old Jaguar. I'm not sure what it was normally used for.'

'Knock off wheel nuts. You hit them to get them loose. By the way, where's that hammer now?'

'She brought it to Delia from where she'd hidden it,' the Colonel intervened. 'It's now deep in the sea, Mr Marklin. No one will ever find it.'

He suddenly picked up the shotgun again. 'Look, Delia, I'm going out to their car to check whether they're speaking the truth about coming alone.'

'But they . . .' she began, but he cut her off.

'They can't get very far without a car. I'll be back anyway, before they can reach another house. If you're worried, I'll wait while you fetch that African bow you told the police about.'

She shook her head. 'I have a feeling they are not our real enemies, anyway, Colonel.'

She looked across at us as if for confirmation.

Arabella and I didn't flex a muscle, even though she was dead right. We weren't their real enemies, but what the hell we were going to do now, I hadn't the slightest idea. Don't get me wrong. I was well aware of what we *should* do and that we might well have to do if . . .

Hawkesworth gave us one last glare for good measure, then left, toting his gun. After we had heard the front door slam, Delia Pettican asked wearily, 'Anything else you two would like to know?'

'One last thing,' Arabella answered. 'Why? Why did Winna, I mean Ella, kill the man you say she loved?'

'Oh . . . so many reasons . . . partly because they had made love, you see, Miss Trench. And she was up to her sweet neck in guilt about it, anyway. She won't tell me all the details, naturally, but I gather she would have waited, had it not been for his insistence.'

'She was still going out with Tony. Still is,' I muttered, as part question, part explanation and part statement.

'Yes, Mr Marklin, I know. She kept that up for appearances, you see. Not that she doesn't love Tony in a way, but not with the consuming love she felt for Alistair.'

'Appearances?'

'Yes. Alistair would of course have lost his position at the school had their affair become public. Continuing to go out with Tony was as good a cover as any – especially for her over-demanding, puritanical father. A cover she would drop when she and Alistair were good and ready.'

I remembered Tony's comments about Ella no longer being willing to make love and I could now see the reason, or rather reasons. For the final clincher must have been her fear that she too might have Aids.

Arabella took my clammy hand and squeezed hard. I squeezed back in agreement.

'And she killed him because he might have given her Aids?' Arabella asked softly.

'Aids was certainly a trigger, Miss Trench. Her father had read her a thousand Riot Acts about Aids and so terrified her about both the mortal and moral consequences of its contraction. And the Aids commercials had set the seal on his words and warnings. But it wasn't just the shock and anger at finding out Alistair had been found HIV positive that drove her to it. I think she'd made such a god of Alistair, come to rely on him so much, that when he too seemed to let her down, it was too much for her emotional state.'

'What about herself?' Arabella enquired. 'She must be worried sick that she's contracted Aids too. Has she gone for any tests?'

'She is. And she won't. I've tried to persuade her but she's terrified the doctors and the hospital won't keep the whole thing quiet if she does. And again, I think she's terrified of what the diagnosis might prove to be. You can see that, can't you?'

I could see the whole damned thing only too well. It was the solution that totally and utterly escaped me. But my self-questioning was rudely interrupted by a kerfuffle from the hall outside. A second later, the Colonel burst back in, his eyes staring wide with anger. But this time, his gun was carried by other hands. The huge, square-cut digits of dear old Gus.

Eighteen

'Call your bloody man off,' Hawkesworth bellowed at me, nodding his head towards the gun in his back.

Flu now having occupied all the floors in my semi-detached brain, I unfortunately said, 'He's not *my* bloody man. He's his own bloody man.' Whereupon Gus shot me an 'Up yours too' look and gave the Colonel another prod that sent him reeling into a chair.

Arabella, luckily, had the sense to go over to Gus and deflect the muzzles to the floor. 'It's all right. Relax, Gus. We're not in any danger. Really. Just talking, that's all.'

Gus turned to me, a frown deep-ploughing his forehead. 'If you're just talking, then what's this overblown fart here doing prowling around the place with a twelve-bore. Luckily, I saw him coming and ducked me head down, otherwise he might have bloody blown it off.'

I saw the Colonel nursing his shoulder and wincing.

Gus laughed. 'Serves him ruddy well right. Got him with the door, I did, just as he was about to peer in.' He turned to Arabella. 'S'all right. Don't think I've done any damage, love. Least, not to your car.'

I looked at Delia Pettican. She looked at me. I looked at Arabella. We all ended up looking at each other. For now, we had an extra problem. A fifth party – who wasn't party to what we four now knew. But we obviously had to tell him something, if only to keep him quiet until we had worked out what our final solution should or could be.

'Well, what have you lot been talking about all this time then?' He grinned. 'Me ears didn't burn, so it can't have been me.'

'Put the gun down first, Gus,' I said, for I did not quite trust Gus's forefinger. It tended to get itchy, when he was frustrated.

Arabella took the twelve-bore from him and propped it up near the door.

'Well then . . . ?' he asked, eyebrows raised.

As if on some heaven-sent cue, the telephone rang in the hall. The Colonel started to get up from his chair, but Miss Pettican stilled him.

'I'll get it.'

We all kept an eerie silence until she came back, her usually tanned face now a mask drained of blood, hope and life.

'What on earth's the matter, Delia?' the Colonel instantly asked, his voice full of concern and, surprisingly, compassion. 'Who was it? Wouldn't be Beamish, would it?'

She shook her head. 'Tony,' she replied, barely above a whisper.

'Tony?' I repeated. 'What's wrong? What the hell's happened?'

She put her head in her hands. 'He's trying to find Ella.'

'Find her?' Hawkesworth went to her side and put his arm around her shoulder. 'What do you mean, find her?'

'Oh God.' She swung round and buried her head in the Colonel's jacket, her body trembling with her tears.

'Come on, Delia, tell me.'

'Tony went round to the garage . . . there was no one there . . . just a note she had left for him . . .'

'A note? Saying what?'

'That she was going board sailing . . . and not to wait for her . . . to come back.'

Hawkesworth grasped her shoulders and swung her round to face him. 'Board sailing? Where? Come on. Don't waste bloody time.'

'Where she keeps her equipment. Down at Studland. Her father owns that little café shop on the beach, up towards the ferry. I know she's got a key.'

'How long's she been gone?'

'That's the trouble. Tony thinks it might be hours. That's why he's been ringing round everybody he knows, just in case she has turned up somewhere. Oh God, I hope she hasn't . . .'

'Has he contacted the coastguard?' Hawkesworth asked.

'Not yet. I told him to ring them right away.'

I went over to Gus, but he'd already got the message.

'I've got a boat,' he grunted, 'over in Studland.'

Hawkesworth looked on him kindly for the first time. 'Ready to go?'

'Ready to go.'

'How many will she hold?'

'All us lot.'

The Colonel took Delia Pettican by the arm and propelled her out of the room. We were close on their heels. As he slammed the front door behind us, he said, 'We'll follow you in my car.'

'Range Rover?' I asked.

'Range Rover.' He looked at me hard, then nodded. 'Thanks,' he said.

I nodded back. He must have read my mind.

By the time we were all on board and parked where Captain Augustus Tribble wanted us, the wind had risen by at least one force, maybe two. And the clouds that lowered upon our unhappy house painted the sea a forbidding grey and were, by no means, in the deep ocean buried. I must say, as I watched old Gus prepare to set sail or, rather, chug out, I was impressed with the quiet efficiency and speed with which he performed each operation. Not that his heavy and old-fashioned day boat was a Virgin Challenger or an Alan Bond special, but all the same . . .

I think everyone else's eyes were scanning the waves around us and the horizon beyond. But other than a few scavenging seagulls, there was nothing to be seen but white horses. As we headed out, Gus at the wheel, cap pulled firmly down on his head, I looked back at the shore line. There was nothing to be seen there either, except the hunched figure of an old man exercising his shaggy dog. I guessed Tony must still be with the coastguard or maybe even out in the lifeboat somewhere. I strained my ears hopefully for the distant beat of a helicopter, but Gus's diesel drowned out everything but its own thumps.

I looked across at Arabella, seated shivering opposite me. For neither of us had had time to pop home and get any really warm clothing. She smiled back wanly and Gus caught her look.

'If she's out here, we'll find her, old love,' he shouted. 'If the whirly-bird hasn't picked her up already.' (Gus has always called choppers 'whirly-birds'. I think he's never got over watching that ancient American TV series of the same name.)

I looked ahead. Hawkesworth and Delia Pettican were up front in the primitive cabin, he sitting, she kneeling on piles of assorted

231

Tribble nautical paraphernalia – coils of rope, fenders, torn oil-skins, oil-soaked rags, dodgy life jackets that *you* would have to hold up, rather than the other way around, and copies of ancient newspapers. Their noses were glued to the scratched and semi-opaque perspex of the windows.

I too was shivering like the proverbial timbers, but it wasn't all from the cold or the flu. At my umpteenth sniff and sneeze, Gus, bless him, offered me his oilskin jacket. Arabella nodded that I should accept, but I didn't. Gus was in the eye of the wind, standing up at the helm and besides, he could give me quite a few years and never miss them. But he would his jacket.

'What's your plan, Gus?' I shouted, above the thumps and the gusts.

He moved his great arm forward and back in a series of zigzags. 'Keep going up and down, old son.'

I cursed the fact that Gus had never managed to afford a two-way radio. At least then we could probably have picked up the coastguard station and learnt what they were doing. But modern aids and inventions had never fascinated him – hence his old Ford Popular and the lime-encrusted ewer and jug in his bedroom.

After two sets of zigzags along the whole width of the bay, I was not only feeling as cold as a Birds Eye prawn, but as sick as a dog. My head had picked up the thumping rhythm of the diesel and my vision seemed to have descended from its usual twenty twenty to as low as two two at times. So I was about as good a lookout as a yuppy is a social worker. In the end, I think I would have actually emitted over the side (and probably fallen in to boot), had Gus not suddenly pointed his great digit towards the west.

I looked where he was pointing. Way, way out, black against the grey, a tiny silhouette hung in the sky, its pregnant shape only just discernible. Arabella, defying Gus's command to stay put, hunched across to me and I made room for her.

'Helicopter?' she shouted above the din.

I nodded.

'Way out, isn't it?'

'Maybe it's done this bit.'

'Hope not.'

'Yea.'

'Maybe it's found her and is going back.'

I pointed. 'It's getting bigger. Not smaller.'

Hawkesworth and Delia Pettican suddenly appeared at the door of the cabin and gazed across to the horizon that held the chopper.

'Whirly-bird,' Gus shouted.

'Whirly what?' the Colonel snapped.

'Bird,' Gus snapped back and raised his onerous eyebrows to the threatening heavens.

'It's not a bloody bird,' I heard the Colonel bellow into Miss Pettican's ear. 'It's a helicopter.' He was back to his irascible self.

Arabella put an arm round my waist, as we watched the chopper's silhouette loom larger. 'How are you feeling?' she asked.

'Like the sea looks,' I forced a smile. 'Rough.'

'You shouldn't be out here.'

I feigned getting up. 'All right, I'll be off. Tell me what happens. On second thoughts, don't.'

She moved closer to me, so that she wouldn't have to shout. 'You don't think we'll find her, do you?'

I didn't answer. I didn't want to. I didn't need to. Her question, in its way, was its own answer. I just sat shivering, as the helicopter's colour turned from black to bright yellow, as it neared us. I could hear another thumping now. From its motor. And then the scything of the blades, as they slashed at the air to remind it to keep them airborne. Soon it was just ahead of us, the waves whipped frothy and flat by its wash.

A figure appeared in the dark of the open doorway. It waved a hand. We all waved back. We could have been trippers on a pleasure steamer at some seaside carnival. But suddenly, and sickeningly, we realized he wasn't waving a greeting, but trying to indicate to us they had already searched and found nothing.

In desperation, we pointed in every direction from horizon to horizon. The figure waved in acknowledgement and we saw the pilot give the thumbs up sign. Then the figure stepped back into the shadows and when he re-emerged, he was holding tightly on to a boy in jeans and a huge life jacket. It was Tony. He recognized us instantly, and in his excitement, would have fallen out of the door, had the Air-Sea Rescue officer not had good hold of him. He shouted something we couldn't hear. The officer waved again. Gus responded with his zigzag gesture. Then as the chopper leant into the wind and whirled away, Gus swung his old lady (as he terms his boat) back for yet another sick-making sweep of the bay.

We were not the lone voyagers for long. Within twenty minutes, as the light started to fade, the Weymouth lifeboat hove into view and pulled as near us as it dared. At last, via their loudhailer, we could learn the latest news, both of their search and that of others on land and sea via their ship to shore radio.

But it availed us little and totally confounded the old maxim about no news being good news. For though we didn't dare admit it to each other, we knew that it was highly unlikely anyone, even of Winna's athletic prowess, would be able to survive on a sailboard or in the water for the length of time she had now been missing. So our only hope was that some other vessel had sighted her and made a pick-up or that she had been washed on shore somewhere on the turning tide.

Whilst still bobbing alongside, the lifeboatmen double-checked on their radio for any news from any quarter, but the only good news they could transmit was that the winds would now abate and the night should prove calm with good visibility. Gus, bless him, lifted his great thumb at this crumb of comfort and gave each individual one of us the reassurance and comfort of his smile. But I knew he knew the seas better than any of us and even after donkey's years of nautical experience, regarded them with gargantuan respect and, it wouldn't surprise me, more than a touch of fear and dread. Maybe that's what allows fishermen to draw the odd old-age pension. Then, with a wave, the lifeboat drew sideways away from us and was gone. Once more we were alone.

I looked at Arabella, now snuggled into my shoulder, more, I suspect, to warm me than herself. But her eyes were tightly closed, the eyelids twitching and I mentally twitched with them for the same terrible reason. Delia Pettican's words, as she recounted Tony's telephone message, came back to me. '. . . she had gone board sailing . . . and not to wait for her . . . to come back.' Nothing about 'Phone me this evening' or 'See you tomorrow.' Or 'I'll pop by your place later.' Just, 'Don't wait for me to come back.' Well, I suppose we hadn't. We had come out to meet her. Come out to the only place where, perhaps, she felt really free. Sans parents, sans pressure, sans pain, sans problems, perhaps even now sans guilt.

I looked out to the horizon. The waves were losing their crests

234

now as the forecasters had promised, and the clouds were thinning enough for the odd glimpse of a nightglow and crescent moon. And suddenly a stillness you could hear and touch and feel seemed to come over all of us. The boat, the sea, the sky, the wind, the air, the everything.

And then I heard a shout, as if from far away. A finger pointed. Heads were turned. And Gus swung the boat's prow in line with the moon. Three minutes that seemed three hours later, we were all crowded on the starboard side of the boat causing a list that must have made Gus's stubble curl, as he throttled back.

Delia Pettican's long, strong fingers were the first to stroke the red and white stripes of the sailcloth, feel the slippery white shine of the board. But it took all of us to recover the sailboard from the covetous waters and lay it on the deck like the body of some magnificent fish that was already wrapped in its own death shroud.

We stayed under that moon until the sea glistened smooth like a mirror for its elegant light and the wind hardly ruffled our hair. Then without a word, Gus slowly swung the prow towards shore and the man-made lights that punctured the shadow of the land like so many fallen stars.

A beachcomber, metal detecting for the odd pennies left behind by the summer crowds, came upon her wetsuited body, some four days later. At Sandbanks. It was wrapped around the worn and weary posts of a breakwater, as if in some terrible final embrace. At first, he thought it was only an old rubber tyre or inner tube and ignored it completely in his preoccupation with every last tourist penny. It was only as he was about to pack up and get to work to earn some more legitimate income – it was still only seven thirty in the morning – that he decided to spare a second to investigate.

The 'accidental' death of Ella Eames was extensively covered by the local media. I grew sick and tired of seeing her father's face on television, hearing his voice on radio and reading his sob stories in print. Only the *Western Gazette* covered the event with any real sensitivity and no prizes for guessing why that was.

After her funeral, which we naturally attended (my flu only just having flown), a separate memorial service was held where the whole of Manners School gathered. But a subsequent suggestion that a plaque in her memory be placed on the wall of the gym was not taken up by the governors or the new headmaster, on the pretext that Manners School did not even have a roll of honour of the dead from either of the two world wars or, for that matter, a plaque for Delia Pettican's father, the founder of the school, George Alfred Manners.

As you may imagine, the tragic death of Winna Eames gave Arabella and me an opportunity to dodge round our moral dilemma about whether we should inform the law of our discoveries. But to this day, our decision to remain silent worries us considerably at times. As, indeed, it should. And we don't mean because Interpol is probably still working away on the case and Digby Whetstone has a file somewhere he can't yet close. But at least the latter now seems to be content to lay the blame for Folland's death solely across the Channel and has stopped worrying Andy Boxall et al in dear Dorset. But both Arabella and I (and of course, the Colonel and Miss Pettican) know that if, eventually, anyone is arrested for killing the teacher, we will all have to come clean. And that will be the end of . . . well, too many things to dare contemplate.

And the headmaster who took one gamble too many? Well, about a week or so after his disappearance, a figure was found slumped against a tombstone in a churchyard near Swanage. Despite considerable loss of weight, it was clear that this was the missing Beamish. Clear, that is, to everyone but Beamish.

The police reckon he must have taken refuge in the belfry of the church, and only descended from his lofty retreat when thirst and hunger drove him down. But no one will ever know for sure what his movements – or thoughts – were over those intervening days. For Beamish has retreated into a land where no one can touch him or harm him ever again. For there is no past where he's gone. And, maybe, no future. Just a staring, incoherent present. Sans memory, sans reason, sans hope, he seems destined to live out his days in an institutional cocoon, protected for ever from the deadly sins which no doubt featured in his scripture lessons at Manners School.

Beside our ever-lingering sadness about the whole Manners School affair, however, lies a tiny personal niggle. Gus reckons, like Digby, that I took on more than I could chew with Manners School, and was bound to fail. And as far as they know, *did*, what's more.

236

'Going to pack it all in now?' Gus had grinned. 'Yer Ercool Parotting?'

I replied with a 'win some, lose some' type remark, to which Gus inevitably retorted, 'Never heard Ercool ever lost any, old son.'

There's no answer to that.

As for Tony Thorn – well, he remains as innocent as the rest of the world. I mean innocent of what really happened that fatal night in the gym. But he still hasn't picked another Winna. Maybe he still mourns Ella, or finds girls too much of a distraction now, until he's made his Loadsamoney. But he has confessed recently that the motorcyclist on the BMW was all his invention to distract attention from poor Andy Boxall. He's well into his A levels now. After Manners School, he plans to go to London University to read economics.

'Not for their ruddy courses, Peter, you understand,' he had grinned. 'But to be near the City, see the mega-financial cheeses at close quarters, hang about in the same wine bars, get a feel of what it's all about, know what I mean?'

Unfortunately, I did. In a few years' time, I'm sure he will be as mega as he wants to be and run a hundred companies and be able to own all those cars he told me about when we first met. One day, I'll be sitting at my counter and there will be a swish and a growl outside the shop window. I'll look up and out of the Porsche will inexorably climb . . .

But talking of cars, I'm very glad to report Gus has stopped doing so. To my knowledge, he hasn't borrowed or test run a car since that old 'Illman H'Avenger. He's well and truly back to swearing by his old upright horror which, nowadays, seems to be displaying some kind of second wind. (I use that word mainly in its latrine sense.) Maybe word of Gus's infidelities got round to it. Who knows? Cars are funny things. Sometimes I'll swear, whatever their price tag, they're almost as strange as people.

Needless to say, Gus was the only one of us to escape the flu. In fact, he seems to be the only breathing being in the whole of Britain who didn't surrender to what turned out to be a new Asian strain. And to make matters worse, we had a Siberian winter to follow that brief Indian summer. Fog, frost, blizzards and blankets of snow aided and abetted the brand new virus and only undertakers still smiled and counted their blessings. Things reached such an ugly pass that one infamous national daily ran the headline, 'BLIZZARDS AND BUG STILL PUNISH BRITAIN'.

I shiver at the thought even today.

M
STE

Steed, Neville.

Clockwork /

$16.95

DATE			